TWO CATS. ONE MOUSE.

Karpov put the headphones back on and set his eye again to the telescope.

"*If I defect . . .*"

As he heard the word, Karpov slipped the last tender mushroom but one into his mouth, savoring it.

"*. . . the possible consequences don't bear thinking of.*"

Down in Gorki Park, the American turned sharply toward Andropov and was gripping his forearm tightly.

"*If you refuse to come over now, you aren't going to like the consequences either.*"

If I were sitting down there, Karpov thought, wearing your shoes, I would not know which way to walk.

"*There's one little chore we'd like you to do for us before you come over. A little information we'd welcome . . .*"

END-GAME

JAMES MANN

PINNACLE BOOKS NEW YORK

ENDGAME

A Pinnacle Books edition, published by special arrangement with New English Library.

NEL edition published in 1982
Pinnacle edition/April 1985

ISBN: 0-523-42491-4

Printed in the United States of America

PINNACLE BOOKS, INC.
1430 Broadway
New York, New York 10018

9 8 7 6 5 4 3 2 1

This is for Nick Webb with gratitude, affection and a greater respect than he perhaps realizes. Remember the words of Samuel Beckett in *Malone Dies:*

> To be buried in lava and not turn a hair, it is then a man shows what stuff he is made of. To know he can do better next time, unrecognizably better, and that there is no next time, and that it is a blessing there is not, there is a thought to be going on with.

· BOOK ONE ·

· CHAPTER 1 ·

It was nearly time.

She saw Mme. LeFrenais coming towards her and sucked in her cheeks, slipping the cover over her machine. Pushing the top drawer of the pedestal desk back into place and turning the small aluminum key in the lock. Mme. LeFrenais was standing over her now, waiting. Lilian could see the smudging of fur at the front of her coat, the loose end of black cotton that dangled several inches below the hem. When she looked up, the other woman's smile was fixed to her face like cheap make-up.

"You haven't forgotten our little evening?"

Lilian noticed a speck of something white and pulpy wedged between Mme. LeFrenais' front teeth, probably a remnant of the lunch which she packed for herself each day and ate at her desk. That and sweet coffee from a thermos, the milk close to curdling.

"We are all expecting you."

Lilian was vaguely aware of several other faces looking in her direction; the rest of Mme. LeFrenais' coterie. One evening a week they would gather in this apartment or that; huddle in the warmth and buzz emptily like so many queens without a hive. They sipped liqueurs and forked at sticky pastries and gossiped about the other women who worked in their section. As the evening wore on they talked about their husbands and former husbands, small gleanings of sex which were never quite alluded to, never quite tasted. On alternate Sundays they went to one of the restaurants in the old quarter of the town for lunch and afterwards they walked by the lakes in front of the Palais Royal and pretended they didn't want to be stared at.

"Eight o'clock."

Lilian tried to stop her lips from tightening. Mme. LeFrenais' hand was resting on the edge of her desk, the knuckles beginning to swell and wrinkle above her rings.

"I'll see." She felt rather than saw the change of expression on the woman's face. "Naturally, I'll be there if I can, only . . ."

She did look up into Mme. LeFrenais' face then and was in time to see the corner of her lip curling away, the raising of the opposite eyebrow, the beginnings of scorn and distaste.

"Only . . . ?" Mme. LeFrenais continued for her, almost goading her into the lie.

"Only I have a headache. I haven't been feeling well all afternoon. I . . ." Lilian heard herself stumbling on, conscious of the flimsiness of her excuse and angry that she had lacked the courage to say outright that she did not want to go.

When she finished speaking the other woman held her ground for a few moments longer, then pulled at the front of her coat as if it were a cloak and spun round as smartly as her overweight, overdressed body would permit. Lilian watched her walk away, the others moving towards her from different parts of the office, heads already beginning to bend forwards.

Lilian placed her fingers to her temple; it was true, her head was aching, not before, but now. She stood up and steadied herself for some seconds against the back of her swivel chair. There was only one other person left in the long rectangular room, its sections partitioned by shoulder-high perspex panels; one of the clerks who had been transferred at around the same time as herself from the main NATO buildings to the northeast, towards the airport. She was young, too young for LeFrenais to sweep into her little group.

Lilian smiled at the girl now. Girl was right: smooth skinned and bright eyed, she lifted her handbag from the desk and smiled back, heading towards the door.

Standing before the mirror in the ladies' room, Lilian was faced with her own coarsening skin, the lines that scratched away from the corners of her eyes and mouth and which no powder could fill in or cover up. Not for long; not for long enough. She took her lipstick from her bag and applied it carefully, knowing all too well the dangers of overdoing it. Of making herself—what had her mother said the last time she had travelled home?—mutton dressed up as lamb.

Lilian brushed her dark hair, still thick and with its shine mostly unimpaired, and as she did so she thought of her mother. Scottish, straight-backed, standing in the doorway of the terraced house in Aberdeen into which she had moved with her Polish husband and in which she had stayed when he had left her five years later. Herself and four-year-old Lilian. Her mother had never been surprised at Lilian's aptitude for languages. "You had to take something from your father, and I suppose it's that; he could talk his way into and out of anything."

Each time that Lilian returned home—from university, from secretarial college, from jobs as a translator in Paris, Berne or Berlin, from her position as a cipher clerk in Brussels—her mother would look the same. Not older, for she had always looked old. Not thinner, for she had always been thin. Not even sadder.

And on each occasion Lilian's ankles were thicker, her shoulders slumped just an inch or two more. The skin beneath her chin slipped down fractionally, her trunk began to thicken, her breasts to sag. She was forty. Other women of forty that Lilian knew had retained the appearance of a person at least ten years younger. But not herself.

She ran the brush across her hair a final time and

dropped it into her bag. One finger ran the length of her eyebrows, left and then right. Lilian pursed her lips, widened them, moved away from the mirror with a small shrug as if to say there is nothing more that I can do. Mutton dressed up as mutton. She opened the door and stepped into the office; all of the desks had been vacated, all the machines were covered, the wastepaper baskets lifted clear, their contents ready for shredding.

Lilian pressed the button for the elevator and waited.

The walls of the lobby were bare, covered in cream lining-paper which gave the impression of waiting to be painted over for so long that it had now begun to fade. Everything else in the lobby was polished and shone, dully or brightly depending upon the material from which it was made. The steel and aluminium and glass of the fluoroscope before which Lilian stood while an image was thrown up on to the screen above. The teak veneer and thicker glass of the desk at which she stopped and showed her pass. The counter upon which she placed her handbag so that its contents could be searched. The rims of the guard's spectacles, the badge on his shirt, the rounded wood and metal of the butt of his gun which swung away from his holster as he stepped out from behind his desk.

"Late tonight."

Lilian looked back into his face, younger than her own but still the cheeks gouged through by deep lines that toppled over his chin and into the flesh of his neck. She said nothing.

"You've been working overtime?"

Lilian's cheeks grew gradually concave. It was absurd. How late was she coming down? Five minutes? Ten at most? But the guard was reaching over the counter into a pile of typed papers, sliding one out from amongst the others.

He adjusted his spectacles on his nose and read down the list, using the index finger of his left hand as a pointer.

"No, no, nothing about overtime here. Not for this evening."

He tapped the paper and it folded back over his hand.

"There was no overtime," said Lilian, keeping her voice low and even.

The guard nodded. "I know. It says here, no overtime."

"I didn't realize the time. I went to the ladies' room." She tried a suggestion of a smile, hoping that he would think, oh yes, women's troubles, I understand.

But instead he glanced again at the sheet of paper and made no move to get out of her way. Lilian looked past his arm at the wall; she could always walk round him. He had no right to be keeping her there, no reason.

"May I go? I have an appointment to keep."

The guard nodded grudgingly and shifted half a pace aside, allowing her to pass so close that her arm brushed against his hip and touched for a moment the bulk of the pistol holstered there. Poor fellow, she thought, her anxiety fading as rapidly as it had come, he probably doesn't have anything better to do than to try and make up some incident, some cause or other for suspicion. Sitting there day after day watching a bunch of women walk in and out, forever searching their bags and finding nothing but lipsticks, combs, tampons, rolls of peppermints and scuffed shopping lists.

Lilian halted facing the wall and looked over her shoulder. Back behind his desk the guard's finger moved over metal buttons, past the green, past the red, pausing over the white and then pressing down. Two sections of the cream-colored wall slid away and Lilian stepped into the space. The wall closed, almost silently, solidly behind her. She was standing inside an elevator, the padded folding attendant's seat pulled out from the side but unoccupied. There was very little dust or dirt on the floor and the sides were unmarked. Although she had never been told, she assumed that the back wall at least, the one through which she had entered, was bulletproof.

There were buttons for ascending or descending but

she did not need these. Instead, she touched the one marked "open doors" and, with a slight jolt and an elongated hiss, they opened. Lilian stepped out of the front of the lift into another lobby, wider than the previous one. There were other elevators to the side, a stairway at the far end. Secretaries and officials moved from these towards the exit, walking quickly alone, or dawdling in pairs or small groups of three or four. Lilian's low heels clicked on the black and white squares of the floor.

A guard, uniformed but unarmed, World War II ribbons on his jacket, glanced at her pass and waved her through. Lilian followed a grey-haired man carrying a smart attaché case through the doors and down the short flight of steps to the street. She had been pleased to be transferred to this smaller building closer to the center of town. Now, instead of catching one of the special buses out along the Avenue Leopold III, she could walk through the residential streets which filtered off from the Rue Royale and reach her apartment close by the Gare Centrale in less than twenty minutes.

The evenings were getting lighter and warmer but still she was glad she was wearing her coat. Nothing ostentatious like Mme. LeFrenais' fur with its high collar which she kept arched up behind her head, but dull brown wool, heavy and unfashionable and warm. She hung her bag from her arm and pushed both hands down into the pockets and, glancing in either direction, crossed the narrow street.

There was a smile on her face again, but different from the false one she had assumed for that officious guard. This, if it was for anybody other than herself, was for Mme. LeFrenais and her cronies. If only they knew the real reasons for her refusal to join them in their soirée; if only they knew about . . .

For a second she hesitated, her right hand pulled free from her pocket, the smile disappearing from her face. Almost immediately she recovered and carried on walking as if nothing had happened. Not hurrying her pace, careful not to alter her normal route. Only when she had to wait for a line of cars to shunt its way along the road that crossed her own did she turn her head. He wasn't in sight, the man who had been standing nonchalantly at the street corner, not reading the newspaper in his hand, staring at her instead. He wasn't there and she didn't expect him to be, there was no reason to suspect—but she was not the kind of woman that men stared at from street corners.

Lilian crossed to the opposite pavement, almost annoyed with herself for being so disturbed by what was certainly nothing.

It was that stupid guard. He had unsettled her with his list and his overtime and his pointless questioning. She looked at her watch. She would make a diversion to one of the stores; there was ample time, and besides, there were things she could buy for the evening ahead.

Very soon, she was smiling again.

· CHAPTER 2 ·

The apartment was small, on the first floor above a dress and lingerie shop that had been advertising a sale ever since Lilian had moved in over two years ago. Whenever she used the door which led on to the narrow corridor, the wooden stairs and then the equally narrow landing which led to the entrance of the apartment, Lilian glanced through the shop window. Between the blank-faced dummies, dressed in clothes that even Lilian considered unfashionable, she sometimes glimpsed Mme. Bertrand, the shop's proprietor and her landlady.

Occasionally she caught sight of Mme. Bertrand's daughter, Louise, a slack-mouthed girl whose skin always looked dirty and who seemed to be permanently smoking. She almost never saw a customer. Lilian wondered from time to time how it was the Mme. Bertrand made the shop pay and then she usually decided that what kept the shop open was the rent paid promptly each month by herself and the two students who shared the apartment above her own.

This evening, a parcel held under her left arm and her handbag dangling from her wrist, Lilian fidgeted her key from the bag and looked casually through the window. There, sitting with her legs crossed and her attention firmly fixed was Mme. Bertrand, talking to a stout man wearing a fawn raincoat and a dark brown trilby hat. Lilian inserted the key into the lock and turned it slowly, more interested in the shopkeeper's visitor than she had reason to be. She did not recognize him. There was nothing about him to excite her interest in any way—save that he was inside the usually empty shop.

She let herself into the dark hallway and switched on the electric light before closing the door. The man could be anybody; a wholesaler, an insurance man, a banker, anyone. Someone buying something a shade indiscreet for a wife or lover. Lilian squeezed the parcel under her arm. She lifted the wooden flap of the mailbox inside the door and picked out the mail. There were three letters, on one of which she recognized her mother's tight, upright handwriting. One was a bill, one she thought was probably some kind of circular. And . . . ?

Lilian pushed the letters into her bag, setting the parcel and bag on the floor, reaching back into the box. Her fingers traced the bottom of the box round and still re-emerged empty. Frowning slightly, she checked the day's date in her head. It should have been there, punctual as ever. As it had been ever since she had moved; as it had always been before. Still frowning she climbed the stairs.

The apartment comprised two rooms. The larger of these living room, dining room and kitchen all in one; the smaller was the bedroom. The toilet and bathroom were at the end of the corridor and these she shared with the couple from upstairs. There were times when Lilian thought she ought to find a larger place, something more private, but that also meant more expensive. With so many trained staff seeking accommodation in Brussels, prices had escalated ahead of the demand. So she always considered moving, got as far as reading the columns in the newspaper, cards in shop windows, and then told herself that she was all right where she was.

If it was neither spacious nor luxurious, the apartment was at least clean and comfortable. The small kitchen area was curtained off with heavy velvet drapes she had found in a second-hand shop in the old quarter. The windows were covered with old Belgian lace bought from the concierge of her previous apartment and mended painstakingly.

Two aging armchairs had been recovered with material Lilian had bought on the first day of the winter sales. She had hemmed squares of lace left over from curtain making and set these on the backs of the chairs; each week she turned them over so that each side should color and darken equally.

There were small pictures on the wall, landscapes. One was of the Highlands, a loch where she had stayed on holiday with her mother as a child; one a view of the Swiss Alps, the peaks crested with bright snow. In a fading photograph a sailor stood at the stern of a departing ship, staring over the railing back towards the port. He was anonymous, nobody whom Lilian could have known, yet there were times when she liked to think that it was her father.

She opened the letter from her mother and read the usual news; facts of a daily existence which scarcely seemed to vary from one week to the next. Lilian supposed that when her mother read her replies she thought the same about her daughter's life. There had been times when her mother had asked her about men friends, but those times had passed. She assumed that her mother no more thought about Lilian with a man than she thought about herself.

Slipping the letter back into the envelope, she left the other two unopened and went down to the bathroom to run a bath. Fifteen minutes later she was standing in her bedroom, unwrapping the parcel she had bought that afternoon; spreading the contents on the bed. It was a lingerie set in soft brown, almost butterscotch; the edges of the pants, the top half of the brassiere cup, the top and hem of the slip, all were worked in patterned lace.

Lilian bent forward and stroked them and they were cool and smooth to the touch.

A shiver ran through her body.

She took her watch from the dressing-table and looked at the face. The tremor that ran through her was not of anxiety now, rather anticipation. Images of other encounters, other evenings flicked across her mind as she sprayed herself with perfume. Her precious Saint Laurent ''Rive Gauche'' in its black and blue atomizer with the gleaming silver top. Sliding new underthings on to her body. Almost, she could feel Gerard's hands cupping her, stroking her, his mouth drifting across the silk, taunting. Through the lace of the curtain she could see the sun setting deep red above the buildings, ridges of dark cloud humping into its color like beached whales. As she looked, the edges of the red spread and thinned out, becoming rose pink and a strange luminous yellow that she had not noticed before.

Quickly, she finished dressing, half-realizing that she had allowed time to pass until she had to hurry, knowing that when he arrived she would be flushed and breathless, damp.

Lilian stood in the center of the room, wearing the black, flared dress that Gerard liked so much and waited for the sound of his key in the downstairs lock.

As usual, there were the tortuous moments when she thought he was not coming; seconds of self-inflicted pain made possible by the underlying certainty that he would be there. Lilian didn't know men very well. She wasn't as experienced as many a girl half her age, but she knew how infatuated Gerard was with her. Blindly infatuated. Any man who could hold her in his arms and tell her to her face, over and over and over, that she was beautiful—well, didn't it have to be infatuation?

Soft, the sound of the key turning in the street door.

Footsteps on the stairs: along the landing towards her room.

Lilian stood there like a young girl about to give herself to the man she loved for the first time.

"Lilian."

His voice was light, with a slight huskiness at the back of it which gave it strength. He was wearing a leather jacket, elasticated above the waist. His gray trousers were tight in the calf, tighter at the crotch. He had on a white shirt with the top four buttons undone and a gold chain showing through. Lilian knew that at the bottom of the chain hung a chunky medallion that had been given to Gerard by a young woman who had loved him in New York. He smiled at her and lifted his cap from his head; the peaked salt-and-pepper cap he had been wearing when he had first spoken to Lilian that Saturday morning they had both been shopping in the same store, buying groceries for the weekend.

After only ten minutes Lilian had felt certain that all of the other shoppers were staring at them. Gerard had winked and lifted two pieces of steak from the meat section and dropped them both into her basket.

She had cooked them that same evening and the meat had not been good, tough and stringy, but that hadn't mattered.

"I was afraid you weren't coming," she said, watching him.

"That's what you always say."

"I always think it."

He put his arms around her and she caught her breath as she felt the hardness of his young body against her own. His lips were at her neck, her ear. His tongue slipped inside her, round her lips. She moaned and said his name and he nipped the side of her ear with his teeth and jumped away.

Lilian cried out and put her hand beneath her dark hair; when she held it out between them it was spotted with blood.

Gerard made sounds to soothe her as if she were a child; he took the hand and kissed the blood away. He smiled from under eyelashes which were really too long and she began to walk towards the bedroom.

Gerard shook his head.

"What is it?"

"Nothing."

"Then . . . ?"

"Here," he said. "Here."

Lilian had not bothered to get fully dressed. The new, shiny slip lay folded over the back of a chair and her dress was bundled against the arch of the old fireplace, now empty save for a vase of dried flowers. She had pulled on her housecoat over her underwear and was standing in the kitchen, making coffee, the darkened water dripping slowly through the filter-paper into the green enamel jug. Gerard was leaning back against the front of one of the chairs, smoking a cigarette. His eyes were all but closed. Ash from the cigarette had fallen in a fine spray across his thigh, drifting on to the carpet. The white line of the scar that ran from belly to hip was ridged like rope. His penis lay limp and curled to one side and it was all Lilian could do to stop herself from kneeling and cradling it in her hand, taking it, soft and flaccid, into her mouth.

She poured the coffee into two small cups and carried them to where Gerard lay. Only one vestige of color remained in the sky, a purple weal rising from the blackness. He opened his eyes—pale blue—as she set the cups down and in that first moment Lilian imagined that she saw there something she had never noticed, yet always dreaded. Something close to scorn; something more than indifference. As if he, too, were seeing her for the first time and noticing the ugliness of her body, the plainness of her face. Lilian pulled the folds of the housecoat tight about her and shivered.

Gerard touched her arm. "You're cold."

"No, it was nothing." She shook her head. "It's all right," she smiled. "Someone just walked over my grave."

He looked puzzled, as if he didn't understand the

idiom she had used. Instead of explaining she pressed up close to him, balancing her cup in her lap.

"I expect I'm tired," she said, apologetically.

He stroked her hair. "Is that all?"

"Oh," she said. "There was a silly business at the end of the day."

Gerard let the arm that was stroking her fall to the back of her neck and his fingers began massaging the muscles; Lilian leaned her head against him and as the pressure slowly increased she made little moaning noises.

"Tell me about it," he said.

"No, it doesn't matter."

"Tell me."

"It was nothing, my sweetheart, honestly."

"Tell."

"Just some foolish man who . . ." She broke off with a cry and turned her head sideways, against his hand. "I can't if you . . . I can't talk like that."

"Okay."

Gerard smiled and nuzzled his mouth against her cheek, sliding the hand away. "Now tell me."

But halfway through her catalogue of half-doubts and coincidences and ill-formed suspicions, Gerard seemed to lose interest and he began stroking her thigh, tips of his fingers barely touching, moving over the skin until they reached the coarse darkness of hair that showed through her new silk pants like a shadow.

Reaching without ever quite touching.

Lilian's story faded into incoherence. When she tried to recall later exactly what she had said, it was impossible to be certain whether she had mentioned the envelope or not—the envelope which had failed to arrive. What did it matter? Gerard only ever asked her about her work out of politeness, in a considerate attempt to make her feel that it mattered to him, when of course it did not. What mattered—she had to believe it: did believe it—was herself. Her ageing, fat body.

Gerard's fingers ceased moving. His cigarette lay stubbed out at the bottom of his coffee cup. Through the ceiling came the sound of two people walking about. Traffic moved lazily along the street outside. As she lay with her head towards the window, Gerard's shoulder arcing out most of the faint light, Lilian could just see the first star through the patterns of Belgian lace.

· CHAPTER 3 ·

Karpov swilled the last of the wine around his mouth as if it were mouthwash. Finally, he swallowed it instead of spitting it out, turning the bottle with his hand and grimacing at the label. He calculated the extra roubles he had paid for a crate of what he had been assured was genuine French Burgundy, estate bottled. The remnants of his meal were spread before him and he eased his chair away from the table and leaned back. When the woman came in she could clear the things away; plenty of time for that.

It had not always been the same: there had not always been plenty of time. Nor had there been the high-ceilinged office, the personally prepared meal, the foreign wine, such as it was. Karpov allowed himself a smile—the fruits of bourgeois capitalism were turning sour! He took a pack of cigarettes from his inside coat pocket, extracting one, snapping off the cardboard filter and lobbing it on to the table. He felt in another pocket for his lighter.

He was a heavy-chested man, with none of the slackening of the belly or stooping of the shoulders which often came past fifty. His jawline was firm and sharply angled, his eyes the gray of slate after rain. For the past twenty years his hair had been white, cropped short and thick and only now beginning to recede at the temples.

While others had fallen prey to factionalism, petty jealousies, had made mistakes which had caused their papers to be removed from their desks within an hour, Karpov had survived. Darwin, he sometimes thought, would have been proud of him.

His first coup had been at the age of twenty-six when he had been one of those responsible for bugging the American embassy in Moscow. Renovations to the building had given Karpov all the excuse he needed. For the following twelve years, up to 1964, every diplomatic cable between Washington and the embassy was intercepted.

When the MGB and MVD were merged in 1953 to form the KGB—the Committee of State Security—Karpov had been well placed for promotion. Since that date he had been careful never to let his star shine too brightly, lest those envious of individual success should decide it was time to snuff him out. Karpov had worked steadfastly, maintained a low profile, prospered.

For a time he had been one of the case officers handling Lieutenant Colonel Whalen, a US Army intelligence officer who had been turned by the KGB and was working in the early sixties for the Joint Chiefs of Staff. Afterwards he had been responsible for high-level penetrations of French intelligence and Swedish and Dutch military security.

Presently Karpov's concern was counterespionage. Specifically, he was concerned with the Soviet Bloc division of the Clandestine Services section of the CIA. Since Karpov had come into this section, there had been no recruitment of significant Soviet agents by the Americans, nor had there been any particularly harmful defections.

When the SB division of the CIA coughed, it was usually because Karpov was gripping its balls.

The Russian stubbed out his cigarette, half-smoked, and walked across the room. He pulled open the top, then the middle drawer of a heavy grey filing cabinet and removed two files.

On his way back to his chair, Karpov looked down through the narrow window on to Lenin Prospekt. The edges of the pavements were still rimed with frost; car tracks patterned on the surface of the road like tractor marks in dark soil. Across the expanse of Gorki Park mist was rising, cold and clogging, off the Moscow River.

The most recent report was on top of the papers in the first file; decoded and typed on flimsy paper with a fading ribbon. He had read it when it had first come in, then again before his meal. Smoke drifted towards the high, decorated ceiling. Nothing had changed: the words still read the same. Brussels, West Berlin, East Berlin, Moscow—the route they had travelled was normal. There was no reason to suspect that the report was anything other than accurate. Karpov sighed, the sour taste of the wine still present in his mouth. He wanted to leave the room and clean his teeth, rinse out his mouth. Later, later. This had to be acted upon first.

Yet it was a shame. He had recruited her himself and it was always worse when it was one of one's own agents. He thought back to that summer he had spent in Switzerland, so different to the cold months of this city—the sunshine, the snow on the surrounding mountains, cups of hot chocolate sprinkled with cinnamon, the gaiety, the intrigue . . . Karpov was chuckling to himself.

He stopped abruptly as the woman who looked after the offices on that floor knocked and entered. He nodded at her as she cleared away the remnants of his meal, closing the door behind her.

Karpov looked at the most recent photograph of his agent. Blurred and grainy, it was clear enough nevertheless to show how quickly she had aged in the few years since Berne; how her flesh had begun to weaken and lose its vitality. Now only her dark hair seemed to have retained any semblance of life or beauty. And this was the woman who had fallen for the flatteries of a man little more than half her age.

There were other photographs, showing the two of them together, presumably taken from a room above. Karpov had no wish to remind himself of those. He closed that file and opened the second, confirming that his memory of contact mechanism for Fedin was correct. For some minutes the thought of Fedin worried him. He remembered that his enthusiasm at the first reports of contact had been tempered by doubts about Fedin's comparative youth, the headstrong jumble of almost adolescent ideas. And yet the skills had been there, the courage, perfect cover. Also, Karpov had learned since, a love of money. Not for the first time, he wondered why the man had chosen for his work name that of a minor writer of the early years of the century. Karpov stubbed out his smouldering cigarette in the corner of the ashtray and reached for a pad. The silver ballpoint pen was a souvenir of another of his visits to the West. He wrote the instruction in neat, rounded letters without needing to refer to the codebook in the table drawer.

There was no wine, no food, in the small room at the back of the fifth floor apartment close to the center of the old industrial area. The window looked out only on to other windows as the big apartment buildings turned heavily in upon themselves, their brickwork and plaster crumbling and in need of repair. The man in the straight-backed chair was no more then medium height, his hair a few wisps flattened across a knife-domed scalp with a mixture of grease and water. He sat with a spiral notepad on his lap, writing in angular letters with a stub of pencil. He sucked in his lower lip as he worked, using the copy of *Madame Bovary* to translate from the book code, transferring the message into a code of his own invention.

He cared nothing for the contents of the message or its meaning; giving no thought to its significance or consequences. He was a transmitter. It was for that that he was paid. And never, he thought, enough.

He folded the reconstituted message in three and

sealed it inside a manila envelope. The envelope he slid between the pages of a paperback novel. *Geierbeute* by John J. McLaglen. On the left of the dog-eared cover was a badge bearing a parody of the Stars and Stripes and the legend: "*Neue Western Aus Amerika*". At the center of the cover picture a man with his pistol drawn stood over the body of a dead or dying man. Vultures, with all the menace of consoling turkeys, surrounded the victim. The picture conveyed nothing of dying or death; nothing of its process.

The man stood up and took his jacket from a hook on the back of the door; slipping the slim book down into one of the side pockets he put the jacket on over his shirt and patched pullover. He took a keyring from his trousers and double locked the door. At the foot of the stairs, he took out the keys once more and unfastened the padlock on his bicycle, chaining it back under the saddle. He took cycle-clips from his inside pocket and attached them round the legs of his trousers.

He cycled through the early afternoon traffic to the Landwehr Canal, dismounting and securing the bicycle to a length of railing protecting a group of recently planted saplings by the canal-side. Without looking round, he walked purposefully over the bridge and entered the U-Bahn station. It was hot and stuffy underground, pieces of discarded newspaper flapping around his feet as the train slowed into the platform. He sat opposite a couple of housewives, scarves on their heads, the smell of fresh fish emanating from the bags they held tightly on their laps.

Out in the fresh air again, he caught a taxi to the Ku-damm, making sure not to overtip the driver for the short distance. At the second pavement cafe he ordered a small black coffee and waited.

When the girl arrived she sat two tables away from him and he heard her order a *Weisse mit Schuss;* while she waited for the drink to arrive she glanced at a magazine, an English-language copy of *Vogue*, the glossy pages sliding one across the other as she leafed through them.

The man sipped his coffee; there was no hurry. When the girl was halfway through her glass he got up with the air of someone who had idled away enough time and squeezed past her table. In a few seconds he was walking back towards the U-Bahn, the straw was still between the girl's lips and the tattered western paperback was between the pages of her fashion magazine.

Van Holst opened out his newspaper and refolded it, in half and then half again. Creasing it across the center and bending it over his hand. The morning in Amsterdam was crisp and bright but there was still a nip in the air and he was grateful for the fawn woollen scarf which was wound about his neck, one end of it splayed across the white metal table at which he was sitting. A dusty sparrow perched on the back of one of the empty wire-backed chairs, otherwise he was alone. He made a point of coming to the small museum on Keizers Gracht every Tuesday and Thursday; he enjoyed the exhibits, even if they were sometimes a little extreme for his personal taste. Also he enjoyed the stillness of the high white walls, the greenish flags of the stone floor, the sense of light and space. And at the rear, the small garden. Areas of lawn on which were sometimes exhibited sculptures, the geraniums coming into bud and the ivy-covered wall. From where he was sitting Van Holst could see through the plate glass which sealed off the museum proper, then the staircase and the upper floor with a pair of doors at the far end which led out on to the street.

In a recess between floors there was a public telephone.

Here, on Tuesdays and Thursdays, Van Holst waited for a call. Some weeks it came. Other weeks the phone remained silent during the half hour in which he mused over the exhibits and his daily paper. Either way, Van Holst was unconcerned. Several calls or none; it affected neither his composure nor the amount paid regularly into his bank.

On this particular morning there was a call. Van Holst walked over the stone floor and up the steps and lifted the receiver. He was not a lightly built man and his footsteps echoed around the empty gallery. As soon as he spoke into the telephone, he recognized the voice that answered. Strange that he had never seen the girl, nor was it likely that he ever would, but he had formed a picture of her in his head which was constant and appealing. Now, as she relayed the the instructions, Van Holst imagined her standing in a telephone booth at the other end of the line, in a distant city, her blonde hair neat and neck length and held in place by a dark ribbon.

This morning she would be wearing a white blouse to celebrate the sun, a floral print dress that was tight at the waist and flared out around the colored tights she wore on her legs. The picture was almost complete when he heard the phone click and the call was over.

Pleased with life, pleased that she had been the one who had called, he fished some coins from his pocket and checked his watch, waiting inside the recess for a little over two minutes before dialing a local Amsterdam number. When the phone was answered on the eighth ring he informed the man that his consignment of Savannah Volunteer Guards in Full Dress had arrived and was ready for collection.

Walking east from the Fodor Museum towards the Amstel River, Van Holst was amused, as always, to pass the imposing front of the Bank of America. It was one of the many little ironies of his life which gave him pleasure.

An orange and white barge was moving slowly down river, a tawny colored tomcat sunning himself on the roof. Van Holst paused on the parapet of the Magere Brug, its archaic wooden structure again in need of paint. He could see the windows of his shop from there, on the corner of Amstel opposite, the thin bamboo blinds pulled not quite to the top of the frames. He rewound the scarf about his neck and began walking again. A brown Toyota sedan was parked outside and through the glass of the door, set into an angle at the edge of the building, he could see Marie dealing with a customer.

Van Holst carried on past and climbed the flight of stone steps which led to the door of the living quarters above the shop. The side entrance allowed him to reach the upper room undisturbed and there he at once settled down to transcribing the orders it was now his duty to pass on. He enjoyed this task, just as he enjoyed everything to do with his tradecraft. Why else, he often thought, did men become involved? Patriotism? Money? Possibly. For himself, as for so many others, it was the pleasure of taking part in a well-disciplined, secret game. It was a way of clinging on to some of the excitement of childhood, with the dangers amplified to suit more sophisticated needs. Small boys were content to play with toy soldiers fashioned from plastic, wood or metal, their weapons and colors having to bear little resemblance to any actual model; grown men played war games with lead soldiers which had been hand-painted with the greatest care, each tiny insignia an exact facsimile of its progenitor.

Van Holst took the pieces, a little over two inches in height, from the shelf adjacent to the window and set them on the broad-leafed oak table before him. The Savannah Volunteer Guard was one of the corps attached to the 18th Battalion Georgia Infantry in the American War Between the States. Tunic and trousers were of gray, the breeches with a stripe of reddish-orange down the outer sides. The jacket was short and belted, finishing well above the hips, with three rows of buttons down the front; its cuffs were the same color as the trouser stripes, surmounted by a design of gold braid. A short length of the orange-red material held the collar taut. There were fringed epaulettes on the shoulders of the tunic. The hats, for all ranks, were high crowned shakoes with a red, white and blue plume.

One of the perfect soldiers was hollow, and it was into this hollow that Van Holst inserted a small roll of paper.

He laid the pieces on a bedding of polystyrene chips, placing more chips on top until the box was full and then closing the lid.

"Marie." He still called her name, even though she was now almost totally deaf. Most of the customers were regulars and they were used to a system of ordering which involved much pointing at catalogues, scribbling on the pages of notebooks and pantomime.

She turned towards the curtain at the foot of the stairs, alerted by a sense of his presence rather than the sound of his voice.

He set the box on the counter before her. "These are for Mijnheer Fedin."

Marie, red-cheeked and fair haired, read his lips and nodded.

To be certain, Van Holst wrote the name on the top page of the notepad on the counter.

She read it and nodded again, even more vigorously.

Van Holst smiled despite himself. Marie resembled a life-size Dutch doll that only needed the winged hat and clogs of the traditional costume to make the illusion complete. The fact that she heard almost nothing and spoke scarcely at all rendered her less human than ever.

She smiled back at him, thinking him pleased with her.

Van Holst turned away and with his quick eye checked the interior of the shop. Columns of model soldiers from the Napoleonic Wars marched down wooden shelves to meet the armies of the Crimean War in combat. Sailors from the days of the Armada were positioned on board a fully-rigged fighting ship anchored in a calm sea of sand. Plains Indians waited for the ill-fated troopers of General Custer's command to reach the spot of their deadly confrontation.

Out beyond the river, Van Holst saw a man who might be Fedin step on to the far end of the wooden bridge. He nodded goodbye to Marie and passed through the curtain and ascended the stairs. From the upper floor window he watched Fedin approach. A slim man, his walk long-legged and athletic, he was wearing a light brown sports jacket and beige trousers in some synthetic material which from time to time caught the reflection of the sun from the water and flicked it faintly back. He was hatless and his hair, long enough to curl up from the base of his neck, drifted out to either side of his head in the breeze. Fedin walked with an easy swing of the arms, fists loosely clenched. His lips were pursed as though he were whistling.

Van Holst stepped back from the window and waited for the sound of the bell as the shop door was snapped open—another relic from the days before he had been able to afford Marie.

"Good day." Fedin's voice was not quite accentless. There was something at the back of his flat Dutch, an almost nasal roll which suggested the man was not speaking his native language.

This was lost on Marie.

She read his greeting easily, nodded and smiled and already she had recognized him from previous visits.

"You have an order for me. Fedin."

Marie was lifting the box from its place beneath the counter; she set it down and reached for the ball of string to tie it, but Fedin stopped her, pointing at the lid.

She smiled again, a little awkwardly this time, and slid the box across the counter towards him. Fedin flicked back the lid, brushed away some packing and looked down at the six model soldiers in their freshly painted uniforms, paraded on polystyrene. He took one from the box and walked with it towards the window. A woman strolling past turned her head towards this handsome young man who was examining a child's toy with such care. Satisfied, Fedin returned the piece to the box and gestured to Marie that she could tie it up.

"You will see that my account is sent in the mail." He spoke facing her so that she could see the words on his lips.

Marie blushed and nodded; the way his brown hair lay against the top of his shoulders gave her a weak feeling at the base of her stomach.

Fedin took the box carefully in his left hand, smiled at Marie, and left the shop. Van Holst moved back to his vantage point above and watched him crossing back over the bridge, his purchase by his side.

De Koffiemoten was round the corner from the *Rembrandthuis*. The faded purple of the slanting tiles outside led to the canal. Fedin went to a table set back from the window. A woman sat up to the small, curved counter and she glanced round as Fedin entered. She looked at him for a moment, large dark eyes widening beneath a heavy fringe of black hair, then went back to her coffee and strudel. A man wearing a striped apron came down the stairs alongside the counter and, seeing Fedin, he raised a hand in greeting.

"Cappuccino," Fedin said, but the man had already slid behind the machine and was preparing it.

The box, gold with a red and blue motif diagonally across it, sat on the dark stained wood of the table. Fedin took a diary from his pocket and leafed through the pages; he made a quick entry in pencil, his writing slightly flamboyant, as flowery as the small pages would allow. The cappuccino was served in a neat white cup, a biscuit on a white plate alongside. Cup, saucer and plate were rimmed in black.

Fedin drank slowly, nibbling the biscuit, forcing himself to take his time and enjoy the feeling of excitement that was building up within him. He was aware of people going past along the main road—not the sight of them but the sound—and he guessed it was a party of students on its way to the Rembrandt Museum. The woman at the counter wiped her mouth, picked up her tote bag, dropped two coins down beside her plate and walked out into the sunlight.

Fedin stopped himself from staring at the box, looking instead at the carnations in slim vases on the tables, pink and red and white. There was the beginnings of numbness along his thighs, a dryness at the center of his palms. He finished his coffee, left money for the man who had gone back upstairs, and stepped casually from the cafe.

There were more people on the street than he had thought and they didn't all seem to be going to the museum. Groups of them, students and hangers-on, were gathering in knots, making their way slowly and noisily along Joden Breestraat towards the flea market. Fedin could see one or two policemen gathering at the end of the street. He quickened his pace a little, not wanting to get mixed up in some absurd incident.

The small block of new apartments overlooked the flea market. Fedin glanced at the blue-gray brickwork on which an artist had drawn a huge phallus and balls in white chalk, prehistoric, like the one he had once seen carved into the chalk of an English hillside.

He pushed open the wooden gate and went through to the stairs. There were only three floors and his apartment was on the top. There were green plants on the window ledges, green plants on the pine table and on top of the stereo speakers at either side of the fireplace. A brightly colored wall-hanging, showing small boats at sea, gulls above them, took up the center of the partition wall.

Fedin set the box of model soldiers on the table and carefully untied the bow Marie had put in the string. He lifted the pieces out of the polystyrene and stood them in an ordered line. Then he took them one by one and weighed them in the palm of his hand. Smiling, he eased the tip of a penknife blade into the bottom of one soldier and a moment later, the thin roll of paper slid down into his hand.

Chanting came through the closed windows, and, above and through it, the sound of officialdom using a loud-hailer. Fedin shut the noise out from his mind and read the note three times. The dry sensation in the palms of his hands increased. He went through into the kitchen and lifted the brown plastic bowl from the sink. Holding the curling sliver of paper in the finger tips of his left hand, Fedin struck a match and applied it to the bottom corner. Flaked ashes drifted down into the sink and the burst of cold water rinsed them away.

Fedin reached into one of the fitted cupboards, between a jar of brown rice and a packet of bran, and brought out a bundle wrapped in blue-black velvet. He unfolded it on the work surface, lifting one flap at a time until the pistol was fully uncovered.

It was a fraction over six inches in length, the rear of the butt ridged to give a firmer grip, the sides crosshatched. It was an SIG-210/5, the original barrel and recoil spring changed to take a clip of eight 7.65mm Parabellum cartridges. The target version of what was already a reliable and accurate weapon. It had a fine-blade sight at the front, a micrometer sight at the rear, above the hammer. The ordinary service model was in use by the West German Border Police and some were in the hands of the Swiss and Danish armies, but as a handgun it was three or four times as expensive as most of its rivals and had priced itself out of the mass armaments market. The pistol in Fedin's hand was even more costly; it was the gun of a connoisseur, an expert, a man who knows one shot may be all he gets.

From the bottom of a metal biscuit tin, Fedin took two clips of ammunition. He carried these and the pistol back into the living room. The noise from the street was more insistent and in the distance Fedin could hear the wailing sounds of sirens. Through the window he saw that a number of mounted police had arrived and were trying to divide the demonstrators in two. Forcing a wedge between them so that helmeted men on foot could begin to disperse them. Fedin craned his neck and at the far end of Joden Breestraat he glimpsed a waiting fire-engine.

He had no idea what the demonstration was about. He tried to read the lettering on one of the banners and at that moment a group of the students decided to rush the shortest of the police lines. Perspex face-shields came snapping down and batons were raised. A man on a dapple gray horse trotted into the marauding group and began to flail left and right with a long truncheon.

The screams and shouts that reached Fedin were muffled by the glass; it was like watching a film.

He stood a foot back from the window and raised his right hand, the pistol moulding to it perfectly. Behind the rear sight his eye was unblinking. Below him a girl with long fair hair was clubbed to the ground and lay still, arms spread, one side of her skirt hiked up on to her thighs. The crowd swelled past her, turning in on itself. Blood was spilling out and staining the girl's hair. Fedin made a further adjustment to the sight until he had it finely focused on her head.

He was smiling.

· CHAPTER 4 ·

The ball struck the ribbon at the top of the net, ran several inches along it like a slack-wire artist, wavered and finally dropped down on Malone's side of the court. Stranded midway, all he could do was watch and groan.

At the opposite side of the net his opponent raised his racket in mock commiseration and called a cheery apology. Malone turned and went back to the base line to receive the next serve. Patterson bounced the ball three, four times, threw it up, swayed back and let it fall. Gave another sign of apology; threw it up again and swivelled his body, feet beginning to move. The racket head came over hard and fast and sent the ball deep into Malone's quarter of the court.

Malone lunged to his right, trying to keep his eye on it, losing sight as it kicked higher than he had anticipated. The ball struck the top edge of his racket frame and went careening over the wire mesh and along the fine gravel path that led between the flowerbeds towards the club house.

A stocky man wearing a dark gray suit stooped and picked the ball up. He glanced at it, advanced with it a couple of paces and lobbed it back into the court. Patterson had already changed ends and now he patted Malone's shoulder with a sweaty hand.

"Not your day, old boy. Still, that's how it goes."

Malone grunted and started to move to the far end of the court.

"How much did we have on this set?" Patterson called after him and laughed.

Malone's eyes narrowed fractionally and he tightened the grip on his racket handle. If it weren't for the fact that the etiquette of his job insisted that he be on reasonable terms with Patterson . . . If it weren't for the fact that these particular grass courts were both exclusive and the best in Brussels. If it . . .

"One!" called Patterson, and hit a loose ball down to Malone's end of the court.

"God," thought Malone. "I'd love to drive that smile clean off your damned face."

He chose two balls carefully, pushed one down into the pocket of his shorts and threw up the other. Ace, he called inside his head. Ace! The serve swerved away from Patterson's forehand, and the return was little more than a lob over the net. Following in, Malone turned his body away from the ball and played a drive volley that landed six inches inside the tram line. With Patterson still chasing hopelessly, Malone was already on his way back to serve again. This time he angled the face of the racket the other way as it came down and the ball swung past Patterson's backhand before he could adjust his balance.

Thirty-love.

Malone threw up the ball and as he began to move beneath it, the stocky man eased into the edge of his vision. Torn between trying to adapt his shot and stepping quickly back and letting the ball bounce, Malone only succeeded in hitting it into the net.

Damn Winstat!

Malone double-faulted and Patterson grinned, rubbing his index finger through the absurdly bushy moustache, moving forward a foot to receive the next service. It was too safe for the server's own comfort;

coming into the net, Malone was easily passed down his backhand side.

Winstat had stopped wandering about like someone who'd found his way into the grounds by accident and was now examining the polish on his left shoe as if it held some intense fascination.

Thank God, thought Malone as he readied his next service, Winstat doesn't have to operate in the field.

With that he had Patterson scrambling for a top spin serve, dipping it back with a drop shot that had Malone running, but running successfully, cross-court to cross-court, forehand to backhand, volley on volley and finally Patterson miscued and lost the point.

Forty-fifteen.

What the hell did Winstat want that was so important?

Fault.

Why couldn't it have waited until he was back at the office? Why not a discreet telephone call?

Fault.

Forty-thirty.

Malone ground his teeth together and snatched at the ball; Patterson drew him forward and lobbed him as though it were the simplest thing in the world.

Deuce.

Operations flicked down inside Malone's mind like train times on a station notice board. Almost before he realized it he was one point away from losing both game and set.

Winstat had switched his attention from his shoe to a bank of rhododendron bushes that had yet to show the first sign of flower. Looking for him from the corner of one eye, Malone lost the ball.

"Bad luck!" With false bonhomie, Patterson was lolloping towards the net, his hand already extended for Malone to shake. "Like I said, old man, not your day."

Malone showered briskly, pleaded an appointment to excuse himself from a drink in the bar, and went to where Winstat was waiting near the foot of the club house steps. While Winstat was short and stockily built, Malone was six foot exactly and weighed one-eighty pounds, spread evenly about his muscular frame. His hair was dark brown with a tendency to curl if he allowed it to grow past a certain length, which he seldom did. His eyes were a bleached blue, his features even, verging towards the anonymous. Under the lines of a forty-year-old there were still the remains of a roundish face that a long time ago would have given a mother cause to say how beautiful he was.

"Well?"

"Something's turned up."

"I dare say."

"A body."

Malone set his head fractionally to one side. "Whose?"

But the shorter man was already walking away and Malone followed him, the two of them passing between the geometric flowerbeds towards the high iron gate and the cars waiting beyond.

"It was passed over at one o'clock. Police turned up a connection with us. We ordered in the Janitors." He paused. "Seems to be your pigeon."

Dead pigeon, Malone thought. He didn't waste his breath with any further questions. Winstat either didn't know or he wasn't prepared to answer. Malone curled his lower lip back against his teeth. They'd be there soon enough.

The offices were in the Saint-Gilles district, sandwiched between a toy warehouse and a building made over to work rooms for a tailoring firm. Malone and Winstat entered by the rear door and climbed the stairs to the second floor. In the first office a fifty-year-old woman was making heavy weather of a manual typewriter, while across the room a man wearing bifocals was scanning a small computer screen. Malone opened the door and Winstat went through first; the pair of them walked along a short distance of corridor and Malone opened another door—they were in his office.

A table topped with formica, three hard chairs, several small filing cabinets made from gray plastic or metal, a floor safe, an electric kettle, a sink in the corner alcove close by the window, cups, coffee, sugar, tea. Piles of newspapers in most European languages, as well as from America and England, stood in neat rows on the floor. A bookcase held a good collection of international telephone directories, train and air company timetables, road and street maps, a section no more than fifteen inches long of novels and plays: Mailer, Styron, Fitzgerald, Albee, Beckett, O'Neil.

There was a manila file on the table and Malone flipped it open and glanced down.

"Oh, shit!" he said. "Oh, shit!"

Winstat slipped a toothpick from his top pocket, tore open the paper, took out the flattened sliver of wood and eased a piece of lunch from between his teeth.

"Someone important?" he asked, only it didn't come out like that and Malone had to guess what Winstat was saying through several fingers and a toothpick.

Malone hesitated a moment, thinking about the subject of the file. His fingers tap danced a little rhythmic line across it. "Lilian Grozcheck," he said, "A NATO cipher clerk. Child of a Polish father and a Scottish mother."

"Divided loyalties," said Winstat.

Malone shrugged. Winstat had a tendency to sum up people in a single phrase, something that would fit snugly into the computer. It was a rush to judgement that Malone distrusted. People were not that easily comprehended.

"She's been working for the KGB for six years," said Malone. "They got to her when she was working as a translator in Berne. We've been on to her for a couple of years, letting her run. She wasn't getting hold of anything important and if she ever did the signs were she'd be too scared to use it."

Winstat nodded, scraped the end of the toothpick on the sleeve of his suit, leaned sideways and dropped the pick into Malone's wastepaper bin.

"We figured if we were patient we'd get the chance to turn her—and we did." He paused. "We were starting to."

"Blackmail?" asked Winstat.

"Uh-uh."

"Money?"

"No."

"Honey trap?"

Malone shook his head. "Not exactly. We got her to fall in love. Gerard. Nice charmer with all the looks of a five-foot-eight Adonis and the morals of a stoat."

"Sounds terrific."

"She thought so."

Winstat stood up. "Shall we go down?"

Malone closed the file. "Okay."

Down was a floor below the normal basement level, reached from a small elevator with a maximum load of four people. The bodies had to be transported feet first. It was always cold and smelled of disinfectant. It reminded Malone of a nurse he'd dated back in Boston.

Mrs. Lambert laid down her patience cards and showed her annoyance clearly on her face. It could have been the first time in three days that she had got right out without succumbing to the temptation to cheat. She picked at a stray cotton thread hanging from the lapel button of her white uniform coat and pushed it down into one of the pockets.

Malone said the number that had been written inside the file.

Mrs. Lambert sighed as if she had quite enough to do without unnecessary interruptions. Once the dead were dead . . .

She was glad it was Malone though. Too smug for her liking. A little too much bounce in his walk. And she was certain that when he didn't think she was looking he stared at the white hairs which curled like the skeleton of a flower from the mole on the left side of her chin.

They went through the rubber-edged swing doors and stopped before a row of trays that filled one wall from floor to ceiling. Mrs. Lambert repeated the number to Malone and he nodded, trying not to look at the hairs curving out of her chin.

Mrs. Lambert turned the key and slid the drawer out. It rode easily on greased ball-bearings and shushed to a stop. Winstat lifted back the sheet and stood away. One pale blue eye hung open, the other blankly shut. The holes at the top of the chest were fist-sized, exit wounds from two bullets placed neatly together at the top of the spinal column. Malone saw the placement of the wounds and something clicked inside his brain, a memory, a pattern. He glanced at the ridge of old scar tissue stretching halfway across the dead man's belly and nodded to Winstat to replace the sheet.

· CHAPTER 5 ·

Gerard slid out from under Lilian's arm and levered himself from the bed. He heard the tempo of her breathing change and glanced down at her face, half-hidden by strands of thick black hair. She pulled up her knees under the covers and made a small grunting sound. Before Gerard was midway through dressing her breathing was back to normal, the coarse deep noise that just fell short of being a snore.

He pulled on his short jacket, brushed his fingers through his hair and stepped softly to the door. Letting himself out of the apartment, he turned left and went along the corridor to the bathroom. Here he squeezed some of Lilian's toothpaste, mint-striped, on to the index finger of his right hand and ran it along his teeth. Bending low over the sink, he ran the cold tap, splashing water up into his face, finally taking a mouthful and gargling with it, head back. He swilled the water round his mouth and spat it down into the basin.

Outside, the street was quiet. From other directions came the faint noise of car engines, but Gerard saw nothing. The light was beginning to spread above the roofs of the buildings and simultaneously the city birdsong faded. Gerard turned southwest towards the Boulevard du Midi and the area around the station and the canal. For stretches of time there was little sound other than his own footsteps. Gerard thought about his target; at the next meeting with his control he would suggest that the time for turning her had come. This business of allowing her to talk more and more about her work and feigning almost complete indifference had gone on long enough. If she harbored any doubts about his intentions in that direction, Gerard was positive they had drifted free.

A black sedan turned ahead of him, proceeding towards him at what could only be called a cautious speed. Instinctively, Gerard checked the number of people in the car, glancing at the street behind. He held himself tense until the driver—a young man much the same age as himself and probably on his way home after a similar night out—had passed him.

Gerard crossed the road, watching for any deviation in the sedan's speed. There was none.

His mind returned to Lilian. Wondering how much longer he could disguise his true feelings for her. His lack of them. The effort to foist upon her flabby body a passion that only other, alternate images could foster. And her own love-making was a mixture of heavy crudities and surprising passages of naive reluctance that he found increasingly infuriating. No wonder that the gestures towards pain had grown more real.

Another set of footsteps merged with his own and Gerard hesitated at the curb, as if uncertain which exact direction to take.

The hum of traffic was rising into the brisk air.

The next time I see control, thought Gerard, I have to insist they bring it to a conclusion.

He doubled back on himself for a few hundred yards, not knowing of any special cause for care, simply taking normal precautions. With the white mist still rising off the canal, he approached one of the smaller factories on the point of disgorging the workers from its night shift. Gerard melted into the groups of men, all eager to be going home, their soiled faces a mixture of tiredness and relief.

Two trams were waiting some seventy yards along the street and Gerard decided that he would take one of them himself; it would drop him close to his own apartment. He could shower and change and then go to a nearby café for breakfast. The best part of the day. His handsome face broke into a smile at the thought.

Men were shuffling on to both trams and Gerard joined a haphazard line for the latter, saw that there were only half a dozen people moving on to the first and changed places. A few men nudged after him. Shoulders and feet touched. The driver sat with his head turned, looking back down the vehicle, counting spaces. Gerard climbed on to the platform, taking money from his trouser pocket as he did so. The workman in front of him stood still instead of moving further forward and Gerard banged against him. The man half-turned and someone else collided lightly with Gerard from behind. Coins spun from his hand.

Frowning, Gerard bent to pick them up. Someone muttered a grudging apology. A blow like a steel hammer drove into the base of Gerard's neck and flattened him to the platform. There was a second blow but he never felt it. Figures around Gerard pushed and swayed. Someone cursed aloud. Hands stooped to help him to his feet and then jerked away from the two close circles of blood that were welling up through the back of his jacket.

The spotlights in the ceiling of the Fodor Museum are arranged diagonally and throw light on to canvases which seem to dribble dried blood. From a tape loop somewhere hidden from sight, an alto sax is playing the middle eight of "Smoke Gets In Your Eyes" over and over again. Van Holst lifts the receiver of the telephone and listens. He leaves the gallery immediately and walks by the canal-side and then back across the wooden bridge.

In his room above the shop he carefully takes an unpainted, featureless model soldier from a cupboard and places it in a special section that he calls, for his own pleasure, Fedin's shelf.

There had been six of the neat, upright anonymous miniatures on the shelf. Now there are seven.

· BOOK TWO ·

· CHAPTER 6 ·

The window by the sink was small and allowed little more than a view of the fire-escape's rusty descent down the wall of the toy factory and a length of alleyway piled high with cardboard boxes and large round bins overstuffed with discarded remnants and misshapen limbs. By twisting his head to the right, Malone could see a triangle of sky. This morning it was just possible to distinguish one shade of gray slowly shuffling across another. The kettle began to whistle and he turned away and poured some of the boiling water into a brown mug—instant coffee which was too expensive and that he drank too often. The report was still on his desk.

Malone stretched and scratched his back through the blue cotton of his shirt. His collar was open and his tie loosened and pulled down. He swung the chair round; tasted the coffee and tasted very little. His thumb riffled the flimsy pages. Two bullets close together, either side of the spine. A pair of 7.65 Parabellum cartridges fired from close range and angled inwards and down. Almost certainly the weapon used was an SIG with a modified barrel—the 210/5.

A target pistol fired at close range.

An assassination carried out in the middle of a crowd

of people when there didn't seem to be any need for such a risk.

The ideas were chasing one another inside Malone's head. Time later for Charlie Huron to check them through his computer. Malone was already reaching for his filing cabinet, the precious stack of six-by-four cards. Names and places came back to him almost without looking, fingering the cards was enough. Rome . . . Orly . . . Stockholm . . . Joinville . . .

In the spring of seventy-eight an undersecretary for trade attached to the Soviet embassy in Rome had been honey-trapped by a particularly pretty boy who worked the north-eastern corner of Vatican Square. Confronted with photographs, cassette recordings, he allowed himself to be turned, thinking all the time that once in the Americans' confidence he would report back to his original masters. The double agent redoubled.

The Russian took too long to play his hand. He was fished out of the Tiber at three in the morning with the aid of searchlights and the clank of winding gear. Two bullet wounds, center of the spine and base of the skull, made by a Walther P-38 firing 9mm Parabellum cartridges.

On May Day of the following year a courier attached to the American Secret Service flew into Orly Airport from London, where he had been partly responsible for the deportation of three Russian diplomats. As soon as he stepped into the crowded baggage check area he was shot twice in the small of the back from close range. The weapon was a Walther P-38.

In August of seventy-nine, a Bulgarian defector had sat drinking his usual mid-morning coffee at a pavement cafe on the Strandvagen in the center of Stockholm. The first shot had driven through the folded pages of the newspaper, the coffee cup, the gold-capped teeth, the mouth. There had been no second shot, just a silver Saab driving swiftly away. The 9mm bullet had also come from a Walther.

Malone's fingers flicked on. He knew there was a

gap. Two years. Nothing until early eight-one. Yes. His hand stilled and he lifted the card above the others. February the fifteenth. Joinville. Malone knew the area, the way the land stretched wide away from the road on either side, the flatness broken here and there by avenues of plane trees. The motorcyclist would have had only seconds in which to register the black car lurching out from between the trees, to take avoiding action. It would not have been enough, not at that speed. As he lay there, face down, a 7.65 Parabellum cartridge tore through the rear of his leather jacket; the second shot drove from close range into the back of his skull.

In that gap of two years something else had changed. This time the weapon was an SIG-5.

Malone's coffee was lukewarm. It was December of eighty-one and a middle-aged woman wearing a fur coat and hat, her stockings swollen over elasticated bandages, got up slowly from her table in Harvey's At the Top on the upper floor of the Harvey Nichols department store in Knightsbridge. It was close to midday and the store was busy with Christmas shoppers. She had several sheets of wrapping paper under one arm; in her handbag were the cards she intended to post that day to relations in Poland.

When she stepped off the first section of the escalator and turned towards the next she collided with a man holding a small Yorkshire terrier under his arm. Murmuring an apology, she bent to retrieve the wrapping paper she had dropped. She was shot twice in the base of the neck with a silenced SIG-5, modified to take 7.65 Parabellum cartridges.

Malone spilled what remained of the coffee jumping up from his desk. His head showed round the door of the outer office.

"Charlie!"

Huron glanced up from behind a computer screen and adjusted his bifocals.

"Run some things through for me."

"Give me . . ." Huron began, pointing at the data already up on the blue-tinted screen.

Malone shook his head. "Now."

He had always been the same. Feeling the need to follow things through immediately, pushing for an answer, a direction, that one reference which would carry him towards a conclusion: all the time closing in.

There had been a time when he had thought that academic research might allow him these kinds of satisfaction. When Harvard Square had seemed the bounds of his visible universe and the smell of wood polish and old books something he imagined he might thrive on forever. All that had been before the conversations had begun, late night discussions in one or another room, a certain professor who gradually emerged as more political than most. One evening there had been a third party waiting to be introduced to Malone, someone who'd flown in specially from Virginia . . .

Charlie Huron brought Winstat with him and from their expressions and the slightly diffident way they entered the room, Malone could tell that they had been plotting together outside.

"It's messy," Winstat began.

"There are inconsistencies," said Charlie.

"And I," said Malone, "don't trust patterns that are too perfect."

Winstat slid the toothpick from his mouth. "Meaning?"

"Meaning that some clever bastard inside an office in Moscow or East Berlin has spent a very long time artfully setting them up. When we find them we pat ourselves on the back and think how clever we are to dig up such a neat set of circumstances."

"We have . . ." Charlie Huron tried again.

"We've done it in the past and those circumstances have cost the Soviets plenty."

"And other times we've been suckered," snapped Malone.

Winstat shrugged, heavy-shouldered. "Some you win, some you . . ."

The flat of Malone's hand hit the desk hard. "This is one I'm not losing, Geoff. Not now. Five bodies and Gerard's six. You can't tell me, either of you . . ." He was staring at them now, staring hard and pointing, ". . . that they don't tie together. The patterns are too close. Almost identical."

Despite himself, Winstat sighed. One of the troubles with Malone was that he'd never got over thinking of himself as a caped bloody crusader.

Malone half-guessed what Winstat was thinking and ignored him. "Well, Charlie, what about it?"

"I'll buy the last two. Joinville and London."

"And Gerard?"

"Yes. And Gerard."

"Three, then?"

Charlie opened his mouth, closed it again. Just nodded.

Malone leaned back in his chair. "We presume one man, working alone, probably at the end of a complex chain of command. He's mobile, highly-trained, he's got more guts than are good for him." Malone let the chair rock forward. "He takes too many risks."

"For his own sake," said Charlie.

"And maybe for his masters'," said Winstat.

For the first time in some while, Malone looked at Geoff Winstat with something approaching respect.

The telephone flashed a green light instead of ringing and Malone switched on the scrambler before lifting the receiver.

"Where the hell have you been, Malone?"

"Here."

"I've been trying to reach you."

"And I've been busy."

"You had your calls stopped!"

"What is it you wanted to talk about?"

"Trondheim."

"Huh?"

"Trondheim, for Christ's sake!"

"What about it?"

"Malone, I swear . . . you want to cut down on the late-night booze. It's your boy, he's through. He's going to make the trip."

"Nido."

"Right. You've got him primed, haven't you? On the boil."

"I'll be in touch."

"Don't hang up on me, Malone!"

Nido was the codename for Dimitri Andropov, a fifty-one-year-old Russian psychologist whose specific field was neurology. American interest had begun in 1959 when the young Russian had visited Norway as a member of the Soviet delegation to a world conference on neural medicine and psychology. A brief, but to Andropov, serious liaison with a female member of the US team had enabled the American security service to keep tabs on him ever since. In 1975 the Nido file had become Malone's responsibility; in 1976 its subject had been seconded to work under the direct auspices of the KGB.

Andropov's initial research had been into the artificial formation of neural patterns and since that time he had specialized in the examination under clinical conditions of the lasting effects which resulted from being exposed to varied sensory experiences. It seemed that such experiences would seriously affect the bases of both memory and personality.

Malone didn't find it difficult to imagine the uses such work might be put to by the KGB. A program of sensory shocks and drugs would enable a skillful team to scour a man's memory to the dregs—or remove from his mind every vestige of the past, even the slightest concern with the future. He didn't need to read the reports of what went on inside Russian psychiatric hospitals to know this: one of the more intensive parts of his CIA training had been concerned with demonstrating the efficiency with which American scientists had mastered the same techniques.

Malone read through the print-out on Andropov that Charlie Huron had set on his desk. He wanted the scientist over and now was the time. The coincidence too fine to be dismissed, left unused. Malone drummed his fingers on the paper. He was wondering if it would be too much to milk Andropov for something else. If the man wanted to come over badly enough, if they could make the gains appear sufficiently strong . . . Malone wanted to nail his theory about the assassin. Nail it hard.

He took a sharpened pencil from one drawer, a memo pad from another, and began drafting the signal.

To: Clan. Ops. (SB division) Berlin Station
For the eyes of Head of Station only
Re: Nido File
Trondheim in April. Essential that bird flies nest.
Suitable letter following via usual channels.
Seek urgently information from subject re. following terminations: Joinville, 81, London, 81, Brussels 82.
All now our code Hedgehopper.
Source: Clan. Ops. (SB division) European Station (Brussels)—Firecrest.

Malone always felt particularly pleased that someone's five minutes with the bird book had resulted in a codename like Firecrest.

· CHAPTER 7 ·

There were ten in the delegation to the 1959 world conference, the majority of them senior neurologists. Andropov was surrounded by professionals with more letters and articles and books after and under their names than he could dream of having. He had been surprised to be selected—no, astonished. At first he had thought it a joke, something conjured up to tease him for all those hours he spent long into the evenings in the library and the laboratory. The notes he amassed in spiral books, page after page covered in figures and letters written in a delicate, sloping hand. More than once Natasha Marakova had found him sleeping, head cradled carelessly on one arm, his pencil blunted and close to his fingers. She made him tea, strong and dark, and woke him with a gentle shake and a shy, turning smile.

They said she loved him. Once they said it to his face and Dimitri Andropov blushed a deep red and knocked his shin painfully against the table leg. They said she watched him whenever he walked across the room. He imagined that they made crude jokes about the pair of them, but these he never heard. Such thoughts plagued his dreams, fuelled by his own unrequited fantasies. Natasha Marakova and himself.

He had only once been with a woman he had not had

to pay for. Two years earlier, his twenty-eighth birthday, a tall brunette with large breasts and a brown and white dog had smiled at him across the wrought iron tables of a Leningrad park cafe. It had been nearing dusk. Andropov's hand had shaken as he lifted cup from saucer; cut through the center of the piece of stale cake. She had smoked a cigarette and petted her dog and smiled. When one of the waiters began to stand chairs upon tables and Andropov got up to leave, the woman had released the animal's lead and the animal had run straight to him, rubbing itself against his legs like some canine Pandarus, easing their meeting.

The woman: he had never known her name.

Only, in his nocturnal dreams, the woman.

She had tied the dog to low, curved railings and led him, his hand shaking, body trembling, through the thickness of bushes. On her breath was the smell of what he later came to recognize as gin. Gin and stale tobacco. Her hands found him urgently, without fumbling. The front of her dress had lifted without his awareness, her coat was spread on the ground beneath them. Inside her padded brassiere lay two shrivelled dugs, like flaccid prunes. Andropov came over her hand as she was squeezing him inside her.

All the while the dog whined.

She loves you, Natasha Marakova.

They had not made her a member of the delegation.

Seated between two of his colleagues Andropov held his memories in check. His thoughts were of Natasha. Watching sets of instruments without his presence to disturb her, returning each evening to the small flat she shared with her mother and father. Hours of silence and the samovar.

The train was slowing down. The journey across the roof of Norway from Oslo was almost over. The head of the delegation removed his spectacles, pinched fingers hard into the bridge of his peaked nose, closed his book and began to lift the blanket from his legs.

Respectfully, the other members followed suit, folding their blankets, readying the cases, setting astrakhan hats at the correct angle to withstand the weather.

There was little wind. The air, as they stepped through the broad station doors and on to the pavement, was dry and brittle so that it was possible to imagine reaching out and touching it as something tangible. Up ahead the tall, stooped figure of the party leader was talking earnestly to the conference representative who had been appointed to welcome them and the Russian security officer travelling with them.

Andropov looked around—a couple of bulky women crossing the bridge over the finger of water; a young man whistling as he cycled, a joiner's triangular bag hoisted over one shoulder; in the small green space to the left a pair of unshaven men drank from a bottle which they kept inside a brown paper bag, passing it from hand to hand. Behind him, the blurt of a whistle and the sound of a train engine pulling away from the platform.

Far to the right—yet not that far—a hill rose, deep in conifers. A single brown line shot downwards at an angle, maybe a ski slope. At the summit, crests of green, steep and dark, perforated the blue wash of the sky.

"Dimitri," one of his colleagues nudged him and he turned.

The Norwegian was moving from person to person, smiling, shaking hands. Andropov looked into the flat, gray face, eyes that seemed to want for color. A ball of skin, like a tight blob of dough, stuck to the side of the man's nose. The handshake was firm, the greeting spoken in an accent that was jarred from the perfect by a grating tone, an iron shovel being scraped over stone.

Three cars drove them through the city. Andropov looked out of the windows, wanting to lean forward and peer but the indifference—or was it tiredness?—of the other passengers prevented him. He noticed a broad crossroads, market stalls in front of the buildings which were set well back. A department store decorated in blue and red ribbon, the windows full with clothes and furniture and children's toys. He noted some of the walls were painted light pastel shades, that some of the streets were paved with wavering rectangular cobbles which glinted pinky-gray when hit by the sun.

One of his fellow scientists had lit a thin cigar and Andropov wanted to open a window, but didn't. Instead he wiped his mouth with a white handkerchief, pretending that the smoke wasn't interfering with him at all, that he was merely clearing his throat.

They seemed to have passed through the center and to be crossing another bridge, high this time, above a river. Away to the left, Andropov glimpsed a white building set alone on a hill, medieval perhaps, a fortress from the way stone walls surrounded it. Deep windows with rounded tops had been carved into the thickness of the white walls.

The car jolted on tramlines.

Andropov fell across the man next to him, flushed quickly and apologized. The car ahead was turning off the main road and coming to a halt. The upper half of the hotel was fronted by wooden planking, recently repainted reddish brown; the lower section was a stippled paint applied directly on to stone, mustard yellow. Andropov got out of the car and held the door open for the others. He observed Kaverin, the security officer, entering the hotel first, the head of the delegation starting after him, then hesitating, waiting, his breath a thin blossom on the bright air.

It was another Norwegian speaking, a similar badge fixed to the lapel of his ill-fitting coat. It was unfortunate about the room, there had been a wholly regrettable confusion concerning the numbers travelling with the delegation. Andropov listened to the pompous phrasing, a tiredness reaching up through his limbs and gradually rendering his mind numb. Through it all he gathered that the rest of the delegation had bedrooms of a reasonable size which they were sharing, two to a room, whereas he was being asked to accept a box room on the attic floor, cramped, yes, but comfortable and clean. Andropov nodded and picked up his bag. If he didn't lie down on something soon, he thought he might faint. All the strain of the journey hit him at once. He followed the man up three flights of stairs and ducked his head to enter a space which barely held a folding bed, a chair and a three-drawer chest. A window too small for a grown man to push head and shoulders through gave out on to the back of the hotel. Andropov dropped his case on the chest-of-drawers and was vaguely aware of the man still talking behind him. It was unfortunate but the bathroom was on the landing of the next floor down. Of course, every effort would be made to find alternative accommodation, but with such an important conference in town it was difficult.

Andropov lay on the narrow bed and after a short while, the man went away. It was quiet. Movements below seemed distant. In his clothes, Andropov fell asleep.

He didn't notice Sarah until the second day. His mind had lost contact with the sterile tones of the simultaneous translator; his pen had ceased to make even the briefest of notes, the backward slanting letters halting abruptly two-thirds of the way down the page. Alongside him another of the Russians was sucking peppermints.

Andropov's head dropped slowly forward and he stifled a grunt. The man next to him stopping sucking on his mint long enough to give him a disparaging look.

Andropov straightened up, leaning back against the wooden rail that ran along behind the bench seats. He rubbed at the inside corners of his eyes. "*Depolarization of the cell thus producing an excitatory post-synaptic potential''* drifted across his brain and he took up his pen and wrote the initials EPSP.

Excitation.

Natasha Marakova walks into the narrow bedroom of her parents' flat and takes off the white cotton uniform, lines and blotches of red and blue biro about the breast pocket. She reaches under the pleating of her skirt and begins to unfasten her stocking.

Excitation.

The scent of peppermint was sickly sweet, strange.

Thinking of Natasha, Andropov turns his head and sees Sarah Jarrett.

''The synthesis, release and restoration of neurotransmitters are all enzyme-dependent.''

She was sitting four rows back, left of center, leaning slightly forward. The first thing he noticed about her was the expression of rapt attention on her face. The second was her hair. A light, bleached red not quite bright enough to be ginger, it was pulled back from a short fringe across her head, the headphones crossing the central parting. A black ribbon—velvet?—was tied high at the back of her head and from that the rest of her hair hung down in a glorious ponytail. A short length of hair, oddly curled, fell down in front of the earpiece Andropov could see, resting against it. She had to be in her mid-twenties, but she looked younger, almost out of place.

He swung his head back, realizing that he had been staring and not knowing for how long. It seemed too long a time. The centers of his palms itched and the back of his throat was dry.

''An excitatory post-synaptic potential. EPSP.''

Andropov looked at her again. She didn't appear to be sitting with the rest of the American delegation, yet surely she was American? Where else would she get that look? Clean and fresh and knowing, as if she confidently expected to inherit the world. He saw now that her face was squarish, her mouth generous and lipsticked, a mellow red that neither drew attention to itself nor clashed with her hair. There were dark lines drawn around her eyes. Blue—he thought—eyes.

She wore a blue linen jacket with a faint check running through it; underneath a blue sweater, matching, not tight. A gold-colored pendant hung from her neck and balanced on the even rise and fall of her breasts.

Suddenly she was looking back at him, directly at him across the many-levelled heads. Her eyes took him frankly and the edges of her mouth widened to show amusement and surprise.

Blood pumped to Andropov's head. He licked his drying lips and fidgeted with his pen until the cap rolled from the writing surface in front of him to the floor. He twisted round and thrust a hand down to retrieve it and his head collided with the shoulder of the man alongside. Andropov jumped back and muttered an apology and kicked the pen top down to the next section of floor.

Before he had retrieved it delegates were pushing past him on their way to coffee and biscuits. Andropov shuffled forward between two ladies wearing tweed suits who maintained a highly technical conversation past his head, speaking in a mixture of Dutch and German. He took his cup and saucer from the woman beside the urn and spilt some of the coffee on to his thumb as he turned to look for the head of red hair.

"Excuse me."

Andropov half-moved, was half-barged aside, more of his coffee overlapping the rim of the cup. He could see the majority of his delegation standing in their usual circle, heads bowed. There was no sign of the security officer with them, presumably the daytime sessions were too boring for him, indecipherable junk. Andropov walked between knots of people, wondering why he wasn't more wrapped up in what was going on. After all those years of late-night study and experiments, this should be a climax of his career so far. It should . . .

"Hello."

Her eyes were blue and they didn't blink or flick away.

"I . . ." Andropov didn't know what to say.

"I'm Sarah Jarrett."

He stared at her stupidly, unmoving until he realized that she was holding out her hand.

"Oh, yes," her fingers surprised him by feeling so small. "I am, my name is . . ."

She read it off his lapel badge, "Dimitri Andropov."

"Yes," he smiled foolishly. "Yes."

She was still holding his hand.

When he realized, Andropov pulled his own away as though he had suddenly realized he was gripping something through which live current runs.

"You understand English?" she asked, lifting her cup to her mouth.

"Yes, if it is not spoken too fast. In Russia . . ." He broke off, fascinated by the lip of faintest red that was now imprinted on the white of her cup.

"What did you think of the lecture?"

"Oh, the lecture, it was, yes, most interesting."

She looked up at him quickly and he was like a small child caught out in a lie.

"You didn't think so! You were fidgeting around in your seat like some kid not out of fifth grade."

"Fifth . . . ? Sorry, I do not . . ."

"It doesn't matter." She moved closer. "You were as bored as I was."

Andropov's protest simmered then faded. His smile was uncertain, yet it was a smile. "Yes. It was not very interesting, the concept of disjunction . . ."

He realized that she was looking at his mouth.

Alarmed, he wondered if he had forgotten to shave. Thirty years of age and no one had ever told him he was an attractive man.

Sarah was pulling her program from her briefcase. "This afternoon's even worse. Dry as old tinder. It isn't until tomorrow that the real exciting stuff begins."

Andropov knew that his cheeks were as red as when they teased him about Natasha Marakova back in the laboratory. Redder. He shifted his weight from one foot to the other and then back again.

"Of course," he tried, "tomorrow is . . ."

But his memory of the program failed him. In desperation he attempted to pull one of the sheaf of papers from the back of his notebook and only succeeded in scattering them over the floor. More coffee limped into the saucer. A wedge-shaped heel pressed down on several of his papers and ground them against the floor.

Sarah bent down and with a quick and easy action, retrieved what he had lost.

Andropov thanked her, clutching the papers to his chest and stammering.

"You don't like the coffee," she said, nodding at his cup and saucer, her eyes bright and mocking.

"No, I . . ."

He was searching the crowded foyer, looking for the rest of his group and an excuse to rejoin them.

"Here." Somehow she had managed to perch her own cup somewhere and relieve him of his notebook and loose papers.

"Go on," she said, "drink it."

Without tasting it, he did so.

"That's better." She whisked away his cup also, set it on a nearby table safely.

Around them, delegates had started to move slowly away, heading back for the conference hall. Andropov turned and began to follow them. Sarah's hand tugged at the underneath of his sleeve.

"No." She spoke softly yet the word seemed to leap out at him amidst the high murmur of conversation.

"I must."

He didn't understand. He did not know what she was suggesting or why. Not to return for the questions. Andropov looked at her and realized that he was staring at the right side of her mouth, where the red of her lipstick had smudged against her cup.

"The lecture was boring," Sarah persisted. "The discussion will be worse."

"No." There was no logic to his thinking. Simply, he knew he had to return, to deny whatever she was suggesting. Behind her, Andropov saw the Soviet delegation heading towards the conference room.

Sarah stood there smiling.

"No," he said again, louder yet his voice uncertain. He shook his head agitatedly. "No."

She laughed and the sound of her laughter spun heads in their direction. Andropov panicked and started to hurry towards the doors. Sarah went after him, touching him on the shoulder just before he entered.

"I'm sorry, I have to . . ."

"Then you'll need these."

She thrust his belongings towards him at arm's length and Andropov seized his notes as a child would a comforter and almost ran back into the conference room.

He made himself wait until the sixth question before looking over his shoulder. In Sarah's place sat a thin-faced man scratching at the inside of his nostril with a propelling pencil.

From the bridge Andropov could see a dribble of schoolchildren reluctantly making their way back to the afternoon's lessons. A solitary man wearing a red knitted hat sat on a small folding seat beside his rod, waiting for the float to bob on the placid water. On the hill beyond the river, the Norwegian flag hung limply down the white flagpole, undisturbed.

For half an hour Andropov had walked, digesting his lunch of pickled fish and smoked meat and salad. He had driven his mind to think of his work. Even to think of Natasha. Anything rather than permit the image of red hair, of blue eyes, of the smudged mouth, to infiltrate their way into his thoughts.

He stood away from the parapet now and checked his

watch. The afternoon session was beginning in a little over fifteen minutes.

Good.

Andropov lowered his arm and turned decisively away. Sarah Jarrett was walking along the opposite side of the street, twenty yards from the beginning of the bridge. A trolley-bus set itself between them and Andropov wiped the palms of his hands down the sides of his trousers and decided that he had been mistaken.

Then the bus passed and she was there, a large leather bag slung over one shoulder, strolling away from the conference center as if she were just a pretty girl with all the time in the world.

Andropov started to walk back over the bridge, hesitated, considered calling out to her, waving nonchalantly, carrying on to his destination.

Waving nonchalantly! It was as much as he could do to set one leg in front of the other and maintain a straight line.

For several moments he thought that Sarah had failed to spot him and that she would carry on walking, regardless. But as he reached the end of the bridge and waited on the curb of the road junction for a car to turn by, he heard her call his name.

"Dimitri! Dimitri!"

There in the middle of that foreign city at midday, amongst office workers and schoolchildren and traffic, to hear his name called aloud by such a woman as Sarah.

Andropov's head was turned; she was hurrying across the broad street towards him, slowing down a line of cars with a raised hand. The hand so white, the hair so red. Her ponytail bobbed as she almost skipped towards him, the white of her petticoats showing under the hem of the coffee and cream dress she was now wearing.

"Where are you going?" she called to him five yards from reaching the pavement, her voice loud and catching on a breath in the break of the last word.

Andropov could only point in the direction of the conference center.

"What? Schwann cells and Myelin Sheaths! That's not your field, surely?"

"Perhaps not, only . . ."

"Anyway, it sounds sort of vulgar doesn't it? Myelin Sheaths."

Andropov didn't understand the reference, didn't know why she laughed, only that her teeth were white and even and that the laugh lines at the edges of her mouth and eyes made her appear a little older than he had first thought.

She had tight hold of his arm and was leading him back across the bridge.

"Let's go down here." Impulsively, Sarah pulled at his arm and they half-ran down the winding slope of a path that took them back towards the river.

Moments later she broke away from him and ran to the top of the bank at the left of the path. At the top she shook her head and the glorious red ponytail jiggled and spun. "Look!" she cried, pointing at something Andropov couldn't see. "There. We can walk over the old bridge, down by the harbor."

Natasha Marakova, Andropov thought as he walked after Sarah, keeping to the path, would never race up hills and shout. Natasha Marakova, dear and gentle as she was, was not fun either.

The old bridge over the Nidelven was wooden and painted brick red. Elaborate carved arches shielded the winding gear which raised the center, allowing tall vessels to pass through.

"Look!" Sarah was calling already. "Will you take a look at that. Isn't that just beautiful!"

Both sides of the river were lined by tall warehouses, their wooden walls painted orange, red, white, yellow. Window frames gleamed, company names shone out from brass plates or climbed the walls in steep lettering. Massed stilts of green and white held the buildings above the flow of the tide.

Today the water scarcely moved. Each bank was double-lined with a reflection of itself, deep colors dipping down beneath the blue, slightly blurred. Sarah slipped her arm through Andropov's and he felt her sudden, impulsive warmth, the pressure of her elbow into his side.

"Isn't that really something?"

Immediately below the bridge, all Andropov could see was Sarah's white, unfocused face, framed in red.

"Beautiful," he said. "Beautiful."

"Isn't this better than listening to some boring old Finn?"

Her blue eyes caught the brightness of the water and brimmed with delight. Andropov heard nothing that she said, seeing only the heart shaped pendant cradled between her breasts, lift and fall.

"Dimitri?"

"Yes."

"Nothing. I just wanted to say your name out loud."

Returning through the city, window shopping, she held his hand and he was surprised at how cold her fingers were, how warm—almost damp—was her palm. In a cafe patronized by middle-aged ladies wearing thick wool coats and stiff, dark hats, they drank sweet rich chocolate and Sarah asked him about his research. Listening, her eyes seemed to change, their brightness faded and for some reason Andropov expected her to take a pair of spectacles from her bag and set them on her nose. But she sat there as she was and looked serious, nodding and occasionally asking a question, from time to time stirring her chocolate with a spoon.

In the midst of one of Andropov's explanations, she darted her eyes round the room then leaned her face into his and kissed him, quickly, on the mouth. Her lower lip slipped for an instant between his. Andropov jerked away and his arm knocked against the table. Sarah saw that his eyes were wide with what she surmised as fear.

"For God's sake!" she said.

He looked at her, withdrawn, clenched in himself.

"It was only a kiss."

Andropov turned his head aside; his hands bunched into fists. As he released them a small shudder ran down his body. When he turned back to her, he was astonished to find that he was shaking.

"I'm sorry. I am not being very polite. You must think me very . . . not gracious."

Sarah tried not to laugh at the formality of his words. She looked at his strong nose, his mouth; she wondered if any woman had ever told him how appealing he was.

"Perhaps it is better that we leave now." He was already standing, hovering from one foot to the other, impatient and awkward.

Sarah finished her drink and gathered up her coat and bag. Out on the street, there were fewer people about and some of the shops seemed to be already closing. She glanced at her watch and it was a few minutes short of four.

"We must walk back," said Andropov, trying not to look at her.

"All right."

This time she did not hold his hand, his arm; only walked beside him, now and then having to hurry her steps to keep up with his lengthening stride. Back across the bridge again he slackened his pace, seeming more at ease.

"It would be best," Andropov said, "if we do not return together."

Sarah nodded. "You go ahead. I'm going back to my apartment anyway."

She moved forward quickly and lifted her arm, fingers touching him on the lapel of his coat. "It was a wonderful afternoon. Thank you."

Her hand pulled him down and her mouth brushed the side of his face and then she was hurrying across the road, almost running, the long ponytail bouncing and skipping behind her. Andropov waited until she was no more than a silhouette among silhouettes, then walked in her wake to the conference hall.

That night Andropov woke up sticky and cold with sweat, the fragmented images of his dream frozen into a tableau that was half-obscene, hardly understood.

"I did not notice you at the afternoon session yesterday, Dimitri." Olga Karenova spoke without looking at him, all of her attention directed to the task of removing pieces of shell from the boiled egg on her plate.

"No, I . . ." Andropov was stranded between a lie and an evasion.

Karenova was the deputy leader of the Soviet delegation, an Academician, Second Assistant to the Chief Psychiatrist of the USSR Ministry of Health. She had iron-gray hair tied in a bun, skin that was freckled and scaled so much in places as to resemble that of a lizard.

"Perhaps you were not well."

The sections of shell were pushed with a finger end to the opposite side of the plate from the two pieces of brown bread.

"Yes, that's right. I was not feeling very well. The food, possibly."

"You went to your bed."

Andropov hesitated too long.

"No."

She looked at him then, a quick dart of the head. He half-expected her tongue to flick out at him forked and greedy.

"No?"

Andropov shook his head. "No. My headache was too strong. Fresh air, I thought, that would do the most good."

The knife sliced away the top of the egg and a clotted stream of dark yolk managed to trickle out after it. Olga Karenova spread some on to one of the pieces of bread and bit into it. A yellow crumb fell to the tablecloth and was brushed away by her sleeve.

"Where did you walk?"
"The river. The harbor. It was most pleasant."
"And your headache?"
"It cleared. Yes, as I walked."
Karenova, her mouth full, nodded.
Andropov hastily finished his own breakfast, anxious to be away. As he was preparing to leave the table, the woman detained him.
"Would you be kind enough, Dimitri Andropov, as to fetch me another cup of coffee?"
Walking back to the table, holding her cup and saucer, he was aware of her looking at him curiously. He tried to read the expression in her eyes but failed. As he bent over the table to set down the coffee she said, almost in a whisper, "Did you meet anyone on your walk, Dimitri?"
"Anyone, Olga Karenova?" Andropov swallowed, prayed his cheeks would not flush and let him down. "Anyone?" he repeated.
"A member of the conference, perhaps. Someone else whose head needed the treatment of fresh air."
Andropov stared at the smears of yolk on her plate. He wondered if he were going to be sick. He managed to shake his head and stand straight and say, "No, Olga Karenova, I met no one."
"Of course," she replied, seeming to lose all interest in him as she spoke. "Of course, that was how it must have been. Who would you have met?"
Andropov made a hasty bow and backed away, turning awkwardly and nearly colliding with another delegate on his way back from the central breakfast table, his plate laden with fish and cheese and eggs.
Inside the conference hall, Andropov sat next to the man who sucked mints and spread his papers across the surface before him, copying the title of the lecture neatly on to his pad. Who would you have met? The question reverberated inside his head, its tone troubling, rhetorical, as though she already knew the answer. Who

would you have met? Andropov looked through the glass doors and saw Olga Karenova walking towards the hall, speaking with one of their colleagues. Just outside the door, she touched the man briefly on the forearm and turned away to talk to someone else.

It was Kaverin. Andropov's stomach turned beneath his ribs and was suddenly cold as spring water. The backs of his legs sang with fear. He was certain that at any moment the man would push open the door and walk to his seat. Questions to ask. Come with me immediately. Come now. The inside of Andropov's head swam. Karenova came through the doors alone. Behind her, Andropov observed Kaverin begin to walk away.

There was a shuffling of feet and then the chairman for the morning session was leading the first speaker up on to the platform.

Sarah settled on to a bench four rows in front of him, a quick shake of the shoulders and a toss of the head that sent her ponytail swinging. Andropov looked at her for as long as he dared and then rearranged the papers in front of him. Olga Karenova was sitting next to the leader of their group, talking to him quickly, precisely, her head bent low.

The lecture passed in a daze. Every few minutes Andropov would write a phrase, a brief note, something to pin him down to the reality of the moment, a gesture towards freeing his mind of the phantoms that chased headlong through it. They had, of course, been warned about the dangers of fraternization, about the traps foreign powers set for the unsuspecting. Any weakness which you show will be seen as a weakness in the Union of Soviet Socialist Republics. Certain countries in particular are dangerous.

The Americans. The Americans. The Americans.

Andropov's throat was dry and he began to cough.

At the coffee break he hurried out with the Russians, making sure that he stood in the middle of their circle, shielding himself within it. If Sarah came out for coffee, he failed to notice her. But back inside the main hall, she was in her seat before him, leaning backwards so that her hair started to spread out over the surface behind. Andropov fiddled with his things and as he did so, he noticed an edge of paper protruding from his pad, the writing not his own.

His breath stopped.

Around him questions had begun.

It was not until after lunch, locked in the cubicle of the toilet and with his feet flat against the inside of the door that Andropov dared to read Sarah's note.

· CHAPTER 8 ·

Sarah Jarrett waited on the seat below the Nidelven bridge for three-quarters of an hour. She had arrived early, knowing that if Andropov got there at the appointed time and saw no one he would turn and run. So she sat, her hands clasped in woollen gloves, legs cold above leather calf-length boots, shivering slightly as she sang the first two verses of the Platters' version of "Smoke Gets In Your Eyes."

After twenty minutes she knew that he was not coming, but still she sat and waited and was stared at briefly by men going home from work across the bridge. Once a woman pushing a pram stopped and spoke to her and Sarah made a face to show that she didn't understand, then looked away. The woman walked on, talking to the child in the pram instead.

A full half hour before his assignation with Sarah, Andropov had knocked on the door of the leader of the Soviet delegation and gained admittance. He had asked—humbly, of course—if he might discuss one or two aspects of the afternoon paper which had left him rather perplexed. The Russian had set down his book, removed his spectacles, pinched the bridge of his nose and invited Andropov to join him in a glass of wine.

They talked for something under two hours, by which time Andropov felt safe and the note in his inside pocket had ceased to infiltrate his heart. He had said thank-you too many times and climbed the stairs to his room, read for over an hour, written some brief notes into his pad, climbed into his fragile bed and slept.

This time he was untroubled by dreams. He woke early, head clear and his brain active. His thoughts were of the morning's lecture; he threw cold water into his face, cleaned his teeth, shaved, all of this thinking about cell structure and irrational stimulation. At breakfast he nodded at Olga Karenova, had the temerity to say a brisk and cheery good morning to his leader, even exchanged words about the weather with the security man as they made their way in opposite directions round the breakfast table. Andropov piled his plate high, chose orange juice as well as coffee and ate and drank heartily.

It was not until three minutes after ten o'clock that he thought of Sarah Jarrett.

She was not in the conference hall.

The lecture had been going a little more than half an hour and Andropov had been taking notes diligently, interested in what the speaker was saying, able to fit it in with his own research at the Serbsky Institute. Suddenly, he was aware of Sarah's absence. It hit him like a blow to the solar plexus; stronger than the presence of all the others.

Sarah was not there.

Andropov's mind flirted with little madnesses. She had stayed all night on the bench waiting for him and had fallen asleep, waking too late to come to the lecture. She had been attacked. The police had arrested her for vagrancy, for prostitution. She had caught cold and been taken ill, even now she was in hospital in a state of fever, calling aloud his name.

At lunchtime his eyes scanned everywhere for her. He hurried from the building after bolting down his food, almost ran to the bridge, terrified that he would see her crumpled form on the grass, her body frozen to the seat.

There was no one.

Neither did she appear all through the afternoon. At dinner, several of the Russians commented on Andropov's abstracted air.

"What do you expect?" asked one of them. "He's missing his little Natasha."

Even Olga Karenova laughed at Andropov's obvious embarrassment. As soon as he could, Dimitri excused himself from the table. In his room at the top of the hotel he looked through the window and tried to quell the feeling that threatened to overpower him. What did it matter? A woman you hardly know. A girl. An American girl. One afternoon you spend with her. One kiss on your mouth and a cup of chocolate shared. Three days ago you never knew she existed and now you don't see her for a day and you behave like a child whose most precious toy has been taken away.

A child—that's what they all think of you, isn't it? Even the American, even Sarah. Little Dimitri. Little Dimitri and his nice little Natasha. Natasha fetching him tea and not daring to smile at him to his face and all the while collecting hopes of him like keepsakes and pasting them in some imaginary album of the soul.

Little soulmates!

Andropov felt sick.

He drank a glass of water from the tap on the next landing and it tasted of rust. Even as he was taking his top coat from the hook behind the door, he told himself that he wasn't going to look for her. How could he? He had no idea where she was staying, where she would be. Simply a stroll across the bridge. A walk to digest his meal, keep his head clear for the reading he intended to do when he returned. He half-realized that he was forming excuses already for the questionings of Olga Karenova the next morning. The sky was beginning to darken, to close in. On the hill away to the right, the white building was little more than a blur. The river was a dark, curving line that never wavered.

The woman sitting on the bench alongside it was Sarah Jarrett.

She looked up at him, surprised, her mouth parting.

Andropov was not surprised. He stood before her, hands thrust down into his pockets, waiting for her to speak.

"What are you doing here?" she said eventually. Her voice betrayed no pleasure at seeing him.

"Your note . . ." he began.

"That was yesterday."

"When you didn't come . . ."

"I came. You were the one who didn't arrive."

"I meant today. At the conference."

Sarah looked past him at the sullen water. "I'm surprised you noticed," she lied.

"I was worried, I thought maybe something had happened."

She raised an eyebrow. "Happened?" She gave a strange little laugh. " Nothing has happened."

"But yesterday. Last evening."

"Nothing happened. I sat on this seat for nearly an hour and got very cold and then I went and found some of my colleagues and drank too much whisky."

"Then today . . ."

Sarah nodded. "Today I was sick. I hope you're satisfied."

"No. No. That you are not well. I am sorry."

She thought how stupid he looked standing in front of her. Stupid and hopeless. She wondered why she had ever fancied him, why she had ever bothered.

"For God's sake," she said, "stop standing there as if you're about to run off, and sit down."

He unwittingly touched her arm with his and when she looked at him she saw his mouth and recognized why she had acted as she had. Her hand closed over his.

"I'm sorry. I didn't mean to be irritable. I'm glad you came." She laughed and this time it was a more pleasant sound. "Even if it is twenty-four hours late."

Sarah looked about her before taking hold of the front of Andropov's coat. He barely had time to move his face towards hers before she was kissing him, not gently this time, but hard and long, the fingers of her other hand pushing up into his hair. She twisted her head sideways, pressing her lips against his and always moving them, increasing the pressure.

Andropov broke away and stood up, looking away from her. She touched the back of his neck and with a cry that caught in his throat he turned to her and his arms were a flurry about her. Her face lifted to him, kissing the front of his neck above his collar, pushing against his cheek, his ears, the top of his head. Sarah was on tiptoe, her arms wound about his neck, feeling the Russian's body shake against her. She sensed power and vulnerability at the same instant. She murmured his name; led him by the hand.

They leaned together underneath the bridge and her tongue slithered into his mouth and Andropov gasped.

Further along the path she took his hand and set it to her breast.

He thought she was seeking only darkness, but it was more.

"Come with me."

"Where?" Not understanding.

"To my apartment."

"What?" Not wishing to understand.

"My apartment, silly." She ruffled his hair and tickled his ear with the tip of her finger.

"We cannot."

"It's safe. You'll see."

"No."

She could feel his fear, there in the half-light. Feel it even though they were no longer touching.

"They will find out," he said.

She shook her head; for her there was no concept of "they." "We aren't in a hotel. It's an apartment block. Separate rooms. Stairs and an elevator. Even a rear entrance." She touched her hand lightly to his mouth. "No one will see us."

He was rigid with fear.

Sarah took his hands again, both of them, and there on the river path she placed them beneath the mohair sweater and lifted them until they covered her breasts. Andropov felt the lightness of cotton, the thin tautness of wire, soft swell of the flesh above. Lift and fall. One of her nipples peaked into the palm of his hand.

Andropov was weak against her, his terror melted by wanting her.

Quickly she drew his hands away and, clutching one of them, she hurried him back on to the road, past the shadow of the conference center. Only buses passed them now, lights shedding yellowy-whiteness fleetingly across pavement and wall as they went noisily past. Sarah pressed her head against Andropov's arm, half-expecting him at every step to pull away and run.

They turned off the road in front of the trolley-bus depot. Andropov read the name on the wall: Elgester Gate. In that light the outside of the apartment block seemed dark green, perhaps brown. Here and there windows scattered haphazardly over the flat front wall were illumined by electric light. They hurried to the back and entered by a door that was heavy and stiff. Ignoring the lift, they took the stairs to the second floor.

Sarah fumbled the key into the lock and pushed him through the door ahead of her. She pulled him backwards and closed the door with her foot, embracing him at the same time. A vein was vibrating at the side of Andropov's head.

"Wait here," Sarah said, and left him in the small hallway while she closed the curtains.

She made him instant coffee without milk, offering him biscuits which he declined to eat. Sarah sat with her legs pulled up beneath her, wide skirt spread over the edge of the armchair. Her belt was buckled tight and held her waist in hard, dragging the material of her sweater down over her breasts. Andropov remembered touching them and tried not to stare; she was wearing the gold pendant still. He wondered if it had been given to her by a sweetheart back home in the United States. Another Natasha.

"Come here."

He knelt in front of her and she stroked his hair and kissed his cheek and the point of his nose, the slight cleft in his chin.

"Kirk Douglas," she said, smiling.

Andropov looked at her, uncomprehending.

Sarah bent over him and kissed his mouth, her tongue pushing against his teeth, wriggling inside him, its tip making patterns on his flesh. He was embarrassed at growing hard, too confused to attempt to disguise it, the bulge that even his loose-fitting trousers could not deny. She saw and smiled and eased him away so that she could get off the chair.

"All right," she said.

The bedroom was painted pink and there was a painting of flowers above the bed. Sarah took off his jacket, loosened his tie and unbuttoned the first three buttons of his shirt. She smoothed her hand over the dark hairs at the top of his chest.

"Don't look," she said, almost giggling. Despite the tiny lines etched on her face, Andropov thought she looked younger than ever.

Don't look—but she obviously didn't care.

Sarah unfastened her belt and let it drop to the floor. She pulled the mohair sweater over her head in one fluid movement and before Andropov had stopped staring at her brassiere, she had hooked her thumbs into the waistband of her skirt and it was spinning down round her feet. She stepped smartly out of it and was standing there facing Andropov in bra and pale blue pants, a matching suspender belt, honeyed stockings.

Andropov didn't know whether to turn away or stare. He coughed, went red, gestured with his hands, gazed at the thickly painted yellow flowers above the green counterpane.

"Dimitri."

Only when he was in nothing other than his underpants, did Sarah unfasten her suspenders and slowly—slowly as though she were enjoying the sensual pleasure of it: a pleasure magnified by his watching—unroll her stockings. She pulled the covers over them and wriggled out of the rest of her clothes. Andropov's hands were cold and uncertain. When she slid one of her legs over him he closed his eyes and threw back his head. Sarah laughed and bit at his nipple with her white teeth. He held her face and traced every contour with his eyes. Again, she put his palms to her breasts and rolled above him. As he felt her, Sarah leaned her body back in an arc and sought him behind her. A smile flooded her face and Andropov caught his breath and once more he closed his eyes.

She slid down him, kissing him, licking his belly as he toyed with her hair.

Later, as she straddled him again, she shook her hair out and it fell forward, covering her breasts almost from his sight.

"Sarah." Her name sounded strange on his lips and she laughed, the sound too loud in the quietness of the room.

She held him and lifted herself up on her knees, sliding down over him so that she encompassed him immediately. Her fingers teased his nipples, mouth, throat, his hair. She rocked above him and he tried to keep himself back but it was useless and he came, crying out, as she arched away from him, strands of red hair trailing to his thighs.

Later he cradled against her as she lay on her back and smoked a cigarette and outside the trolley-buses clanked into the semi-circle of turning track.

Andropov didn't know how long he had slept. Waking, momentarily uncertain of where he was or why, his upward jolt of the bed stirred Sarah and her yawning arm claimed him and led him back down. He was already hard and she took him half-awake and this time Andropov controlled himself—thought he did, though it was more likely her instinctual response—until Sarah came.

She fell away almost at once and Andropov lay there with lines of red hair stickily across his mouth and neck. For hours, so it seemed, he listened to the metallic coupling of buses, the hiss of doors.

"Dimitri." Her whispered voice, urgent, broke him from the cocoon of helplessness. "Dimitri, you ought to leave."

He dressed hastily while Sarah made him coffee that was too hot to drink. Panic made his socks too tight, his buttons too large, his shoes too small. Sarah pulled his top coat about him, fastened it, kissed him on the corner of the mouth as he stumbled towards the door.

"Tomorrow," she said quietly. "You'll come again tomorrow. "Meet me on the bench. The same time."

In the dim light of the landing, Sarah's hair looked darker, her face was shrouded in shadow. It was not till much later that Andropov would regret that this parting was so messy, clumsy; they had not lingered and kissed or talked of love. He found his own way down the stairs, guiding his steps with a hand sweeping the cold wall. Already he knew that he would not go to the bench beside the river the next evening and that if he did she would not be there.

For the remaining two days of the conference, Andropov studied hard, wrote copious notes which he transferred each evening on to neat cards and filed alphabetically. At mealtimes he studiously sought the company of the other members of his delegation, dreading the moment when the security officer's hand would descend upon his shoulder, or he would look up, turn a corner and there would be Sarah, facing him. He was uncertain which of these encounters he feared most.

Neither occurred.

On the final morning, as he prepared to board the

Oslo train, Andropov's eyes checked the platform, wondering if by any chance Sarah might be there. One last glimpse of that head of red hair. The carriage door slammed behind him and he took his seat next to Olga Karenova and immediately pulled a book from his case. He had no way of knowing that Sarah had got as far as the station entrance, prompted by some last minute feeling of regret. It had not been strong enough to make her walk through the barrier and out on to the crowded platform. She had considered going into the cafeteria and ordering coffee, deciding against it, lingering instead in front of the bookstall, leafing through month-old copies of *Life* and *Time*. Soon, she knew, the whistle would sound and release her from whatever shreds of responsibility she dimly felt.

As it shrilled, she turned on her heel and it was then that the two men came towards her. They walked steadily, approaching from different parts of the station foyer, angling towards her. Light gray suits, white shirts and plain ties; their hair was fair and cut short, almost a crew cut. One of them wore glasses with a tortoiseshell frame and he removed these before he spoke.

"Miss Jarrett."

Sarah staggered slightly, one part of her mind trying to place the accent, some part of the mid-west. She nodded, said something without knowing what it was.

"Let's have some coffee, Miss Jarrett."

The other man reached out and held her arm.

· CHAPTER 9 ·

3 NOVEMBER 1962

Dearest Sarah,

If only you knew how much your letters mean to me. However brief, however infrequent, they breathe life into me as I read them. Especially now, this is so. The weather here is cold and drab. There is snow on the ground and more in the sky. Walking round the park earlier, letting your words run through my mind, my fingers were chill to the point of numbness and the air was damp with mist and a faint drizzle of rain. But, my darling Sarah, the thought of you warmed my heart as nothing else ever can. I returned to my desk and set my new paper aside in order to write back to you while your words were still fresh and new.

How can it be so long since I saw you and yet your face is so clear and beautiful to me? All I need to do to summon it is close my eyes.

My research seems to have reached a stalemate and for the past month or so, little has gone right. How cruel it would be if after all this time, any real breakthrough were to elude me. I only hope that your own work is progressing as well as when you last wrote of it. Perhaps it will be written up in one of the journals which the Institute subscribes to? I long to read of it in detail—the excitement of seeing your name there in print!

I overheard the Chief Psychiatric Specialist here talking the other week and from what he said, it seems that certain personnel might be transferred to one or other of the psychiatric hospitals for short periods. There were no names mentioned within my hearing and I hope that if it comes about, I will be omitted from the list. To be forced to leave my work at this stage would be unthinkable.

Keep well, my beloved, and know that all my loving thoughts are for you.

As ever, your Dimitri.

17 June 1964

My dearest Sarah,

Forgive me speaking of myself immediately, but this morning's news threatened to drive even the pleasure of your long-awaited letter from my mind. As I told you before, I had hoped that the three months I spent attached to the staff of the hospital at Kaluga would be all that was expected of me. Now I find I have been posted to Leningrad for an indefinite period.

I pointed out to the Director that it was more than a matter of personal preference and that I had reached a stage in my research that was truly vital. He was very understanding, he is, in fact, a charming man in his own way, but there was nothing that he could do.

So from next week I shall be in Leningrad and I have no idea for how long. More than anything else I shall feel deprived of your letters. I shall not be able to write to you and that is like depriving me of air. Sarah, my darling, think of me as I think of you and cling to the hope that one day, somehow, we shall be once again together.

Your own, as ever, Dimitri.

28 January 1968

Darling Sarah,

Your words were cruel. Of course I want our relationship to continue. It is the only thing which keeps me working, the only true reason for living. You must understand what I meant when I said I would rather end our correspondence than go through a lengthy period of not hearing from you. I was only trying to convey the desperation I feel when months pass without a letter, without anything. But you must know, deep in your heart, that the knowledge that I would never hear from you again would be unbearable. Without that, without the slightest chance that one day we will meet and touch, my life would be pointless. It would be over.

I love you with all my soul,
Dimitri

9 September 1969

My dearest Sarah,

Even your letter failed to cheer me. I have been ill for several weeks with pneumonia and confined to my bed as I was, I could not help but review what a miserable failure my life has been. Next year I shall be forty! Forty years of age with only one significant piece of research published. Articles and papers enough, but piecemeal work, nothing of substance. All those years seemed to have passed in a maze of experiments and tabulations and filing cards leaving me dry and useless on the other side.

I am forty years old nearly and I have loved one woman in all my life and that for one night. Not even so long. I have not married and now I never will. I have no children. Sarah, if only I had a son! Someone to live on after me, someone of my blood, who I could make proud of me as a son should be of a father. Instead what has there been? A succession of secret letters posted in secret places and delivered by how many strange hands.

Sarah, I do not think I can go on, not in the same way. Please do not reply to this letter. It is best that we say nothing more to each other. I no longer feel I have the spirit, the energy to love anyone, especially someone as dear and as beautiful as you.

Goodbye, your loving Dimitri.

The motel was off the Boston Turnpike and to reach it Sarah had had to drive through the center of the city, her five-year-old Ford getting clogged in the traffic for interminable stretches of time. She had fiddled with the radio and cursed as it dipped from station to station and was ploughed under by static. Angrily, she switched it off and lit another cigarette, glancing at yesterday's copy of the *Globe* on the seat next to her. "Calley" leapt out at her from the headlines: "Lieutenant William Calley charged with the responsibility for the massacre of . . ."

The car ahead of her lurched forward a few yards and Sarah swerved clumsily, frowning at her own ineptness, stubbing out her cigarette and already wanting another. Her hair was long and straight, the red darker for having recently been hennaed. There was only a touch of lipstick on her mouth, make-up on the rest of her face lightly applied so that the age lines clearly showed. She was wearing a panelled print skirt; a green blouse with a few scraps of token embroidery which were supposed to be ethnic. Ethnic what, Sarah didn't know. The sleeve of the white linen jacket she had taken from the wardrobe was smudged with paint and she supposed she should have put it back and chosen something else, but even then she had been running short of time.

Cabin fourteen was at the end of a line, a black Pontiac with Virginia plates parked at an acute angle outside. Sarah drew up alongside, checked her face in the rear-view mirror, slipped her bag over her shoulder and got out. The door opened before she could knock.

Turner she recognized. She supposed that wasn't his real name but that was what she had always called him; he was already back by the low table, fixing her a drink. The second man—there always had to be a second man—was new. A young black, with an uplifted nose and eyes that seemed too large for his face, leaning back against the wall close to the back windows and watching her.

"Vodka and tonic," said Turner, handing her the glass.

"Thanks."

She drank half of it immediately, then toyed with the stem of the glass as she waited for the men to begin.

"Won't you sit down, Mrs. Radcliff?" This from the newcomer.

"Sit down, Sarah," said Turner. "Tell us what's on your mind."

She pulled a padded seat out from the dressing-table and sat there, one leg crossed over the other. She set down her drink, opened her bag and took out a packet of cigarettes. The men watched her light one, draw on it, slip packet and lighter back into her bag.

Sarah let her head fall back as she blew smoke towards the ceiling.

"Mrs. Radcliff?"

The stranger was still standing, his back no longer touching the wall: Turner was sitting on the corner of the bed.

"It's this last letter."

They continued to look at her, their expressions giving away nothing.

"You've seen it?"

"Naturally."

"Well, then you see . . ."

"I'm afraid . . ."

"It's so damned difficult." Sarah stood up, reached for her drink, her hand far from steady. "I just don't know what to do."

"What to do?" echoed the man by the wall.

"That's what I said," Sarah snapped.

"Now, Sarah," said the man she knew as Turner, "it was you who requested this meeting. We're simply trying to establish which area it is that's bothering you."

"Jesus!" the word hissed between Sarah's lips as she sat back down.

"You want another drink?" asked Turner.

Sarah tossed her head. "Sure. Why not? It all comes out of my taxes, doesn't it?"

Turner nodded towards the black, who walked over and took Sarah's glass and refilled it. When he handed it back to her, she was conscious of him looking at her breasts beneath the green blouse. Instinctively, she tugged at the front of her lined jacket.

"I don't know how to answer," she said after a few moments.

Turner gestured vaguely with his hands. "There shouldn't be any need to stray from the agreed pattern, unless . . ."

"Damn it, you said you'd read the letter!"

"Mrs. Radcliff, take it easy."

"Take it easy!" Sarah scoffed, stubbing out her cigarette angrily.

"Reassure him, Sarah, tell him you understand what he's feeling. That you've experienced time when you've felt much the same yourself. Point out to him that he's wrong to say he has no one. Tell him he's got you."

The second man stopped looking at Sarah's legs and said, "Try and make him see how empty your life would be without him, without his letters. Give him the old malarky about how you're sure it'll become possible for you to be with each other again."

"Just convince him you've still got each other, Sarah, that's all you've got to do."

Sarah began coughing and that evoked tears for some fool reason she was unsure of. At first she imagined she was crying for that poor, dumb scientist she'd fancied taking to her bed in a strange city all those years ago.

But as she dried her eyes on a handful of Kleenex she thought maybe she was only crying for herself. Crying for herself on account of she felt like a whore. Being looked over by two gray-suited pimps who were selling her body—more than her body—to another man two continents distant. And selling herself was what she was doing, what she had been doing for the past ten years. A regular chek, too small to raise eyebrows, paid into her account—interest on the legacy invested for her by the executors of her late uncle's estate.

Whore!

Sarah renewed her lipstick and blinked the word from her mind.

"There is one possibility," began the stranger, glancing over at Turner as if for permission.

"Yes," Turner continued for him, leaning forward on the bed, hands clasped in front of him, elbows on his knees, "you could tell him about the boy."

Sarah reached for the sides of the stool; her head was starting to swim. She'd drunk that damned vodka too quickly. It was always the same, drinking in the late afternoon.

"This might be the time," said the wide-eyed man, leaning back now against the wall.

"It'll be the hook," said Turner. "The thing that'll hold him, whatever else."

"After all, it's what he's crying out for, isn't it, a son?"

Turner nodded, tapping the ends of his fingers together. "So, Sarah, you give him his son."

"No!"

"Mrs. Radcliff, circumstances . . ."

"No!"

"Sarah." Turner got up from the bed, shot his black colleague a glance that told him to keep quiet, set both hands on Sarah's shoulders. Not ungently. "Sarah, it's what he wants. What he needs, you know that. You read his letter, the things he was saying. How much a son is missing from his life." He was stroking her shoulders now, his fingers reaching the bare skin at the back of her neck. "Sarah, you can give him that son. Just by putting pen to paper you can do that."

Her head began to shake sideways and for an instant Turner's hands were stilled, their pressure sudden but marked.

"You can!"

Sarah's eyes closed; her head drooped forward. "After all this time."

"Explain it to him. Tell him that up until now you thought it cruel to let him know. Better that he should be ignorant. But now, now that you've realized his need is so great, his fears so strong. Well, isn't it the least you can do?"

Turner released his hands and stepped back.

"The least you can do," repeated the man by the wall.

Turner didn't thank him for it. He stood where he was until Sarah's head had come up and then he gave her a smile and asked her if she wanted another drink. And when she said no but took a cigarette from her bag he lit it for her and let her have another of his smiles. When she thought about the meeting later, Sarah realized that in all those years it was the first time she had seen him smile. She knew then how important it was to him that she did as she was told.

"You'll be okay?" Turner asked as Sarah stood by the cabin door.

She nodded, too exhausted to speak.

"You drive safely now."

She sat behind the wheel of her car for fully ten minutes before turning the key in the ignition and backing out of the lot. The traffic would have built up even more now that she was trying to reach home.

Andropov came out of the Metro and walked across Dzerzkinsky Square, the letter so heavy in his jacket pocket that he was certain it must be weighing him down. Surely people could tell from the way he moved the magnitude of what he was carrying? He had read it walking across Gorki Park, pigeons wandering the bare expanse of grass. In the distance the iron wheels of the amusement area were rimed with frost. He re-read the letter on the subway, jostled by workers, shoppers, a smattering of visitors.

Richard . . . Richard . . .

The name came rushing into his ears like the sea.

Richard Jarrett. Richard Andropov. He did not know Richard Radcliff. Her marriage in 1963, another of the little details Sarah had neglected to mention.

But Richard—and she said she called him Rick. Ricky sometimes. She said he was strong and wiry, tall for his age. For his age: he was almost ten. Andropov walked through the nearest door to the ground floor of GUM and at once he was lost in a crowd of people, white, wide faces, fur hats and scarves, a domination of black.

Ricky's hair was black, Sarah had said, black and fine. He was a handsome boy with a mouth just like his father's. A woman in a headscarf barged into Andropov's back and apologized loudly before joining the end of a long queue. He nodded and went towards the stairs, climbing past the first gallery to the second and losing some of the mass of shoppers on the way. The sky was heavy gray through the vaulted glass roof. Andropov fingered a boiled sweet from his pocket and put it in his mouth as he slowly walked.

"You will love him when you see him, Dimitri. Every time I hold him in my arms he reminds me of his father. He reminds me of you."

Snow had begun to fall, softly, on to the curve of glass above his head.

"Every time I hold him . . ."

Andropov was standing in front of a window sparsely filled with children's toys: yellow and blue balls and red and yellow plastic fire engines, curly-headed dolls with bright staring eyes. Suspended from candy-striped hoops, two monkeys, brown and orange, hung in grotesque embrace. He had never seen his child. For ten years he had not even been a footnote to letters, he had not even existed. Andropov had never sent him anything to hold, cling to, build or cast aside unwanted. In his mind a picture formed. Between two trees, the grass still a little damp from dew, a man bends to retrieve a ball then rolls it down the sloping ground towards a boy who runs at it and kicks it with a small shout of pleasure. He does not know the child's face even from photographs, only Sarah's words. The man's face should be his own, but who has seen his own face clearly in a dream?

Two women, bulky, their coats belted tightly across, pause and stare at the man who is leaning against the front of the window, forehead touching, eyes closed, breath smearing the glass.

· CHAPTER 10 ·

It was 1978, the radio was playing "Baby Stop Crying" and Dylan seemed to have got third wind. Malone turned left on to 95. He had pulled into the South Shore Shopping Plaza outside of Braintree and bought a tuna melt and a Coke. Now the sandwich was laying heavily on his stomach and all that remained of the drink were pebbles of crushed ice at the bottom of the carton.

For late fall it was warm. The trees back from the highway were mostly free of leaves and brown and gold heaps were piled at the sides of the road like drifts of colored snow.

It was almost enough to quell Malone's anger—anger with himself. Disillusion and regret. He had spent an hour being hauled over the coals and the worst thing about it had been knowing that his superiors were right and he was wrong. Malone's bleached-out eyes flicked blue across an intersection as it flashed by. He released his foot on the gas, knowing he was driving too fast. His fingers loosened on the wheel and he arched his head backwards. There hadn't been enough in Malone's life to prepare him for failure. The faces of the men at the Agency's headquarters at Langley hovered into his mind.

"We're sure you appreciate the seriousness . . ."

"Some bastard in the Kremlin . . ."

"Steven, the issue at stake here is one of credibility . . ."

"What we're saying is, everybody's allowed to foul up the once."

It had been a Thursday morning and Malone had been shadowing a Czech professor whose visit to England was due to finish within two days. The professor had let it become known—but not widely—that a change in those travel arrangements would not be unwelcome. Negotiations were underway. The CIA and MI5 together were responsible for keeping an eye on the Czech to ensure that nothing frightened him into changing his mind. It wasn't really Malone's affair, certainly not his file. But men with field experience of the right kind were low on the ground and so he was drafted in.

Malone had taken the change within sight of King's College Chapel, drifted two sides of the outdoor market and finally lodged himself in the A-B literature alcove in Heffer's bookshop. His man spent almost an hour, peering at titles with his head so steeply angled to one side that it seemed his spectacles must topple from his pallid face. Every now and then he would pluck a book free and lean sideways against the shelves while his fingers pushed the pages back and forth.

Malone's eyes fixed at a point on one of the alcove shelves, read with a jolt the lettering along the spine:

Malone Dies.

Malone took the slim paperback down. From the center of a black-framed cover the sketch of a skull stared eyeless off a gray field.

Samuel Beckett: *Malone Dies*.

He copied his quarry, Malone, reading a sentence here, a paragraph there.

This tangle of gray bodies is they. Silent, dim, perhaps clinging to one another, their heads buried in their cloaks, they lie together in a heap, in the night. They are far out in the bay. Lemuel has shipped his oars, the oars trail in the water. The night is strewn with absurd . . .

Malone closed the book but the image persisted—this tangle of gray bodies . . . Watching the professor lift his bundle of purchases towards the cash desk with difficulty, Malone followed with his single, slim novel held between the fingers and thumb of his left hand.

Turning left out of Trumpington Street less than three minutes later, Malone lost him. Suddenly, simply, the Czech was no longer there. Instead there was a delivery van, black and maroon with gold lettering spidering the sides; two cars pulling round it but at no great speed, both seemingly full. A narrow alleyway which angled to the right and then cut back sharply towards the main road.

Within the hour, the professor had been bundled into a plane amidst a covey of diplomats and flown back behind the Iron Curtain. Before that day was out, Malone underwent a number of intensive and awkward interviews, the first with a bald and perspiring section head of MI5 and an inspector from the Special Branch. Next a gruelling session with two Agency operatives in Room 388 of the American Embassy in London. The final debriefing was carried out down the corridor by the Chief of the Political Liaison Section himself, the Head of the CIA section in London.

The next morning the cable had come through from Langley, bringing Malone's recall. A room in which natural light never shone and the temperature never varied. A room in which every hesitation of the heart, every cough and shuffle and each faltering of breath were picked up and recorded and stored.

A room of grey men.

"What we're saying is, everybody's allowed to foul up once."

Malone checked his rear-view mirror and indicated that he was pulling in, slowing and stopping by the side of the road. The car tires shushed through leaves, brown and curling. He had a friend he played tennis with whenever he was in Paris, a good player, outside

Malone's normal range. When he'd been back in the US, he'd played qualifiers for the tournaments, picked up a wild card or two. Malone had gone to watch him one time and seen his friend go down one and love in less than twenty-five minutes.

"How do you start to handle that?" Malone had asked him, quite a while later.

He could remember the answer clearly. "You do two things. You forget all about it and you live with it etched inside your brain. The same as every time you lose a point, you forget you've lost it and you keep why you lost it clear as diamond. You tell yourself you're never going to lose a point again."

That, Malone decided, sitting there on the side of Highway 95, was what you did. You told yourself you were never going to lose again, not another point, another game, not another man. While he was in the States and as long as there had been a margin of time, he had opted to move on the Andropov file himself. Besides, there had been sentimental reasons enough for stopping off in Boston.

Earlier that day he had walked across Harvard Square and the earth had been soft underfoot, sunlight had broken down the ivy covered walls. He had browsed in a couple of bookstores and tried to shake the memory of what had happened in England from his mind. Finally he had treated himself to coffee and a croissant, pleased to be able to sit with that morning's edition of the *Globe* and the sight of two female music students talking their way excitedly through a Charles Ives score.

Now he was on his way to see Sarah Jarrett.

Malone looked over his shoulder and waited as a truck rumbled past. He pulled out and drove in its wake, letting the features of the Andropov file filter down through his mind. Andropov and Sarah. Closing out everything else—anger, annoyance, everything. In ten miles, he hung a left on to 27 and the houses began to thicken. He was drawing into the suburb of Sharon.

She wasn't Sarah Jarrett any more. Only to Andropov

and—in part because he saw her as the Russian did—to Malone. The Radcliff house was a large wood-frame building off the side road. The sloping lawn needed cutting. Around it were low bare bushes and a hump-backed tree against the trunk of which a russet-colored cat with fluffy hair tested its claws. When Malone turned his car into the drive, the cat tensed and then ran up the stunted tree and perched across the hump.

There were lace curtains at the front windows, a water hose slackly coiled on the edge of the porch. The green paint of the front door needed attention. Malone shut the car door and sensed rather than saw the movement back of the left-side window. Instinctively, he unbuttoned the front of his light gray jacket with his right hand.

Sarah answered the door almost as soon as Malone's finger had released its pressure from the bell push.

"Yes?" The voice was sharp, edged. The door was open no more than necessary for Sarah to look out and speak.

"Mrs. Radcliff?"

"Yes."

"My name is Malone. I'd like to talk to you, if I may."

"You'd like to sell me something?"

Malone shook his head and she looked at him properly for perhaps the first time. She noticed the color of his eyes and the way they didn't let her go, the signs of strain on the otherwise blandly handsome face. She guessed him to be six or so years her junior, sensed that under his off-the-rack suit he had a body that was in no way slack or loose.

"You're not selling anything?"

"No, ma'am."

Sarah opened the door a little wider. She was wearing a fawn cardigan over a white sweater, faded denim jeans with bottoms and grubby white sneakers.

"We have a mutual friend," said Malone. "Two mutual friends."

Sarah put her head to one side and automatically picked at a strand of red hair that fell out of its grip. She parted her lips slightly and pushed her teeth together as she slid the hair back into place.

"I think you know a Mr. Turner," said Malone, anxious to be inside now, thinking that if he stayed there on the porch much longer the neighbors would not shrug and figure he was an old family friend who'd just dropped in to pass an hour and drink instant coffee.

"Turner?" Sarah's eyes, a brighter blue than Malone's but beginning to lose their shine, widened.

"He's an associate," said Malone, his tone trying to reassure her.

Sarah still hesitated. Behind her, Malone could see a Hoover leaning against the white staircase, a yellow duster draped over the bannister end.

"The other friend we have in common," said Malone, "comes from further away. A long way off. He's, let's say, our Russian friend."

Sarah was aware of weakness flooding her stomach. Her bladder ached; for an instant she thought she might be going to wet herself. There, in front of him, this man she didn't know but whose light gray suit she should have recognized. This—what was it?—Malone.

As soon as he stepped inside, Sarah shut the door behind him and ushered him through into the lounge. She didn't seem to have got that far in her cleaning. Dust lined the surfaces and several half-filled ashtrays gave off a smell like stale, gray sweat. The photograph of a serious-looking teenager wearing a lettered sweat shirt dominated the mantelpiece.

"Is that Ricky?" asked Malone pointing.

"Who are you?" Fear and anger were mixed in her voice.

"He's grown into a fine-looking young man."

"I said who are you?" Sarah's voice was marginally below a shout.

Malone set the picture down and turned back towards

her. "Malone," he said. "Steven Malone. You don't need to know anything else."

Sarah went across the room and took a cigarette from a silver-colored box, lighting it with a gas lighter. Neither of her hands was steady. Malone thought how much she'd aged since the last shot he'd seen of her; how her waist and hips had thickened. He stared as she blew smoke towards the ceiling and saw that no matter how she'd changed she was still an attractive woman. There was something about her that reeked to him of sex.

Sarah sat down on a hessian-covered chair and ran her tongue across the underside of her top lip. "What happened to Turner?" she asked, looking at a stain on the carpet.

"Nothing happened. I wanted to meet you myself."

She shot him a glance and he tried a smile which broke against her distrust.

"Dimitri," Malone explained, "he's my responsibility."

"Responsibility?"

"I keep a watch of his file."

"And mine?"

Malone nodded. "In so far as it concerns him."

Sarah stood up. "D'you want a drink?"

"You mean coffee?"

"No."

Sarah was looking towards the liquor bottles standing on a trolley at the far side of the room.

"I'd enjoy a cup of coffee," Malone said.

"You wouldn't. It's cheap and awful."

He shrugged and Sarah poured herself a shot of gin, wiping the rim of the glass with her fingers first. He watched to see if she were going to dilute it with tonic, but she brought it back to her chair as it was.

"Don't worry, Mr. Malone," she said with the beginnings of a wry smile, "I'm not the alcoholic in the family."

Malone assured her he wasn't worried and thought about the remark. He presumed Richard wasn't the alcoholic either.

"So what do you want?" Sarah asked a few moments later. "What exciting news have you got of my beloved Dimitri? My long lost love from across the sea."

"There is some news," answered Malone, "but it didn't come in a letter."

Sarah looked at him through a wreath of smoke and waited.

"It seems Dimitri's time spent working in psychiatric prison hospitals has not passed unrewarded."

"What do you mean?"

"He has been permanently assigned to assist the KGB."

"The . . . ?"

"The Soviet security force."

"Dimitri!" Sarah laughed. "That's ridiculous!"

"Apparently not."

"A spy?"

"Not that. But they'd find use enough for him in other areas. Memory—assembling it and taking it apart—isn't that one of his main fields?"

Sarah nodded her head, stubbed her cigarette into the ashtray, grinding it down in the other butts and the accumulation of ash. She made a face at the glass of gin as though it were sour. Another strand of hair fell loose and this time she left it. She looked, Malone thought, the way disappointed women who've passed forty are supposed to look.

"What does all this have to do with me?"

"It means Dimitri is more important to the Soviets. It also means that he'll come in contact with information which may be useful."

Sarah sat back. "And you want me to ask him for it," she sneered. "Love letters full of nice juicy secrets."

"No." Malone sat forward on his chair, hands clenched

over his knees. Sarah was thinking how muscular his legs would be beneath the neat gray of his trousers. "Nothing as crude as that."

"What then?" She drank some more gin. Considered lighting another cigarette but decided against it.

Malone opened his hands wide, keeping the fingers interlocked. "We'd like you to plant the idea of defection."

Sarah let the implications of the word seep in. When they had she slammed her glass down on a low table and stood up, shaking her head. "Jesus Christ! What do you take me for? What do you take him for? Darling Dimitri, after all this time I've decided I can't live without you. Pack your bags tonight and climb over the Berlin Wall tomorrow. If you don't get shot to pieces this nice Mr. Malone will smuggle you over to America. P.S. Don't forget to bring lots of secrets with you."

Sarah folded her arms across her chest and swung away from him, her cheeks flushed and the blood racing through her. Malone stood behind her, close enough to get the scent of her body. He touched her on the top of the arm and she jumped beneath his fingers.

"We're not about to throw away seventeen years of patient work by being hasty or stupid. Above all, we don't want to throw our Dimitri into a panic. All I want you to do is let the idea germinate. Slowly. Let it take its own time. Mention the possibility in one letter and if he doesn't pick up on it let it fall. Try again in a letter's time. You know him well enough now to judge the tone of his response." His hand was still on her arm, unmoving but there. "Once he's picked up the idea let him make the running. Get him simmering on the back burner and hold him there. We'll burn him down when he's good and ready."

After a short while Malone sensed Sarah relax beneath his hand and he removed it. At the trolley he offered her the bottle and asked her if he could pour her another drink. She declined and reached for another cigarette instead. On the bookshelf close to where Malone was standing there was another photograph of Richard, this time with the man he presumably thought of as his father. The other man was smiling proudly, the son just managing a grin; both were holding rifles.

"Your husband a good shot?" asked Malone.

"Huh!" Sarah snorted with laughter. "That's a joke! He hasn't got off a good shot since . . ." She stopped abruptly, fidgeting with her hair. "He was the one that got Ricky interested. Took him out hunting when he wasn't big enough to hold more than a popgun. That was before Ricky got a mind of his own and turned against it."

"Against guns?" Malone asked.

"No. Against hunting. That boy's conservation crazy. Go to squash a spider in the bath and he'll bawl you out as though you were clubbing a baby seal to death. He's always reading books and writing letters to the papers and to his congressman. Going to lectures and conventions and Lord knows what else. Right now, instead of going straight to college, he's trying to persuade his father to pay for him to spend a year with some ecological set-up over in Europe."

Malone nodded. "Uh-huh. That's the way the kids get. Some kids. Enough ideals to save the world twice over."

He and Sarah stood, saying nothing, staring at one another.

"He's given up on his shooting, then," said Malone, moving towards the door, nodding at the photograph on the mantelpiece.

"Oh, no. Only it's target shooting now. Ricky's the best in his high school. More cups and junk up in his room than there's shelf space for."

Malone stopped by the door and turned back to face her.

"You'll do it?"

Sarah drew breath slowly. "Do I have any choice?"

Malone shook his head. "I guess if it comes down to it . . ."

At the front door she paused with her hand on the latch. "Maybe the coffee isn't as bad as I said. I could make you one in a couple of seconds."

Her eyes were brighter again, her voice rising.

"No thanks. I'll be on my way."

On the porch he held out his hand. "Nice to have met you after all this time."

She looked at the outstretched hand but made no move to take it. Malone nodded shortly and walked over to his car. When the door closed he didn't look round.

Malone dropped the coin in the slot and dialled. When the voice answered he said "Firecrest" and then a five digit number followed by three letters. There followed the click of a switch-board connection being made, followed by the briefest of pauses during which Malone assumed that the scrambler switch was being depressed, the tape machines switched on. He recognized Turner's voice instantly.

"Steven."

"Hi."

"You talk to her?"

"Sure."

"How'd she seem?"

"She's holding up. She's strong."

"Only?"

"Only what?"

"Your voice sounded an 'only' that didn't get said."

Malone hesitated fractionally. "Something's getting her down and I don't think it's our man."

"Oh."

"More like hers."

"Her old man?"

"Yes."

It was Turner's time for hesitation.

"You surprised or not?" Malone persisted.

"No, not really."

Malone waited.

"Year or so back," Turner started slowly, "seems a friend of Radcliff's saw Sarah's car outside the motel . . ."

"The motel," Malone almost shouted. "You're not telling me you used the same . . ."

"Steven, Steven, calm down. Of course we didn't. You know what standard procedures are. It was a chance thing. He may even have been humping a bit on the sly himself. Whatever, he told Radcliff about it and of course Radcliff went bananas."

"What happened?"

"I don't know."

"You don't . . ."

"Sarah wouldn't say. Only that it was okay. Maybe she talked him out of it, maybe she took a fall, I don't know."

"You mean she could have let him think she was in there screwing around?"

"It's possible. I didn't want to push too hard, rock the . . ."

"You didn't report it," said Malone accusingly.

"Sure, we kicked it around. Didn't seem to amount to much. The letters went on like before. I guess it didn't get out of the section."

You know damned well it didn't get out of the section, thought Malone. He said, "You know he drinks?"

"Everyone drinks, Steven."

"I mean *drinks*." Malone emphasized the word heavily.

A pause, then, "You certain?"

"Sarah said something, a couple of things. She may be putting it back herself in sympathy."

Turner whistled lightly down the phone. "What d'you want us to do?"

"Check it out. See if anything needs to be done."

"Okay." Turner cleared his throat. "Steven, what if it's bad?"

"I don't want this one fouled up."

He put the receiver down hard and left the booth.

Half an hour later, Malone dredged another number from his memory and found another callbox.

There was a short silence at the other end of the line and then a woman's voice asked uncertainly, "Did you say Stephanie Harold?"

Malone assured her that he had.

The woman asked him who he was and Malone said he was just an old friend who happened to be passing through Boston and he thought he'd give Stephanie a call.

"I guess you must be quite an old friend, indeed," said the voice. "Stephanie was married three years back. She's Stephanie Esher now. She's got a little girl, name of Debbie."

Malone said nothing.

"I can give you the Eshers' number. I'm sure Stephanie will be pleased to hear from you."

"Thank you, it doesn't matter."

"Very well. But who shall I say called?"

Malone was already hanging up, backing out on to the street. It was as well he hadn't rearranged his flight. Now there was no more than an hour to kill.

Driving home in the December dark after spending the Happy Hour drinking Jack Daniels on the rocks with some friends, Howard Radcliff was going too fast along Highway 95 when his headlights suddenly cut out. In a moment of panic he cursed and reached clumsily for the switch, his coordination poor and worsening. His foot pushed down on the gas instead of relaxing. He couldn't find the brake.

"Fuckin' lights!"

Before he could bring the car under control and pull into the side, a grain truck, seeing nothing in the fast darkness, collided with him head on. It was five days short of Christmas.

Sarah wore black through to the New Year and sent Richard over to the conservation conference in Amsterdam on the insurance.

· CHAPTER 11 ·

Mushrooms were his delicacy. Blue buttons, tinned and flown to Eastern Europe, bought in quantity and at considerable expense, hoarded against those special occasions which demanded something different for the palate. Karpov drank a little of the chilled white wine and forked another of the blue buttons into his mouth. Biting into it gently, savoring the taste. Another sip of the dry wine and he broke off a piece of dark bread and dipped it into the garlic butter sauce. There were only four mushrooms remaining. Never mind, they had been good—all the better for the waiting—and now the meal was going to be made complete.

Karpov looked at his watch and then glanced towards the heavy wood door. An easy chair had already been set by the window, a small table beside it. A high-power telescope stood on its tripod in front of the table, adjacent to the chair. By sitting forward Karpov would be able to observe with clarity and comfort. Unless . . . he checked his watch again and stood up, his mouth set in a hard line . . . unless there was some last minute difficulty of which he had not been informed.

But before he could settle into his window seat, the senior technical officer had knocked. Entering the room promptly on Karpov's response. Mikhilavin was slender and soft-eyed, twenty or more years younger than Karpov.

He was one of the rising generation of new technocrats whose abilities and ingenuities were transforming the old tradecraft upon which Karpov had cut his teeth. This operation, however, was one that Karpov admired for it called for a mixture of the old crafts and the new; the street-wise and the technologically assured.

"You are ready?" Karpov asked, almost nonchalantly over his shoulder.

"Minutes only."

Karpov nodded and settled into his chair. "Proceed."

Mikhilavin summoned two of his men who hustled like bees around the window, arranging wires, a small receiver, a junction box into which they plugged two sets of headphones. While this was being done, Mikhilavin focused the telescope and Karpov, leaning back, fastidiously ate another blue button mushroom.

The minions murmured and buzzed and backed towards the door. The senior technician made a final adjustment to the telescope and unwound his slender body until he was above and beside Karpov, his eyes redolent of excitement.

Karpov poured the last of the wine; there was only one glass.

"Now?" he asked.

Mikhilavin's tongue slid wet and pink over his lower lip. "Yes, Comrade Karpov."

Karpov nodded and moved to the front edge of the chair, closing his right eye and squinting through the lens. Strange, he always thought, that being right handed he had always had to fire a rifle with the left hand; his left eye would not shut independently. The thought faded from his mind as the two men walking slowly across the expanse of Gorki Park, turned towards one of the paths and were suddenly facing him. Karpov felt a little jump of pleasure which transmitted itself to the man alongside him.

"You have them?" asked Mikhilavin, his voice rising.

Karpov moved his head away far enough to nod, then resumed his watch.

Dimitri Andropov walked with both hands crossed at his back, as if he felt a need to keep himself upright. The fur collar of his coat was pulled high and the black astrakhan hat jammed down on to his head so that it almost reached his arching eyebrows. He spoke little as he walked, staring straight ahead as if to look sideways would be to recognize what he was doing, who he was walking with.

Andropov's companion in this lunchtime stroll across the park was shorter and stouter. Wearing rimless glasses with angled edges, hands pushed deep into the pockets of his dark blue overcoat, a fur hat sloping backwards from his head. He talked in short bursts of sentences, making points quickly and then allowing Andropov time to assimilate what he was saying. From time to time, he glanced round, trying to assess what the Russian scientist was thinking.

"You know him?" asked Mikhilavin.

"Andrew Carver, a junior cultural attaché at the American embassy."

Both men smiled to themselves and Karpov finished his wine.

Andropov and Carver were approaching one of the park's squares now and as they did so a woman wearing a green headscarf got up from her seat on the bench and began to push her pram towards them. It was the first Streetwalker. Mikhilavin's fingers twitched over the controls of the receiver. The woman leaned forward as she was walking and readjusted the blankets covering her child. Mikhilavin nodded hastily and handed one set of headphones to Karpov, slipping the other over his head.

On the left side of the receiver a panel of parallel circles began to dance with red. Mikhilavin's lips were parted, the soft tongue pushed into one corner. Inside Karpov's head a sound like that produced by a synthesizer wriggled and refused to be pinned down.

"What's happening?" Karpov demanded, turning. "What's going wrong?"

But the technical officer could not hear—only the

same snake of sound that slithered across the cold air carrying the chill of the Moscow River.

In the room that sheltered between the chimney stacks and minarets of the roof—strange in its aluminium and double-glazed windows—technicians made minute adjustments and read figures off columns. Deft fingers flicked up a cut-out here and here and here, lifted the decibel count through another fifteen degrees and pushed in another pair of compensating filters. Behind them a bank of reel-to-reel tape machines silently turned and rolled.

The woman in the headscarf bent low over her pram and shushed the baby warmly wrapped inside. As she straightened up, her hands lowered the folding roof by several inches and at that moment Andropov and Andrew Carver came within thirty yards of where she was.

Mere sounds became words.

". . . spoken to my people about this, Dimitri, and I know that . . . this move at the correct time. Now . . . prevaricating exactly when you should be being decisive and . . ."

The voice changed. Andropov's now, more hesitant, weighing his responses as if he knew that with each phrase his life was more in the balance.

". . . so long. You have to under . . . lived with a memory for as long as myself, there is something so frightening about the prospect of confronting the reality that . . ."

"Dimitri, you have to see that it's perfect. We'll never get an opportunity like this again. Surely you can see . . ."

Through the telescope Karpov saw the two men come to a halt at the left-hand corner of the square, half-facing one another. Andropov's expression was one of doubt edged with the beginnings of despair, like a portrait bordered in black. Behind them, too far behind now, the pram was being joggled up and down as the green headscarf bent over its contents.

Karpov pulled the headphone away from one ear and,

seeing this, the technical officer lifted his set from his head, holding it so that one of the earpieces was close to the left side of his head. His gentle brown eyes looked at Karpov questioningly.

"That isn't the only Streetwalker you've put down there?"

The eyes smiled slyly; the mouth formed the word, no, as though the men were still sealed off from the actual sounds of the room. Mikhilavin pointed through the window to a point that only the telescope would pick up.

Karpov nodded, replaced the headphones and set his eye to the circle of glass. Andropov and the American had settled on one of the benches and opposite them a short man with ear muffs and a tattered fur hat was getting his equally small, short-haired dog to sit up on its hind legs and beg. Every time the dog reared back and up, the man reached into the capacious pockets of his overcoat and took out a piece of broken biscuit. He teased the dog with this until the animal started to growl in the back of its throat, whereupon the scrap was tossed into the air and the dog jumped backwards and caught it. The man leaned forward and patted it, readying another biscuit in his pocket.

"I'll think about it."

"Seventy-two hours."

Andropov's face was shot through with pain. The piece of biscuit bounced off the dog's nose and the short man laughed and scratched his ear through the worn fur muff.

". . . impossible . . ."

The volume leapt so that the words roared into Karpov's ears and beside him the technician regulated the controls on the receiver and the top two pairs of circles ceased to bounce with red.

"You've had time enough to consider. Years enough. If you don't make up your mind now, there won't be another chance."

"I don't see how . . ."

"Dimitri . . ."

The American had turned sharply towards Andropov and was gripping his forearm tight through the heavy material of his coat. Through the angled, rimless spectacles the younger man's eyes held him clearly to the bench.

". . . let's be clear what the consequences will be."

"If I defect . . ."

As he heard the word, Karpov slipped the last but one blue button into his mouth, savoring it.

". . . the possible consequences don't bear thinking of."

"If you refuse to come over now, you aren't going to like the consequences either."

If the Russian's face showed premonitions of fear before, it was suffused now with the reality. Carver's hand dwelt on his sleeve a few seconds longer and then returned to his pocket. The woman in the headscarf was slowly wheeling her pram back through the square. On the roof, fingers turned and pushed and flicked as dials read off at differing levels. A third Streetwalker pushed his food trolley into the square and kicked down the stabilizing legs no more than twenty-five yards to the right of the bench occupied by Andropov and Carver. One of the technicians switched on the third recorder and the spool began to unwind, another track sliding into the mixer. Below the bank of machines, another technician watched the controls of the mixer, ensuring that the master tape achieved the best possible merging of the recordings. It was this master recording that was being fed down into Karpov's office.

"You want something to eat?"

Karpov watched as Andropov shook his head. He broke off another piece of bread and dipped it into the sauce. Carver shrugged and stood up, walking over to the food stand. Karpov heard him order a *chebureki* while keeping the telescope trained on the Soviet scientist. If I were sitting down there, he thought, wearing your shoes, I would not know which way to walk.

"There's one thing, one little chore we'd like you to do for us before you come over. A little information we'd welcome."

"No, no, this is . . ."

"Call it establishing your bona fides."

"Impossible!"

The wiry little dog missed his biscuit altogether and the hand of the technician on the roof was not quite fast enough to prevent Karpov's head being filled with high-pitched yaps of disappointment and frustration.

Both men stood up from the bench. Carver still biting into his hot pastry, the meat and gravy with a tendency to slide down his fingers. The American looked at Andropov as he licked them clean.

"Let's take a walk."

Hangdog, Andropov nodded agreement.

Karpov glanced round at Mikhilavin and gave him a questioning look. The officer smiled back at him confidently and at that exact moment the operative at the master control switched in pick-ups for four and five. They were positioned and ready, directional microphones three feet in length, fitted with telescopic sights through which the operators tracked their quarry. One was on the same roof as the control room, slotted between the chimney stacks, pointing down over the park. The second was clamped to the top of the now immobile great wheel in the amusement park, on the river side of where the two men were now walking.

Mikhilavin licked his lips. Karpov hesitated over his last mushroom. The sound jolted through the headphones, broke into a flutter of static, fell and rose and levelled out. It had taken perhaps seven seconds.

". . . ation concerning an agent operating in Western Europe."

The American's voice rose to cover and stifle Andropov's interruption.

"This boy's something special, out of the ordinary. He's an assassin, we think freelance though operating under KGB direction. We want something concrete that'll

help us clip his wings. He's been operative for too long without our being able to pick up much of a trace.''

''I have nothing to do with such operations, you must understand this.''

''Sure, but you do debrief agents returning from the West. You're involved in that—amongst other things. It shouldn't be too difficult for you to turn up something.''

''I . . .''

''Three terminations at least. One this year, two last. Brussels the most recent, the others London and Joinville, France.''

The air hummed with static. Both operators held their breath, watched movements, mouths. The silence clung like the debris of a dream, drawing every listener into its center.

''This is essential?''

''Let's say, you'll be made a whole lot more welcome with it rather than without it.''

''And the information—if I can find anything—I commit to memory and bring with me.''

''All but the ear.''

''The ear? I don't understand this.''

''Hold someone hostage and sooner or later you have to send proof. Something more than a letter, a signature. So you send a lock of hair, but maybe that's too easy to fake, so you come up with something else—a little finger, an ear maybe.''

''You want . . . ?''

''We want an ear, proof. We want something we can hang on to till you give us the rest. Like I said, think of it as your bona fides.''

The two men stopped walking. The sound burped down one channel. Carver had screwed up the piece of paper in which he had carried his *chebureki*, and now he held this tightly in his left hand. With his right, he clasped Andropov as if this were a parting of old friends.

''Seventy-two hours.''

''I should come here?''

Carver swung round and lifted his head and for several seconds he was staring directly into the lens of Karpov's telescope. The Russian held his breath.

". . . risky. Use the fall-back. I'll initiate it my end."

With a quick handshake, the two men parted and began to walk across Gorki Park in different directions. Mikhilavin was already using Karpov's telephone, checking figures.

"Seventy per cent from the directional pick-up on the wheel." He nodded and smiled, eyes shining. Quickly he returned to the window, where Karpov was ridding himself of the headset.

"It was good," he said. "When all three Streetwalkers were within range, we were getting between ninety and ninety-five per cent. Once the first pick-up had been made, we never dropped below thirty." He wet his mouth and stepped away. "There'll be a clear mix on your desk within forty minutes."

Karpov nodded. "That's fine, Comrade Mikhilavin. And sometime later today, we'd best discuss that other matter."

Mikhilavin unplugged the headphones from the receiver, ready for his men to collect. "Of course."

While the apparatus was being taken from the room, Karpov went back to his desk, Fedin's file in hand. Once the door had been closed he read the contents of the file absorbedly. So the Americans were getting anxious about Fedin, were they? Well, they weren't the only ones. He bit into the soft, blue-gray flesh of his last mushroom. It tasted very good.

As the dates in Fedin's file noted, this last contract had been entered into more quickly after the last than was usual. Normally the killing of the lover of a middle-aged cipher clerk, carried out on one of the early morning Brussels trams, would have signalled a lengthy period of inactivity for the assassin. But, as the signal eminating from Karpov had made clear, there were reasons for acting quickly.

A high-ranking Polish diplomat—their number three at the Hague—had been discovered leaving information about Warsaw Pact defence plans in a letter drop which had been cleared by a member of the British Secret Service. This leak had been confirmed during a random satellite interception of coded messages sent to the British GCHQ at Cheltenham. The cause of the urgency, though, was that the diplomat had suddenly become jumpy; something, someone had warned him that he was on the edge of being blown. The Poles were uncertain exactly how much classified information their man had access to and asked the Soviets for a little comradely assistance. Hence Fedin. Besides, it afforded Karpov an excellent opportunity to watch his freelance assassin in the field.

Karpov timed the contract through the chain of transmitters—the wispy-haired Berliner with his paperback westerns, the girl with long legs and fashion clothes, Van Holst with his shop full of model soldiers on the river Amstel. If Fedin accepted the contract he would have little time for manoeuvre.

The diplomat visited Amsterdam from the Hague for professional reasons on the first Monday of each month. His business finished by the end of the morning, the Pole had established a regular routine. First he would be driven towards the harbor and visit one of the several Indonesian restaurants on Storm Steeg. There were five in the street altogether but the diplomat always lunched at the same one. After a leisurely wallow in an eighteen dish *rijsttafel* washed down with half a dozen glasses of Dutch beer, he would climb a trifle unsteadily back into his car and travel the short distance to the red light district which flourished between the National Monument and the Old Church. His apparent predilection was for a hefty-thighed redhead who sat in her window wearing thigh-length black boots over fishnet tights, a white satin blouse unbuttoned over her half-cup brassiere and a studded dog-collar tight at her throat. A riding crop dangled nonchalantly from the back of her chair as she sat with legs crossed, contemptuous of the gawkers and windows shoppers and intently reading Virginia Woolf.

Fedin would have to carry out his contract in the restaurant, in the prostitute's tiny basement room or during the journey in between. When he removed the tightly furled piece of paper from the hollow center of a replica model of a Commander of the United States Navy in Summer Campaign Dress of 1862, Fedin's orders made it clear that he was to take the diplomat in the restaurant if at all possible, the first fall-back being the whore's room. The assassination was only to be carried out on the intervening journey if there appeared to be no other alternatives.

Karpov tapped the papers of the file into alignment. He wondered whether the young killer knew that he was being squeezed and why; he was interested to see how he would react. If Fedin was losing all sense of caution, then even skills such as his were too dangerous to use. And if that helped to provide Comrade Andropov with his bona fides . . .

The phone rang as Karpov was lighting a cigarette and looking down through the narrow window on to Lenin Prospekt. He dropped his lighter back down into his coat pocket and lifted the receiver on the third ring. Nodding his white hair, he listened to the duty officer on the operations desk. His face toyed with a smile which never arrived. The gray of Karpov's eyes darkened and went flat.

He set down that telephone and picked up the one next to it. Mikhilavin answered himself.

"Yes," assured the voice, velour-smooth. "Yes, naturally. And by special courier?"

"Of course, special courier!"

"Then the print will be edited and ready for viewing tomorrow afternoon."

"Morning."

"By that time only a rough cut . . ."

"Morning!"

"Very well."

Karpov heard the receiver click down and ground out his cigarette, not trusting the reasons for his own anger.

The viewing theater was in the basement. There were a dozen chairs, comfortably upholstered, a small wooden surface between each to facilitate note making. Every desk was equipped with an independently controlled lamp. A glass of vodka waited beside the center seat in the rear row. Karpov noticed this and ignored it. He sat to the right of the central line of four chairs and crossed one leg over the other, leaning round as Mikhilavin came down from the projection box.

"We had good time on the dispatch, but as I suggested would be the case, the print is hardly more than a rough cut." He made a slight bow of the head which Karpov tried not to think of as facetious. "I trust you will find it conveys the necessary information adequately."

Karpov nodded curtly. "You have a field plan?"

"Of course."

Milhilavin gestured towards the box and the theater lights dimmed down; a map showing the center of Amsterdam was projected on to the screen. The technical officer used a pointer.

"Here is the restaurant, on the north side of Storm Steeg, two hundred meters from the canal. We had two cameras set up inside, the first positioned at the rear of the curtains leading to the toilets at the back of the building. The second was operated by remote control from a van parked around the corner in Zeedijk and positioned inside the air conditioning duct on the front wall."

Mikhilavin moved his pointer eastwards.

"To cover the journey across the bridge and around the church square into the red light district, we placed a camera with telescopic zoom lens at the top of this tower, seventy-five meters above the ground." Mikhilavin smiled and corrected himself. "Seventy-six."

Karpov tapped his fingers on his cigarette case, unimpressed.

"We were also using two Streetwalkers, one with a camera concealed inside a briefcase, the other a Japanese taking home movies. The first of these was detailed to follow the car on foot before taking a short cut alongside the canal to the place our quarry frequented. Once the woman is reached things became slightly more difficult due to the conditions under which these people work. The rooms are small and heavily used and those renting them out proved very reluctant to cooperate. However, we put in a camera on the third floor across the canal, here, with a more or less unimpeded view of the front of the building we were interested in. We eventually positioned a remote control eight millimeter camera inside the woman's room, but only with a partly obscured view."

He nodded towards the projection box and spoke to Karpov at the same time. "Naturally, we were expecting the contract to be fulfilled in the restaurant. All the time our man was inside there were never more than three other customers and two waiters, with two more men in the kitchen," He smiled. "It was the obvious choice."

Karpov broke the filter from a cigarette and dropped it into the metal ashtray clipped to the seatback in front of him.

Mikhilavin signalled to the box and the map flicked from the screen. A moment's blackness was broken by an image of a man in a dark suit sitting alone at a table, numerous small dishes spread out before him. This changed almost immediately to a close-up from what appeared to be the opposite side of the room, but angled more towards the center of his face. Karpov's stomach churned its juices in sympathetic but vicarious pleasure as a small piece of pork was dipped into a mustard sauce and then deposited inside the narrow mouth. As the remote-control worked the zoom, Karpov saw with increasing clarity the dark hairs which curled from the diplomat's nostrils, the tiny veins across the nose.

The film cut raggedly to the street outside, an unsteady sequence showing the man coming out of the restaurant and climbing slowly into the rear of the car, the door held open for him by a female chauffeur wearing a peaked cap and a light gray trouser suit. One of the Streetwalkers managed a good medium close-up of the diplomat's hand patting her thigh as she turned away. The door shut faster than etiquette called for. The screen was blank for an instant, a short sequence of numbers flashed up and was replaced by an out-of-focus shot down on to the roof of the car. A wavering pan followed the vehicle into the shelter of the Old Church and then there was a subliminal second of black before the car reappeared on the far side of the square, the indicator signalling a left turn towards the canal.

Karpov's eyes narrowed as, partly veiled by the branches of one of the trees that lined the canal, a different camera closed on the prostitute sitting in the window, a red light above her head ostentatiously advertizing her trade at the same time as it allowed her to read her book resting on her booted thighs. Another woman walked slowly through the frame, younger, her hair a coil that hung down to the small of her back. She seemed to be wearing nothing more than high-heeled shoes, stockings supported by a red suspender belt and a gauzy see-through top with matching knickers.

In the closeness of the small viewing theater, Karpov could feel the intensity of Mikhilavin's contempt.

It was broken by a flurried movement of the camera and the appearance of the Pole at the corner of the street. He was walking steadily enough now, heading directly for the woman targeted in the window. The whore in the red suspender belt came towards him and tried to intercept, but the diplomat brushed her away. At the top of the frame, the woman's hand closed her book and set it on the floor. Heavy thighs stretched and then there were heeled boots which seemed to be standing for one surreal instant on the diplomat's shoulders.

The picture fluttered and the screen went blank.

Karpov swore and Mikhilavin let his tongue caress his lips as he leaned slowly back in his chair, one leg hoisted over the seat in front.

Images flickered and were never still, Karpov thought he was looking then at an empty screen, but something inside the emptiness moved and he realized these frames were from the camera hidden inside the room. Grainy, black and white images like a worn peep show. The man's hands unbuttoning his trousers from the striped braces he wore beneath his suit jacket, fumbling with the fly. The camera picked out behind him only the whore's right leg stretched out along the narrow bed, the riding crop being struck impatiently against it.

What a farce it is, thought Karpov, a man struggling out of his trousers into the embarrassment of a dwindling erection and short, dark socks.

A hand, claw-nailed, plucked at the front of his white briefs dismissively.

Pulling off his left shoe the Pole lost balance and staggered into a sideways hop which carried half of him out of camera. The riding crop swished down the screen.

There was a rapid cut to clear color film as the Streetwalker arrived in perfect time to catch the limber shape of Fedin entering through the folds of material which hung over the short flight of steps leading down to the prostitute's room.

Karpov hunched forward in his seat, arms hugging the chair back.

The diplomat seemed to be standing, splay-legged, at the side of the bed, the whore's head partly shielded by his arm. There was a sudden twisting apart of the bodies and then the open-shirted chest of the Pole filled the screen. Moved backwards until there was nowhere else to go. Karpov could not prevent the start that jogged his own body as the chest on the screen rocked forward and back and then seemed to burst apart with black blood.

The woman rushed, scrambling, across the camera.

Then it was Fedin's arm extending, the pistol angling down.

Dark spots of blood struck against the camera lens.

Fedin stooped across the body and the screen revealed one side of his face, in front of the fall of brown hair, apparently speckled with blood.

Color soaked the screen with a quick cross-cutting of images from the room across the street and the Streetwalker on the narrow bridge. Men and women running without rhyme or reason. A close-up of the young whore against the wall, hands raking her face as tears of fear fell. A party of middle-aged tourists grabbing at one another as they retreated to the iron railings alongside the canal.

The prostitute in the boots was standing hard against her window, her mouth open in a succession of silent screams, the fist which held the riding crop hammering uselessly against the pane. Suddenly, as one of the cameras tightened on her silent screaming mouth, the face broke through the plate glass of the window. The editor had slowed the frames to stop motion. Shards of glass rainbowed out and fragments of dark matter, like pulped fruit, erupted from the back of the woman's head as she plunged forward into the street.

"Enough!" Karpov pushed himself back in his seat and gripped the arms tight.

Mikhilavin signalled over his head and the remaining frames of the film cut to nothing as the theater lights dimmed up. The technical officer stood, one hand pressed loosely against the front of his thigh, waiting. Karpov remained where he was, staring forward with eyes as dark and blank as the screen itself.

· CHAPTER 12 ·

Andropov sat with his head between his hands and the image of the son he had never seen clenched inside his brain. The moments, he thought, the hours and the days—time that he could never recover, even with the benefit of memory. A childhood and a fatherhood which he had never known. That he would never remember. He drew his arms down and set them on the desk in front of him, his face gray from being left in the dark for too long. He leaned back in his chair and gazed around his room. Details of experiments, case studies, the results of countless encephalograms, papers which he had written but never delivered. Memory, Andropov thought, was the one thing that for him would never fade and could never be taken away; it had never existed. Not for Richard and himself. Hardly, now, for Sarah either. What was there? A rattling of trams as they turned through the night, the hiss of doors that sought confusion with the hiss of a woman's breath. That memory was so slight, it yielded him so little comfort, that there was nothing he could do to keep it close.

He looked again at the files and drawers and shelves and thought about the men and women fragmented there. And their memories? Gradually, Andropov had developed the techniques necessary for obliterating them, blanking them out, destroying the neurograms that mapped the whole of a person's past. Either that, or opening it up, freeing from behind whatever locks the names and the occasions that had become sealed. Information which was beneficial to the State and obtained from friend and foe alike. Agents who needed deep debriefing: those suspected of spying or subversion—defectors.

Andropov's right hand wiped away the beginnings of sweat from his temple. What techniques, he wondered, would the security forces of those smart and self-assured young men have at their disposal? How would they unlock his mind? And when they did, would they discover what he himself most wanted to find—the twenty years which had never been his? The years in which his son had grown to manhood. Would they have the penetration of technique to discover those? The bright young people of his new country. The home of his wife and child. His new fatherland.

He stood up and paced the room, fear of what he had to do making his nerve ends jingle and drying the back of his throat until he was parched. In the old days, he thought, Natasha Marakova would have made him tea. But she was married, with four children, to a doctor who specialized in the treatment of geriatrics and who was researching into the biological nature of ageing. The last time he had seen her was four years earlier, queuing on a cold and blustery day to buy meat. The wind had tugged at her hair and she had set her hand to it and half-turned her head so that she was facing him directly. Andropov had halted, brought to a standstill by that movement, that moment, by the realization of a life which might have been that was encapsulated within it. She had not recognized him. Later, Andropov had been glad.

Now, on the third floor of the Serbsky Institute of Forensic Psychiatry, he boiled a kettleful of water and made his own tea.

Since his attachment to the KGB he had acted as a liaison between their officials and the Institute staff. A man with a round, reddish peasant face and a gold-capped front tooth had smiled across a desk and handed him a copy of "Regulations on the Emergency Hospitalization of Mentally Ill Persons who are a Public Danger."

"Read it," he had said, his smile widening, "read it, comrade. Lest there should be any doubt."

There were no doubts, Experience had put paid to that. Patients forwarded from Kaluga, from Leningrad and Kazan. Occasionally prisoners graded "strict" or "special"—those with whom maximum precautions had to be taken. Andropov had become used to signing reports which labelled men and women as suffering from "incipient schizophrenia," suffering from "an overestimation of their own personality," from a state of mind which had brought about "a major deterioration in the quality of their work," from making "a poor adaptation to the social environment."

It all came down to a simple equation. These people were critical of the machinery and ideology of the State and anyone who was critical of the State had to be insane. Clinically insane. Those dissidents, all of the letter-writers and journalists who complained about the abuse of psychiatry and neurology in Russian hospitals, failed to understand that simple fact—to find fault in what was right was nothing more than a clear sign of a fault in one's own mind.

Andropov no longer referred to the Regulations; there was no longer any need. He understood the mechanics of his job and he carried them out with a minimum of regret. Without, almost, thinking.

"And now . . ."

The tea was bitter, large dark leaves adhering to the side of the white china cup.

And now he was about to make his move against the State. He was on the verge of acting in a way which could only be construed as positively hostile. Like those he dealt with every day, those whose pasts and futures he assigned away with a quick flourish of his signature and the smear of a rubber stamp, he was putting himself beyond the pale.

He was about to go insane.

There were five cases still awaiting a definite decision from Andropov. Two men and a woman whose actions and whose carefully monitored conversations had led them to be labelled dangerous. A sleeper whose reactivation after seven years had produced results which were sufficiently unusual to merit close study; a woman who had worked in the KGB coding offices for fifteen years before showing subversive tendencies. That the first three would be committed to one of the psychiatric prison-hospitals was not in doubt—the delay was caused solely by the need to formulate the most adequate reason. As for the two remaining instances, there was one mind which had to be layed open, another which, after examination, would have to be closed. The whole gamut of scientific advance was at Andropov's disposal. Psychosurgery, hypnosis, the varying of depressant drugs with hallucinogenics, electroshock, sleep therapy, periodic insulin shock.

Andropov opened a card index file and flicked back through a number of cards. The woman's name was Andrushka, she was thirty-nine years of age. So far she had been under hospitalized surveillance for seventeen days. The unlocking was still in process, each statement cross-checked and verified against the known facts and circumstances. This the easiest part. Later would come intensive medication from which the patient would be aroused for electroshock, doses of over one hundred volts lasting less than a second and administered by means of electrodes soaked in a saline solution. Both medication and shock treatment would be strengthened as the days stretched from twenty to thirty, from thirty to sixty. First, her in-depth memory would fade and break, leaving an awareness of where she was, who she was, who the doctors and nurses around her were; gradually, the next stage would be reached in which those simple questions were unanswerable and the woman would be pressured by an intense anxiety about her identity; the final state relieved her of this anxiety. She would exist solely in the here and now. There would no longer live within her any concept of self, any memory. She would be, at thirty-nine years of age, a complete amnesiac, each second forgotten the instant the next was reached.

As Andropov checked through the findings on her cards, part of him tried to erect a motive of humanitarianism which would justify and define what he was going to do. He was fleeing to the West to escape from the corruption of science in the Eastern bloc. He wanted to testify to the way in which neurology had been harnessed by the secret forces of the State for its own ends. He was a propagandist for Human Rights, a Solzhenitsyn come to judgement.

He was none of these things. He wanted to see again the woman whose image he had loved for so many years; he wanted to see his son.

Andropov took his topcoat from the peg at the back of the door and changed the comfortable shoes he wore indoors for a pair of short rubber boots. His hat was leaning against a pile of books and he set it on his head and pulled it low. It was early evening. There would be few people remaining at the building on Lenin Prospekt. He could use his pass and gain access to the files in the registry; there need be no questions about what he was doing. The cross-checking of classified information came within his brief.

It was late enough for cars to be travelling from the center of the city with their headlights burning. The purple-black of the sky was cracked through here and there with lines of white that appeared to Andropov as markings on a chart. Sarah. The name, the head of red hair, the almost insolent beauty of her face burst in upon him with such force that he stopped in his tracks, all breath driven from his body. Men stepped around him, a woman hesitated, her round face staring up into his. Andropov felt the edges of panic and knew that his forehead was beaded with sweat. The woman spoke to another passer-by, who glanced at Andropov hastily but carried on walking. She took a step closer, then another, peering at him. At any moment, thought Andropov, there is going to be a crowd, a scene.

"Do you want," the woman asked, touching his arm delicately as if half-afraid that his illness might be contagious, "a doctor?" Through the film of perspiration that was running over his eyes, Andropov managed a smile.

"No," he assured her. "No, I'm all right. It will pass. If I stand for a minute or two. Everything will be all right." He made a motion of dismissal with his hand. "No. No doctor."

The woman started to back away, anxious yet unsettled by his response to her inquiries. Eventually she carried on her way, glancing round every fifteen or so yards, until he must have been indistinguishable to her.

Still on the same spot, still holding Sarah's name in the hollow of his mouth like the host at Communion, afraid for that moment to swallow, afraid of the transformation, the body and the blood.

He had to show his pass three times before gaining access to the Registry. Twice he signed his name, the second time at the bottom of a slip of stationery on which he had written the code numbers for the files he wished to examine. The duty clerk was a young man whose breath smelt of sour cheese and who had been doodling little stick men in between the columns of *Pravda*.

The man looked at Andropov's request negligently, sliding slim-hipped from his stool and setting his pencil down across the newspaper.

Andropov set himself to wait. He had made sure to ask for a cross-section of material, the references all relating to the testimony of the former coding clerk and recorded on tape. She had mentioned a number of messages which related to assassination, a routing which included Berlin and Amsterdam, incidents in London and Brussels. More than that, she had spoken a name. Fedin.

The young man returned with four files and handed them to Andropov.

"You know you must refer to these here?" he said.

Andropov nodded, counting the files, fingering them apart so that he could see.

"They're not all here."

The clerk pushed his newspaper aside irritably. "No."

"The missing file, someone else is using is perhaps?"

The clerk shook his head.

"Then . . . ?" Andropov waited for an explanation.

"That file needs special clearance."

"Why? I need it. I must see it for my work. You can't block what I am doing because of some bureaucratic nonsense . . ." Andropov broke off, aware that his voice was becoming increasingly high-pitched and rattled. He waited, controlled himself and spoke again, trying to sound authoritative and assured. "From where must I obtain clearance?"

The clerk checked a column of initials and numbers. "Room 332. Comrade Karpov."

Andropov's throat moved in and out as he hastily drew in air. The stink of sour cheese made him cough, doubling him over and bringing tears to his eyes. The duty clerk watched, dispassionately. When he had wiped his face, Andropov said, "Please telephone him."

"He'll have left the building."

"Please."

"It's too late. Try again tomorrow."

"How long will it take you to try now?"

The two men stared at one another and Andropov wondered if he was being foolish to make a scene. After all, one day was all that was at stake. Less. He could return in the morning promptly and ask for permission to read the file, sure then that he could rationalize the necessity of checking crucial information that Andrushka had revealed.

He was turning away when the young man said, "Wait. I'll see what I can do."

Karpov's voice was steady at the other end of the phone, almost bored. He seemed to listen to the registry clerk's request patiently enough, as if nodding his head a little as he did so.

"Which file did you say?"

"FA7111."

"Subject?"

The clerk glanced down. Andropov's heart came near to stopping. "Fedin."

"And he is making reference to other files, this . . . this Andropov?"

The clerk told him.

Karpov stifled a yawn. "Ask him which case at the Institute the examination of these files concerns."

The young man put one hand over the receiver, asked and received the information. He transmitted it along the line and waited while Karpov apparently considered.

"Very well. Let him have access."

"Excuse me," said the clerk quickly, "I shall need a written authority."

"Tomorrow," replied Karpov, sounding more disinterested than ever.

"With respect, authorization cannot be retrospective. If you refer to memorandum . . ."

"My God!" Karpov exploded. "Send a messenger. Send me a form. Let the man have his damned file!"

Andropov rocked back on to the heels of his rubber boots, clutching the wall, certain that if he did not he might faint.

The lights of the big wheel in the amusement park turned and spun. A thin film of rain hung from the sky like gauze. The sound against the window panes was faint and distant. Karpov watched as the slightly stooped figure of Dimitri Andropov hunched his shoulders into the rain and looked querulously around before starting to walk towards the city center. After a dozen yards Andropov stopped and fidgeted with his gloves, pulled the collar of his coat back up. Watching, Karpov shook his head; the cigarette in his hand smouldered. He wondered whether the scientist had made written notes or if he had decided to commit what he could to memory. The latter, he decided—at this moment the man is too scared to take the least additional risk. It was all there milling around his brain along with the other facts and half-facts, the formula and data, the lame fantasy of a life into which his need for love had drawn him. There, and they would drag it out, the Americans. They would untumble the poor bastard's brain using the very methods he had helped to invent.

Karpov blew smoke against the window; the pitiable rabbit of a man was out of sight.

The Russian continued to stare out over the dark expanses of the park, the colored lights of the wheel becoming increasingly blurred as the pressure of the rain increased. Slowly, he smiled. The Americans would broadcast a fanfare about the defection of a prominent Soviet scientist; they would play on the work that he did, calling it a violation of human rights and a mockery of science and medicine, all the while to mask the fact that their CIA was making use of the self-same techniques. Then when the headlines had died down and their experts began to sift through the plethora of information Andropov had brought them, it would lead them along sufficient blind alleys and into enough dead ends to confuse their already mazed minds still further. And out of the mist of all the colored glass and fake jewels which were Andropov's prize, they would find one diamond, hard and real. A killer who no longer obeyed orders was expendable. He was about to sever the links in the chain: no more controls, no money. Let him hang free—it was no more than he deserved. Karpov had decided to let them have Fedin.

* * *

It was past midnight and the duty officer sounded as if he were already fighting off the beginnings of sleep when Karpov summoned him. The memorandum to his superiors had not taken long to draft and would take even less time to transmit. Karpov rubbed his hand with satisfaction against the firmness of his belly and poured a small amount of brandy into the glass. Alas, it was not French. Not five star, or even three. Karpov smiled into the emptiness of his office; this night it didn't matter.

Memorandum AK39/42(Ref: FA7111)
Andropov, Dimitri
The rabbit has been fed, now let him run with the fox.
Karpov

· BOOK THREE ·

· CHAPTER 13 ·

The light shifted through the first green leaves, patterning the woman's shoulders, the darkening red of her hair. She moved awkwardly, as if the brown slats of the wooden seat were too hard. Glancing round for a waitress, she felt inside her leather bag and took out a packet of cigarettes. Lighting one, she turned her head aside to exhale smoke on to the clear air. When the waitress came, she ordered coffee, speaking in English and assuming that she would be understood. Across her shoulders, the morning bit cold.

Two young men sat a dozen feet away ostentatiously leaning back against the bench seating which partitioned off the café area from the street. Their shirts were open at the neck and unbuttoned midway down their chests; one of them wore a silver chain and cross, the Christ figure on its crucifix suffocating in the dark curl of hair. Their jeans were too tight and they spoke too loud. They had given her the briefest of glances as she entered and then dismissed her from their thoughts.

Sarah was conscious of the lines that crow-footed away from the corners of her eyes and mouth, the looseness of skin below her cheekbones and chin. However she treated it, her red hair had lost its shine. The hands that held the coffee cup were suddenly pudgy and worn.

For Christ's sake, they were old woman's hands!

Sarah rattled her cup down against its saucer hard and one of the young men looked at her questioningly before dismissing her once again.

Nearly fifty years old.

I am, thought Sarah, nearly fifty years old.

Sarah drew on the cigarette and shifted sideways, crossing one leg over the other. The light was bright enough to make her shade her eyes with the flat of her hand. They had forced her back to Trondheim, forced her and bought her, and following a life-long pattern, she had allowed herself to be forced and bought.

Sarah's throat was dry and she ground the cigarette into the bottom of the ashtray; she considered ordering another coffee, but instead she dropped some coins on to the table and stood up. For so many years of her life, she thought, those young men would have turned their heads to watch her go. Now they ignored her as she stepped on to the pavement and turned to cross the street.

How was Dimitri going to see her? What was she going to be to him? A fantasy that he had nurtured and grown until no reality could hope to correspond. She began to walk briskly, dreading the moment of their first meeting and the look she was certain would come to his eyes when he saw how she had changed, how she had faded and aged, worn by life.

On Thomas Angells Gate a busker stood in the middle of the pedestrian precinct, a small crowd loose about him. People stayed for a few minutes and then walked on, some of them coming closer to throw coins into the guitar case which lay open on the ground, a red carnation resting inside its neck. Sarah stopped and leaned against the plate glass window of a clothes shop, hanging baskets of flowers and yellow welcome signs tapering away towards the end of the street. Beyond that the wooded slope reached up to a flat blue sky; flat like a piece of stage scenery.

Sarah toyed with her lighter and watched the man

with the guitar. He wore loose green cords and a faded blue T-shirt, his hair long and frizzed out at the ends. Ten, fifteen years ago he would have been standing outside the flower market in Boston singing the same songs. There was a smattering of applause and he gave a laughing bow and swept his arm around and then above his head. He is, thought Sarah, so thin. And her mind began to flirt with images of his body, fragments of sexuality that broke across the clear cold of mid-morning.

The young man began playing something which Sarah recognized and gradually she realized it was some Bob Dylan thing and then she knew it as "Don't Think Twice, it's All Right." The voice was too strained, too strongly accented, but the harmonica, clamped in a harness round his skinny young neck, was note-for-note perfect. As the song went on, his legs started to make awkward dancing steps.

"We never did too much talking anyway."

Sarah's fingers drew tight around the small silver cigarette lighter and she stood clear of the window. She took a couple of paces away but something held her, the singer or that foolish song, the whine of the harmonica and the high nasal call of the words.

"You just kinda wasted my precious time."

The last chord rang and echoed and Sarah didn't feel that she could move on until it had faded fully away. She was applauding along with the rest and she realized that the busker had noticed her, was smiling at her specifically, showing that he was aware of her attention. As she stood there, his smile began to mean something else; he was guessing at the shape of her body beneath her coat, at other things.

Sarah dropped the lighter down into her bag, pushed up at her hair. She walked diagonally across the street, pretending to be interested in the shoes and boots on display in front of her. It was the singer's final look which remained true for her, not the words he had been singing. The reflection which looked back at her from the shop window was of a still-attractive woman, red hair borrowing from the sun.

"I never wanted to do this." She spun round on Malone, almost spilling the drink in her hand, anger bright in her blue eyes.

"Sarah, we've been over all this before. There is no point in rehearsing the same old positions."

She pulled back her head and looked at him, finally relinquishing him to stare down into the central square instead. The stores and shops had all closed at four o'clock and already the city had the air of a place which has been prematurely deserted. Across from the entrance to Malone's hotel, statues stood at strange intervals in a broad paved space that was otherwise empty. By eight o'clock it would be alive with cars, a shrink-wrapped version of small town America in the early sixties. Men wearing black or denim blue would be sitting on the hoods of one another's customized vehicles, occasionally walking across to the canopied bar for a beer or climbing behind the wheel to cruise the few streets, engines tuned to a rasp. Sometimes they would allow the girls to stand close, but usually they left them to lean on walls, on the backs of benches, or to loiter around the tables of the bar. Not all the girls are fair, but they are all tall and slim, high breasted. They are young and chew gum.

Sarah can remember nights like that: she can remember being young.

Malone loosened his tie and poured himself a drink, a whisky cut with water. Somewhere in the back of his mind was a memory of being in a hotel room in New York—a sad-eyed hooker with a coarse laugh and bad breath who had tucked the dollar bills he had handed her down into the top of the stockings she was still wearing.

"This your first time, honey?"

He realized that Sarah was talking to him.

". . . goes wrong, then it's not my fault. I'm not

going to be responsible for everything getting fouled up. You hear me?"

Malone nodded, took a little of his drink, noticed that Sarah had still not touched hers; was just using it as a prop.

He sat down. "You don't have to worry. All he has to do is see you . . ."

"See me!"

"That's right."

"One look at me and he'll freak out and jump the first damned plane back to Moscow."

"That's ridiculous."

"You're damned right it's ridiculous! He doesn't want to see me. He wants to see some kid in her early twenties with bright red hair and tight little tits who likes to ball her ass off."

Malone raised his hands towards her, fingers spread. If she hadn't been drinking earlier, her adrenalin was certainly flowing fast of its own accord.

"Sarah, you aren't the only one who's changed. It isn't just you who's got older. What do you think's happened to Dimitri? How about him? He's fifty-three for Christ's sake! You think he's going to be looking for some woman half his age?"

Sarah laughed. "Isn't that what most men of fifty are looking for?"

Malone shook his head. "Not this one."

Sarah shook her head. "No, maybe he's dumb enough."

"And anyway, you've got no reason to run yourself down."

"Meaning?"

"Meaning you're still an attractive woman."

Sarah curled her bottom lip a little. "You mean, for my age."

"No."

"You do. Say it."

"I don't mean that."

"You said, still."

"What?"

"Still an attractive woman, that's what you said. Still."

Malone stood up, balancing the whisky glass on the flat of his palm. "Come on, Sarah, that was just a figure of speech. You know that."

"Like Hell I do."

He touched her cheek with his other hand and she pulled her head around as if she'd been stung.

"He isn't going to be disappointed."

She looked at him scornfully. "You mean when we hit the sack."

"I didn't . . ."

"But that's it, isn't it? That's what I'm here for. To give Dimitri a quick roll in the hay, a taste of the good life, a fuck for Uncle Sam!"

"No."

Malone finished his drink and set down the glass. He'd always considered that bringing Sarah out to Norway was a mistake, running an unnecessary risk. But Andropov had insisted, his one condition, the one thing at which the Moscow contact thought he might baulk. Sarah has to be in Trondheim. Malone unstoppered the bottle and shook his head at the sentimental rightness of it. The damned conference couldn't be in Stockholm or Paris or even London. No, it had to be Trondheim's turn again. The perfect resolution. So much easier to forget the twenty-three years that had somehow slipped in between—or did it make them stand out all the more clearly? Like the lines on Sarah's face.

And yet, thought Malone, looking at her as she stood by the window, a cigarette in her mouth, whatever time has done to her it has not made her unattractive. There was still something sensual about her, something of the flesh. A feeling that her body would come alive in the way that few others did.

"No," he said, "we don't want that to happen."

She raised an eyebrow. "I don't go to bed with him?"

"Not now. And not here."

Sarah looked at Malone for a few moments longer, as if she didn't quite understand what he was saying. Then she started to laugh; she laughed until she was shaking and Malone had to go over and take the drink from her hand. Ash from her cigarette drifted towards the carpet.

"Okay, okay. I understand. You fly me out here, having made me spend God knows how many hours in the library at MIT so I won't look too obvious a ringer at the conference. All of this with the intention of turning me into a choice piece of bait. The only thing is, poor Dimitri doesn't get to swallow until he makes a few thousand more miles of air time."

Sarah shook her head and a length of red hair unwound.

"My God, Malone, you really do it, you know that? You may look as nice and harmless as a guy coming to the door to peddle bibles, but that's just a front. That handsome face and those clothes and those pretty powder-blue eyes that look straight at one as if you were telling the truth. Huh! You do it, Malone, I know that now. Whatever it is, whatever it takes, you *do* it. Even if it means turning me into a stupid little cock-teaser. One of those kids down on the street who gets into your car and kisses you without taking the gum out of her mouth and all the time she's got her legs crossed tight on account of she's saving her precious little ass!"

Malone offered her back her drink and she nodded and took it from his hand and threw it down in one gulp.

"Give me another."

Malone looked doubtful. "Don't worry, Malone. This is one family that's learned its lessons about drinking too heavily. Especially drinking and driving. But if you think I'm going to get through this completely sober . . ."

He poured her a fresh vodka and she took it away before he could dilute it with too much of anything else.

Malone wondered how well she would hold up over the five days before they intended to fly Andropov out, halfway through the conference. He hoped that she would do okay—because if anything else happened then his chances of accomplishing the Russian's defection would be restricted. And because, pointless as it was, he liked her. She'd drunk too much too early and she'd grown up a little wild. Screwed around more than women were supposed to at the time she was doing it *and* you could tell that she'd enjoyed it; she had married a man she'd never particularly cared for and had a son for whom she seemed to care even less; the husband had died and she didn't see much of the son any more and still she carried on in her own way, coping as best as she could. She was forty-eight years old and when the light hit her right she was attractive enough to make Malone itch. And, anyway, as much as his job allowed him, he liked her.

"Here's to it," said Sarah, lifting her glass and smiling cynically, roguishly.

"Sure," agreed Malone, "here's to it."

On the plane Andropov had developed a nervous twitch at the corner of his right eye, an irritating tic that started up suddenly and continued until he thought it would never stop. Andropov remembered the story he'd heard about the man who died from the hiccups. Thirty-six hours, or was it more, and then he died. Was it possible, he wondered, gazing out at bank upon bank of white cloud, to die from a ticking nerve at the corner of the eye? And then he realized that it had stopped.

Twenty minutes later, as the voice over the intercom was instructing them to fasten their seat belts and return all seats to an upright position, it began again.

"Nervous, comrade?" asked the man sitting alongside. "About the descent?"

Andropov nodded clumsily and covered his eye with the fingers of his hand.

"Always it is worse coming down than at take off. Always so. I remember when I was with the delegation which flew to Vienna in seventy-five—or was that seventy-six? I don't think you were present, comrade. Well, as we . . ."

Andropov was no longer listening. The air in the cabin seemed to be thickening, he pulled at the collar of his shirt, felt himself reddening, but not with embarrassment. The pulse at his eye corner increased. He gasped in a mouthful of air and it was like chewing cardboard. As his head twisted sideways, he saw Olga Karenova staring along the row from her seat across the aisle. If she had appeared to be an old woman to Andropov in fifty-nine, now she was strangely preserved, fossilized perhaps. Her hair was the same color, worn in the identical manner. None of her clothes suggested the slightest concession to fashion or change. It was as if she had stepped out of Satis House, a refurbished Miss Havisham who was all the more macabre for ridding herself of all those cobwebs and the smell of must. It was only when you were close enough to see her skin that it became clear how much she had indeed aged. It was like the skin of a lizard, patched and reptillian, dry enough to flake at the merest touch.

She spoke to Andropov as they descended from the plane, her voice no more than a dry rasp. "Something troubles you, Dimitri?"

"No . . . no, the flight. It was not comfortable. And coming into land was . . ."

His words became parched before her staring, bead-like eyes.

"Something about returning here after so many years." It was as if she had heard nothing of his garbled excuses. "I can see that it makes you nervous. Poor little Dimitri . . ." He realized that she was touching him, that the bent fingers of her hand were plucking at his sleeve, and bile rose in the back of his throat. ". . . I remember when you came as our baby, so young, such a frightened little rabbit."

Her fingers lifted away and for a moment both Andropov and Olga Karenova stared at them as if they were disembodied and acting of their own volition.

"If you are worried, Dimitri, if you are troubled, come to me." Her head nodded so vigorously that for an absurd second Andropov was afraid that it might topple off. "Come to me."

Every minute his eyes searched for Sarah, around every new corner, along each corridor and inside every lift; he saw her in every turning back, every shape materializing from shadow. Each voice or footfall brought her to him, every tread upon the stairs. So many times he was terrified that he had been in her presence and not noticed her. How much would she have changed? Supposing that she had dyed her hair, cut it short, done something to alter her appearance so much that . . .

But when she stepped into the large room in which the opening reception was being held, he knew her instantly. It was as if he had some premonition that she was about to arrive, a sense of her which angled his head towards the doorway at the exact moment she was to step through the double doors.

She came with the rest of the American delegation, sixteen of them—men in solid middle age for the most part, hair either cut close or allowed to grow too long as if declaring some freedom, some commitment to the student youth of their past. The women—there were five of them—were younger, slimmer, their appearance that of people who knew they were an advertisement for the vitality and good grooming of their country. One woman, the youngest of all, her hair a long coil of black, was dressed in a green pants suit and held a black leather case tight under one arm. The impression was that if she became bored—and she certainly expected to—she would break out a batch of papers and get down to some serious reading.

Andropov was aware that the twitching had returned to his head and for an instant he glanced round to see if Olga Karenova was watching him. That was the only time his attention shifted away from Sarah, his eyes following her as close as a guiding hand. He watched her incline her head towards one of the men and nod agreement, turn the other way and smile at one of the women; another of the men stopped before her and pointed at something, his remark causing Sarah to laugh.

Andropov was fierce with jealousy.

He fought to prevent himself from hurrying across the room. He wanted to take her in his arms. This woman who had kept a love alive through few enough letters and a handful of blurred photographs, through a succession of letter drops and secret meeting places, twenty years of fear at being discovered and exposed. He wanted to touch her face with his own, wanted the warmth of that red hair against his mouth.

See seemed to see him, her head hesitated fractionally in its curving movement and then passed on. He was certain she would have been given the same warnings as himself. There was to be nothing suspicious in their behavior, they were not to seek one another out unnecessarily; at this stage to throw everything away because of a stupid risk would be an absurd waste.

Andropov made himself turn back into his own group. He hovered around the edges of a discussion on nerve tissue replacement, a glass of sherry warming in his hand. Sarah in his eye. She was wearing a green dress, loose at the waist, a hanging belt that tightened nothing, an arc of flesh above the bodice, one gold bracelet all the jewelry she wore. He wondered if she had picked him out. Certain that she had, positive that her perception of him was as finely tuned as his or her. He knew that she wanted to hurry through the milling crowd of people and be with him: knew that her feelings were identical to his own.

It was twenty minutes before, by chance, they crossed one another's paths.

"Dimitri."

At first he didn't hear her voice, thought it a snatch of someone else's conversation, a quiet sound that had slid out from the guilt of conversation. Sarah had slipped from his sight; the broad backs of two members of the Romanian delegation, identical twins, had shielded her and Andropov had taken his glass of barely tasted sherry and stood on the fringes of the Soviet group, half-listening.

"Dimitri."

There was no mistaking the voice. He turned and she was there; his mouth opened, his hand jerked outwards, the glass seemed to spiral in slow-motion to the floor. The brittle crash was muffled from all but those standing close. Andropov stared, not at the fragments of glass, the winding lane of sherry, but at Sarah. At her face, rounder now than he remembered, than in her photographs. He stared at the blue of her eyes and the fullness of her mouth. He was giddy with joy.

"Sarah!"

She jumped back as if struck. Her elbow collided with the delegate behind her, causing him to grunt and half-turn. Half a dozen of the Russians were silent, watching, their expressions varying from amusement to annoyance.

"Sarah."

The name echoed around the tight group, from the hapless Andropov to the dried mask of Olga Karenova's face, to the accusing eyes of the square-shouldered security officer, Kulyagin, the partly-smothered giggle of the youngest member of the party, on to the now-pale features of Sarah Jarrett.

"Dimitri," she said, stepping back towards him. "Dimitri Andropov." Her voice was faltering, but she was in no doubt as to what she must do. "After all this time. Well, this is a wonderful surprise."

And she gave him the smile she saved for members of her late husband's family on the rare occasions they came to call. Smiled and held out her hand. Andropov hesitated, feeling so many eyes watching him. Finally he reached out his arm and took her hand in his. His fingers convulsed, jumped as if he had touched, suddenly, unknowingly, a live wire. Sarah, smiling, clenched her hand round his and held him fast.

"How long has it been?" she was asking.

And ". . . really, can it have been so long."

And ". . . naturally, I read with a lot of interest your paper . . ."

And ". . . perhaps we can find a moment to talk later when . . ."

She had shaken his hand once again, brisk and business-like now, nodded in the direction of the few Russians who were still showing an interest in their conversation, and then she was lost amidst the throng.

Andropov felt sick. He stood with his colleagues for what seemed a long time, aware that to behave in any manner which might be interpreted as strange would mean the end of everything. He could sense that Kulyagin was watching him, peering through his thick-framed glasses as he smoked yet another of the black Russian cigarettes which he fixed into a short ivory holder and lit from a stubby gas lighter whose flame leapt a little too high.

Olga Karenova moved so that she was next to him, drew him slightly to one side. "How nice, Dimitri, that you should renew an acquaintanceship from so long ago. How charming." And she gave Andropov a smile that threatened to shake a flake or two down from the dry hide of her face.

As soon as he felt it was safe, Andropov excused himself and went to the men's room. Inside a cubicle he sat down without lowering his trousers, elbows on his knees, head bowed into his hands, the pulsing breaking more and more emphatically against his fingers.

When he finally went upstairs he found Kulyagin in his room. It was small, on the second floor of a hotel in Kongens Gate, close to the main square. A tiny entrance hall leading into a space which barely held a single bed, a folding table and bedside cabinet, a narrow set of drawers. Adjacent to the hallway there was a shower and sink, shielded by a plastic curtain. The security man sat cross-legged on the bed. From the amount of smoke in the room, the thick, slightly sweet smell of tobacco, it was clear that he had been there for some time. When Andropov entered the room, Kulyagin put down his cigarette holder, resting it on the glass ashtray, and took his spectacle case from the inside pocket of his coat. He peered up at Andropov through thick lenses and returned the cigarette holder to his mouth.

"Why . . . why are you here?"

Andropov was aware that his voice sounded weak in the closeness of the room. He wished more strength for it, for himself.

"I thought," Kulyagin began, "a little talk. Please . . ." He motioned with his hand. ". . . sit down."

So many times, Andropov was thinking, I have heard phrases like that from men like this one. So many of the patients I have dealt with have begun their journey to the hospital with exactly such a visit, exactly such a man, such an invitation to sit down and talk.

He remained standing, not finding it easy, yet conscious of the need to retain some sign of independence, of not caring. After all, wasn't he a senior member of the delegation?

"What did you wish to say to me?" There was still a tremor in his voice and Andropov clenched his hands at his sides, saw that Kulyagin had noticed and willed them to relax again.

"I thought . . ." The security man made an elaborate pantomime of using his cigarette holder. ". . . that you were, what shall I say, unusually nervous this evening."

Andropov held on, said nothing: waited.

Somewhere outside the hotel a church clock began striking, but Andropov was unable to count the chimes.

"The encounter with the American . . ."

Kulyagin smiled behind his glasses, letting the sentence remain unfinished.

"The American, yes," Andropov heard himself saying, "what of her?"

"You seemed startled by her presence."

"Of course," countered Andropov quickly, wondering even as he was talking if he hadn't spoken too soon, appeared too anxious, "after so many years, who would expect to . . ." He paused, coughed into the back of his hand. "We were fellow delegates here in nineteen fifty-nine. It was inconceivable that she should be here. Naturally I was startled."

"Yes," agreed Kulyagin, "but not inconceivable since she is here."

"But how was I to know, what was I to think?"

Kulyagin stood up, his legs unfolding with a fluidity which somehow belied the stolidness of his appearance. "Of course, I understand."

"That is all you wished to say?" asked Andropov as the security officer moved towards the door.

In the narrow space their bodies almost touched.

"I was concerned, nothing more."

"Of course."

Hand on the door, Kulyagin turned as Andropov had known he must. "One of our comrades reported that you seemed unwell during the flight. He said you appeared nervous, apprehensive."

"It was the thought of landing. It always affects me that way. Nothing more."

Kulyagin nodded: "Of course."

When he had gone, Andropov threw up the window to clear the room of the smell of cigarettes. For some time, he leaned against the sill and watched the cars slowly cruising the street.

Since the last time she had met him, when he had visited her at her home outside of Boston, Malone had let his hair grow that much more fashionably long. Now its ends were beginning to curl where they touched the nape of his neck and hung over his ears. He was, Sarah thought, an attractive man and yet . . . for a moment she tried to imagine herself in bed with him, but the image balked at the edge of her mind. It wasn't that he was sexless, nor that his body lacked either beauty or strength—he did have very good legs—it was the bleached blue of his eyes that held her imagination at bay. The thought of coming back into full consciousness and seeing them staring down; seeing that and knowing that they had never been anything less than alert.

She stamped out her cigarette and noticed with a fleck of annoyance that the red of her lipstick was clear on the stub. She was certain Malone would notice too and find it offensive.

She said: "You'll have to change your plan."

Malone leaned back in the chair. Coffee and orange juice stood on the table in the center of the room. The first plenary session of the conference was due to commence in a little less than half an hour. When he had looked out of the window and towards the wooded hills earlier, Malone had thought there was snow in the air. If it had been Connecticut, there would have been snow for sure.

"No."

For some inexplicable reason, Sarah felt relaxed, more so than she had since leaving the States. It was as though, somehow, she had gained the edge—a space ahead of the game in which she could feel good and rest. She had been feeling the same way all those years before when she had first noticed Andropov sliding nervously into his seat, wide rabbit eyes twitching.

"Malone," she said, beginning to smile, "this is no time for you to be stubborn."

"It isn't a case of that."

"Isn't it? I thought you boys were supposed to be adept at changing fast to meet new situations." She raised an eyebrow and let a shade more exaggerated Southern drawl slide into her voice. Hadn't she been brought up in Virginia? "That's the way it always is on TV."

"This isn't . . ." Malone began and quickly realized she was teasing him.

Sarah laughed and asked if there was more coffee. Malone fetched it, adding sugar and cream, wondering what the hell she was doing being so damned attractive at breakfast time and her forty-eight years of age.

Sarah took the cup and the brightness of her eyes told them both that she knew what he was thinking.

"You don't think he'll hold?"

"That business last night, dropping his glass and behaving like a fool in front of all those Russians—are you kidding me, Malone?"

Malone sighed and drummed a brief tattoo on the chair arm. "I heard about that," he said. "I also heard you handled yourself pretty well."

Sarah grinned. "Living alone, a woman has to learn how."

Malone was brought up short by the ambiguity, glanced at her to make sure it hadn't been intended. Of course, it had.

"He'll crack," she said.

"He'll have to hold on. Speak to him. This evening, lunchtime perhaps."

Sarah was shaking her head. "You don't know him."

Malone shifted his weight. He didn't like the way Sarah seemed to be getting on top of the conversation. He said briskly, a little too briskly, "One night hardly qualifies you for knowing him."

"What about the letters, Malone? The years of letters. I was the only one he talked to, the only one he felt was close and maybe understood. Maybe. I know him, know how much this means to him."

Malone was about to interrupt, but something in Sarah's face inhibited him. He drank some orange juice and waited for her to continue.

"It isn't even me," she was saying. "Not now it isn't. That's not what he wants, me, even though he might say it is." She made a tossing movement of her head and her hair caught the light from the lamp that was switched on in the corner of the room. "It's Richard."

Malone nodded, mouthed, silently, "Yes."

"I never asked," said Malone, leaning back in his chair. "When did you tell him? Tell Richard, I mean."

Sarah reached for her packet of cigarettes, took one

out and let it lay on the lap of her skirt. "I told him after the funeral. Howard's funeral. We were standing in the kitchen. Everyone else had gone. Ricky was helping me stack dishes in the washer and I just told him. Richard, I said, he wasn't your father. I know, mother, he said right back. I think I've always known." Sarah set the cigarette between her lips but still didn't light it. "That night he came into my room. It was late, past one. He just sat on the bed and I told him who his father was. I told him about here and the poky apartment with the trolley buses outside and . . ."

Malone grasped her wrist between his fingers and forced her to look at him.

"It's all right," she said before he could ask. "I didn't tell him anything else. None of the rest. He doesn't know about the letters, about this; he knows nothing."

"You're sure?"

"How could he?"

Malone stood up. "I guess not." He glanced at the watch on his wrist.

"All right," Sarah said, settling the unlit cigarette back into the packet, "I'm on my way."

He held her arm a moment longer than was necessary. "Thanks for what you did the other night, the way you handled things, it was . . ."

"It was what I'm being paid for."

Malone's hand dropped away.

"You'll think about what I said."

He nodded. "I'll think about it, but at the moment day five looks good to me."

"Still?"

"Still."

"Okay," Sarah shrugged and Malone opened the door for her. He watched her walk toward the lift, wondering how many women of nearly fifty had legs that good.

* * *

Kulyagin sat on Andropov like a hawk tight to the glove. Every time the Soviet scientist turned his head, raised his eyes from his notepad or his plate of scarcely touched food, there was the pair of spectacles focused towards him. In the men's room Kulyagin used the urinal and basin next to Andropov's; waiting patiently to share the same towel.

From a distance Sarah saw what was happening and hoped that Malone saw it too. The security officer was pushing Andropov hard, making him sweat, watching until he broke. Once, coming into the conference hall, she saw Andropov's eyes seeking her out. Save me, they said, help me. Get me out!

It was after dinner that Malone made his move. The dining room of the hotel the Soviets were using was on the ground floor, along a broad, L-shaped corridor from the reception desk. There were several Eastern bloc countries staying at the hotel and what seats remained in the restaurant were taken by other visitors. The town was always overcrowded at conference time. Kulyagin came through the dining room doors with less than five yards between Andropov and himself. Two more of the Soviet delegation were following the security officer; they approached the doors as he passed through. The waitress turned from the coffee table in the corner of the room and her arm collided with the nearest of the two following Russians. Coffee leapt across the front of his gray suit, the sleeve and leg of the man alongside him. At once the waitress, flustered, began to dab at the men with a cloth, apologizing loudly. A customer from the nearest table hurried to help, interposing himself between the two men and the still lightly swinging doors.

Outside, at the beginning of the corridor, Kulyagin began to swivel round, hearing the sound of the cup and saucer as they shattered. His spectacles were halfway to his inside pocket. Two men came around the L of the corridor fast. For fractionally longer than it should have taken, Kulyagin saw them as diners at the hotel. One hand trapped his wrist hard against the front of his jacket, another gripped the muscle of his upper arm expertly, so that when he tried to struggle the pain was sharp and intense. Between the heads and shoulders of the men, he could see Andropov being hustled away. He managed to open his fingers wide enough to let his spectacles fall to the floor, but nothing more.

"There's a car out front," said Malone urgently. "Walk to it now. Get into the rear seat and lie flat."

Andropov's eyes were wide and startled. Malone could see the nerve ticking fast and then faster.

"My baggage . . . ?" he began.

"In the car."

"Sarah . . . ?"

"She'll be on a later flight."

Still Andropov stared, transfixed in the lobby like a startled animal caught in the oncoming headlights of a car.

Malone could hear voices around the corner of the corridor. He knew that his delaying tactics only allowed so much time; his instructions had been to make as little fuss as possible, to avoid an incident from which the Soviets would feel unable to back down.

"Go!"

He half-pushed, half-pulled Andropov through the glass doors and on to the pavement; the rear door of the Opel was already open wide. Andropov lost his footing and Malone caught him. Outside the cafeteria next door, a couple of women nudged one another and began to point. Through the doors, Malone saw Kulyagin run into the lobby.

"In!"

He threw Andropov into the rear of the car and the scientist fell, half along the back seat, one arm and leg sprawled awkwardly across the floor. Malone slammed the door shut and pulled open the passenger door. The car was already swinging away. As he shut the door behind him, Malone realized that Kulyagin was standing directly in the path of the car, his hands resting on the top of the hood.

The driver looked at Malone hastily, questioningly.

A few more people were beginning to gather; several of the Soviets were pressed against the inside of the glass doors like visitors to the aquarium. Malone clenched in his breath tightly and climbed back out into the street. The Russian made no attempt to move, except that when Malone came towards him, he lifted his hands from the car and squared his shoulders.

"You know that what you are doing is in violation . . ."

Malone set his left hand on the man's shoulder, close enough for the fingers to trap the nerve at the base of the neck. His other hand darted low with a speed which Kulyagin couldn't match. He grasped the Russian's testicles and twisted hard. A strangled sound escaped from Kulyagin's throat and immediately his eyes began to water; both of his arms made desperate swimming motions, as of a man drowning.

The Opel had backed away and now it came alongside Malone, its passenger door flung wide. In a second Malone was inside and the car was jumping away, leaving Kulyagin on his knees in the gutter, both hands clasped between his legs.

Olga Karenova's cable to Karpov was brief:

"The fox has got the rabbit."

· CHAPTER 14 ·

Moose Head was a rocky wooded bluff that jutted out into the Atlantic between Quoddy Head and Machias. It was high up the Maine coast so that the next thing you came to, almost, was Canada. Back from the Head was a narrow inlet like a beckoning finger, the tip at low tide a spread of gray-brown mud that sucked at a man's boots when he walked. When the tide was up, the water level widened out until it came within spitting distance of the tree line: thick green spruce.

Across to the south of the channel there was a dilapidated canning factory, the walls of the main building collapsing inward but never quite falling; the legs of the loading jetty tall like a flock of pale gray herons, quite still by the shore. On the north side there was a timbered boatshed with a brick chimney off to one flank. A smaller shed stood behind on stilts, and then a short, high jetty whose supports hung dark green two-thirds of the way up. Moose Head Haven was the sign at the front of the boatshed, but several of the letters had fallen away and the imagination had to read them back in.

A dirt track road, wide enough for a single car or pick-up, ran down between the boathouse and a slope of rough green that spread back for some thirty yards into the trees. In the middle of that space there was a shingle hut with a steep sloping roof and a single window and door which were painted red and padlocked. A power cable ran from the hut to the boathouse and then tracked back again to the house by the side of the dirt road.

It was inside the house that they were holding Andropov.

A large house, a foundation of bricks and cement holding it level above the uneven ground. Like so many of the houses that were passed on the drive off Highway 1, it was made from overlapping boards and shingles, all painted white. The roofing was a deep rose-red and all of the windows were fitted with white linen shades; those facing out on to the inlet were pulled down. A short flight of steps led up to what might have been a conservatory had there been any sign of plants or flowers inside: instead model sailing ships stood along each ledge and sill. They were set on shelves which had been specially fitted to the rear walls to take the tea clippers and schooners with comfort. Where there were no ships there were books or china—small leather-bound volumes with colored page ends that showed dully through a film of dust, bone china cups and saucers, sauce pots and plates, hand-painted with flowers and foxes and fishes with open mouths and large heads. Almost every room in the house was the same confusion of bric-a-brac. And underneath it, running the whole length, was a cellar crammed with three generations of collecting and never throwing away.

They called the Petersons the magpies when they drove in each week to the store in Lubec. Called them that to their backs and nodded to their faces and exchanged a few words about the fog or the sardine catch or whose house had been the latest victim of arson. Herbert Peterson, he hired his boats through the season and took people out himself, showing them where to make the really big catches and making them pay for it something special. Millie, she cooked for the visitors and made their beds and in between times she went round the place dusting her knick-knacks with a feather duster and singing old hymns to herself under her breath. They'd been like it for forty or more years, and no one figured they'd be any different till they died.

Andropov was in the parlor room at the center of the house, sitting in a polished wooden rocker with a blue padded cushion tied to its back. Behind him was a glass-fronted mahogany chest crammed with cups and pieces of gold and silver plate, colored vases and willow-patterned bowls.

The screen door didn't fasten properly unless it was locked from the outside, and now it was banging with the wind.

Millie looked into the room to see if their visitor wanted a cup of tea. Andropov's head lolled to one side and his eyes were closed as if he were asleep; one hand was loosely gripped about the smooth arm of the chair, the other resting on his lap. He hadn't shaved that day, his skin the color of grime that contrasted harshly with the contents of the room.

The screen door banged loudly. The Russian's hand tightened on the chair and his head jerked up, eyes opening and immediately flickering across the room with fear. When he saw it was the woman he relaxed slightly. He heard her voice faintly, as if through layers of lace. He nodded his head, as much to send her out of the room as anything. There was a clock on one of the small tables, a small black and whiteface set into the head of a china dog. Andropov leaned over and peered at it—seven minutes past eleven. He guessed that they would return at midday, the same two men who had been questioning him since his arrival on the previous afternoon. First there had been the doctor whose breath had smelled of peppermints and who had reminded him of the conference hall in Trondheim the first morning he had seen Sarah. Then his interrogators, a burly man with a cast in his left eye who had introduced himself as Pyle and the fresh-faced youngster who looked little more than twenty and spoke with a soft drawl which Andropov had difficulty in understanding. The second man was called Duvall. So far they had been polite and patient, understanding.

But a remark Pyle had made when they were leaving the room the last time had told Andropov clearly enough that this patience had limits. They had told him about the building between the house and the trees. Obligingly, Duvall had held the screen door open long enough for him to see the shuttered window, the electricity cables. He did not need to be told what facilities would be kept there; neither did it have to be spelled out to him which techniques would be used. It was all a matter of time: time and cooperation.

Millie Peterson shuffled in with the tea. She walked without lifting her feet from the ground, her backless carpet slippers worn and comfortable and many years old. The tea was strong and sweet and Andropov drank it slowly, trying to think out the correct strategy. Not to tell them everything he knew too soon, that was the thing. To make them believe that he had information which was of great interest which he would divulge as soon as . . .

As soon as they allowed him to see Sarah.

Sarah and Richard.

The phone rang in one of the other rooms. Andropov looked again at the dog which was a clock: eleven fifteen. They called in every two hours, day and night, whether his interrogators were there or not. Andropov guessed that there was some kind of control post in the nearest town, perhaps a house in which the American who had brought him into the country, in which Malone waited and listened to the tapes of the debriefing. There would be someone with him, Andropov thought, an expert in the transmission and assimilation of information. They would have access to a computer terminal, the business of collation would be continuous. What Andropov gave them would be checked against what they already knew, what they suspected, what they wanted to know.

They had talked little on the plane, the tall American

with faded blue eyes and himself, but enough for Andropov to know that Malone was more than a little interested in Fedin. He had tried to hide it, kept his face as immobile as ever, his hands as still, yet there had been something—a quickening of the pulse which Andropov had sensed almost vibrating through the tight space between them as they sat side by side at the rear of the aircraft.

Yes, Malone wanted Fedin more than anything: and for himself, he wanted Richard. Sarah and Richard: Richard and Sarah.

Well, then, let both of them get what they wanted.

But Andropov knew that if he let Malone have Fedin too soon he was unlikely to be allowed to see either Sarah or Richard until the whole process was over and done. He knew that could be a matter of many weeks, months even. And he did not want to wait that long.

"He's holding out."

"You're sure?"

"No doubt about it."

Pyle was sitting beside the window, the brightness of the clear light making one side of his face shine and covering the cast in his eye completely. Duvall leaned forward on the center of the settee, slightly uncomfortable in Malone's presence, still in awe of seniority, especially the kind which had been gained in the field.

Malone himself sat at a darkened pine table in his shirt sleeves, the light burnishing the hairs on his forearms. Every now and again he would drum a quick rhythm on the wood, punctuating the conversaton, his own thoughts.

"Sir, he has been involved in this kind of thing. I mean, the debriefing of defectors and such like. He must be aware of the procedure better than most."

Duvall looked up at Malone as he was speaking, his tone deferential.

"You mean he's playing the game for his own ends?"

"Yes, sir, I think so."

Malone pushed his chair back from the table, seemed about to stand up but didn't. "What have we got to lose if we play it his way?"

"Time, sir?" asked Duvall, uncertain whether it was the answer Malone wanted.

Pyle shook his head.

"Well?" Malone asked.

"The initiative," Pyle answered. "We lose the initiative."

"Fine. So what do you suggest?"

Pyle shrugged, sat round away from the light. "I think he's going to keep pussyfooting about for weeks if we do it this way. Talk for an hour, ask questions. Bring the answers in, find out which questions we have to ask next, build up a dossier little by little." He shook his head. "It'll take too long and we can never be sure how much he's holding back on purpose."

Malone's fingers executed a neat paradiddle and he nodded towards Pyle, telling him to continue.

"We can give him a couple of shots of Pentathol. That'll open him up enough to begin with. Then when he's thrown out a whole lot more than is coming already, we can take him into the shack. Shoot a few volts through him and bust him wide open."

Malone stood up so fast that Duvall rocked back on the settee in surprise. Pyle did no more than blink his bad eye and open one hand flat against the wall.

"You know what we've got here, don't you?" Malone said. "I mean, you do know what we're dealing with? This is a friendly defector. An expert in Soviet methods of using psychiatric methods on all manner of people, all kinds of what they call enemies of the state. Well this isn't an enemy of the state. Not this state. Not the U.S. This is a man we've persuaded to come over to us after a lot of effort and a lot of energy. We want to be able to parade him in front of the media boys without them picking up on the fact that we've been shooting him full of dope and sticking saline electrodes to his head. We want him to work side by side with our own scientists and tell them what he knows of his own accord. Now do you understand that?''

Duvall mumbled that he did, certainly he did.

Pyle took his time because he wasn't going to show that he was allowing himself to be railroaded by rank, but he eventually nodded and shifted his feet a little and said if that was how Malone wanted it . . .

''You're damn right that's how I want it!''

Pyle pushed himself up from the chair and glanced out at the street. There wasn't a soul in sight. Just more of these clapboard places that looked to Pyle like they'd been built for a movie that had never been made and been left standing. He was certain no one lived in the things. No one normal, anyway. What he wouldn't give for some solid brick and concrete, even a good old tenement or two. Some skyline, not this picture book stuff.

''You're going to let him see his kid, then?'' Pyle said.

Malone shook his head.

''Play it your way, you've got to give him something.''

''The son's out of the country. He works for this conservation organization. Goes all over. He wasn't supposed to be out but he is.''

''We bringing him back?''

''No.''

''Then it's the woman.''

Malone didn't like it, was still uncertain how far he could trust Sarah not to crack, but in the circumstances . . . ''Sure,'' he said, ''the woman.''

''You'll get her flown up here?''

''Tonight.''

''We can tell him?''

Malone nodded. ''You tell him.''

''Okay.'' Pyle glanced across at Duvall. ''Let's go.''

Malone watched them walk down the drive and into the Buick. Something in his gut told him that bringing Sarah up to Maine wasn't the ideal solution, that Richard would have been better. But Richard was in Europe and if it was a choice between Sarah and games out in the woodshed he guessed it had to be Sarah.

He made the call and when it was over he was certain that Sarah had been drinking. Real drinking.

"What's that?" asked Duvall, looking at the small leather case Pyle lifted from the trunk.

"This?" Pyle grinned. He snapped it open and showed the syringe, the two small stoppered bottles. "What the hell you think it is?"

"But you can't . . ."

Pyle rested a hand, not lightly, on the front of Duvall's jacket. "I always said, the trouble with all you good old Southern boys is you have too much respect for authority."

Herb Peterson was a big man and the weather had eaten into his skin and left it brown and strong like old leather. His eyes were still as clear and as keen as they had been when he was seventeen. His appetites were still as strong. Just once in a while there'd be a woman who came up to the place for one of the fishing holidays he and Millie ran, and then, boy, he'd show her something she never looked to be getting, even though the brochure did advertise the week as being all inclusive.

Peterson laughed at the memory of it, the last time, that grade teacher from Iowa some place who didn't know which hour of the night it was or where it was coming from next. Old Millie's ornaments clinking and tinkling and falling to the floor, one by one.

Pyle came walking over towards him from the Buick and Peterson set down the lobster pot he'd been fixing, waiting to see what he wanted.

"That wife of yours," Pyle began.

"Millie. What of her?"

"She's been in there again, talking to him."

Herb Peterson took his time about clearing his throat; spat down on to one of the thick planks which formed the way up to the boatshed. Behind him the channel was running narrow, gray-brown mud stretched wide towards the trees. A bird scooped low over the water with a flourish of wings.

"So what if she has?"

"You know what."

Peterson stared across at him, saying nothing.

"Keep her away from there. Tell her to leave him be."

"What goes on in the house ain't none of my business. That's Millie's in there. You talk to her."

"We already did."

"Sometimes she don't hear too good."

Pyle wasn't sure enough that Peterson was goading him, not sure enough to do something about it.

"You tell her," he said pointing at Peterson. "Tell her to keep well clear."

Herb Peterson hawked up some more phlegm and swished it around in his mouth a little. He knew Pyle was thinking about taking a swing at him and every ounce of him wished the man would. But all Pyle did was fix him with as hard a look as he could with that funny eye of his and then stomp off towards the house, the other one joining on after him like a tame hound. Peterson laughed and went back to his work.

Andropov was leafing through a small, bound book, a collection of Puritan sermons by Jonathan Edwards. He set it down on the shelf when he heard the men at the screen door and was sitting back in his chair by the time they entered the room. Duvall was carrying the tape machine; Pyle a small leather case which he held almost delicately in his left hand. He set the case down on the round table between them and looked at it for only a moment—but it was long enough, specific enough, for Andropov to guess at its significance.

"You asked about Richard?" Andropov said. "You asked about my son? About Sarah?"

"What we'd like to talk about," said Duvall, talking quietly and as if the Russian had never spoken, "is the man whom you claim worked under the codename of Fedin."

"We already . . ."

"Of course," Duvall continued, "we are still checking the information about this man which you gave us and there appears to be some difficulty in matching up what you say with information already known to us."

"I assure you everything I said was true."

Pyle laughed, short and brusque.

"The name, for instance . . ."

"The name is on the man's file. His codename. There is no doubt about the facts I gave you. I . . ."

"Hey, now, stop playing games, huh?" Pyle's voice was rougher than Duvall's, louder. He had remained standing close to the wall while his partner sat close. Now he made a couple of paces forward, pointing a finger towards Andropov's chest.

"You read this Fedin's file, right?"

"Yes, I told . . ."

"Then you must know his name?"

Andropov shook his head. "No. There was no name."

"Nationality?"

"No."

"Age?"

"No."

Pyle slapped his hands against his thighs with digust. "Some file!"

Andropov willed himself to interrupt. "I wish to talk of Richard."

"He's in Europe." Pyle's voice was savage, final.

"You bring me out of Europe to America and then you tell me that the son I have never seen is not here but there."

Andropov was half out his chair, hands pushing down on the polished wood of the arms, the strain showing clearly on his face.

"You weren't due to come over for days yet, he would have been here by the time you arrived."

"You say," Andropov shouted, staring across the

room at Pyle. Through the door to the left came the indistinct sound of Millie Peterson singing of going down to the river.

"That's it, buddy, I say."

The two men stared at one another until Andropov slowly subsided into his chair.

"And Sarah?" he asked finally, his eyes on the floor.

"Tell us about the man in Berlin."

"I told you!" Anguish broke from the edges of Andropov's voice. His throat seemed to be swelling; it was beginning to be an effort to speak. He rubbed his neck and swivilled his head. "I must have something to drink."

The two men looked back at him impassively.

"Please," he implored Duvall.

"Sure," said Pyle, "get him some water. No, make coffee. Tell that old woman to make coffee. We'll all take it easy and drink coffee while the professor here tells us all about the man in the little room in Berlin with his paperback westerns stacked wall to wall."

The dog-clock told Andropov it was several minutes short of two hours before the session finished. He was having difficulty keeping his eyes open, his throat still seemed to be swelling up. More than anything—almost anything—he wanted to sleep.

"Sure," said Pyle, "you get some rest. After all, with that Sarah you keep jammering on about arriving tonight, I guess you're going to need it."

Andropov's arm slipped from the chair; his face tightened sharply, "Sarah? Tonight she will be here?"

"Take it easy. Take it easy. You wanted to see her, she's coming. What did you think, we're holding out on you? You carry on being a good professor and there's no telling what you'll end up getting."

Andropov's mind was still off-balance. He looked at Duvall for confirmation of what the other man had said and Duvall nodded that it was true.

"One thing," said Pyle and pointed at the leather

case that was still on the table. "You know what's in there, don't you?"

Andropov hesitated. "Perhaps, I am not sure, only . . ."

"I'm going to leave that where it is for you to look at every once in a while until we come back. If we find you've been holding out on us then a shot of that is what you're going to get and that'll only be the beginning. You understand me, don't you, professor?"

Andropov nodded and looked away; he understood all too well.

The screen door banged shut and a few minutes later the car engine started up. It was some moments before the sound of the Buick had faded away. Tonight, Andropov was thinking. Sarah was coming that night. Millie Peterson came into the room with a faraway smile and began to flick a yellow feather duster along the shelves and over the tops of the tables, singing snatches of tunes as she went, praising the Lord and giving him thanks.

Herb Peterson drove Sarah from the grass air strip at Lubec. He had been waiting with Malone when the single-engine Bar Harbor plane had landed at the end of its charter flight from Bangor. Mist had risen above the landing lights and hovered there like yellow fog. Peterson had rolled a cigarette and struck a match on the underside of his boot, a quick dry rasp against the scored leather. As soon as Sarah had gone out Malone took her in his own car, while Peterson waited by his pick-up truck, the light of his cigarette like a stationary glow-worm in the dusk.

Malone gave her coffee, black, and laced it with brandy from a flask. He told her to be as natural as she could, to help Andropov relax and let him think everything was going to be all right between them as soon as the debriefing was over. Tell him about the house in Sharon; tell him about Richard and the work he's doing. Just make him feel that it's okay.

Malone saw Sarah shiver and hoped it was the cold; he gave her another tot of brandy and then told her to keep the flask. If she was drinking anyway, this wasn't going to make any difference.

"I'm glad you come up, " Malone said.

"Did I have any choice?"

Malone watched her climb into Peterson's pick-up and thought that she looked good. He just hoped she'd be good enough to go some way towards fulfilling Andropov's fantasy. Part of it. He waited until the tail lights of the pick-up had faded away and then drove back to the house, wanting to sleep himself but knowing there was a lot of the material Pyle and Duvall had gathered which need sifting.

Herb Peterson chatted away as they drove along 191, used to passing the time with the holidaymakers he took out into the ocean, sensing something of Sarah's taut nervousness but passing it over, letting the words fall as easily as the night did around them. When they drove down the dirt track towards the house, its lights shone out strongly against the backdrop of trees.

Peterson carried her suitcase up the steps and through the kitchen to the back room on the first floor where they were going to sleep. Andropov took Sarah tight into his arms and rocked her there for so long that her arms grew numb, imprisoned under his. Finally she had to tell him to let her go and when he did she saw that the tears had already started to dry on his face.

Millie Peterson served them up a fried clam supper and as they ate Sarah and Herb Peterson kept up a rather desultory conversation, Andropov not listening, not taking his eyes for more than a few seconds at a time from Sarah's face.

"I guess you folks are tired out," said Herb, lighting a roll-up as Millie cleared the table. "Why don't you get on up?"

The phone rang in the next room and he went stiffly to answer it, assuring the caller that everything was all right.

Andropov's eyes checked the clock.

"Come, Sarah," he said.

She submitted to his kisses and then made him sit on the bed while she sat in the easy chair with its intricate lace antimacassar and poured them both brandy into the glasses that had stood on either side of the washstand.

"Drink up, Dimitri," she said, forcing a smile. "Drink to us. After all those goddamn years! All those miserable goddamn years!"

Andropov moved to comfort her, but she flung out her arm and kept him at bay and shook her head. "You mustn't . . . you mustn't rush me. I can't . . . I don't . . . Oh, God!"

She swallowed down the brandy and poured another immediately. All those years living with Howard had made it an automatic process for her as well. The only thing was that until recently, until now, she had been able to keep the need for it at bay. The need for so many things.

"Sarah, what is it?"

She was the one who was crying now, gulping sobs which rocked her body in the chair. Andropov reaching forward each time as if afraid she might fall out of the chair and on to the floor. Even through the tears, even with the distortions of her face, she looked beautiful.

"Sarah." He was on his knees before her, holding her arms gently and moving with the slow swaying of her body. "Sarah, it is all right. We are here, together. We love each other. It is all right."

She collapsed against him and he fell with her to the floor, the pair of them jammed awkwardly between bed and chair. Andropov kissed her face, her hair; he ran his hands over her back, her arms, pressed her to his chest and felt fresh tears as they ran on to his cheek and neck. The smell of brandy was warm and strong on her breath.

"Sarah!"

He lifted her on to the bed, laid her diagonally across it, trying not to look at the tear-strewn face now, the blotch of powder and the smearing of lipstick. Pushing against her side, his hands starting nervously, compulsively, to unfasten her clothing.

She tried to roll away but he had to pull her back, so much pent-up feeling, so much desire for her pressed tight into a ball which her presence had begun to unwind and which now would not be stopped.

Sarah mumbled his name until it became an incoherence, a jabbering which rose and fell as he moved himself above her and struggled to rid himself of his own clothing. She cried out as he entered her, unready, unwilling even, part of her mind wishing herself to be miles away, the rest not even knowing where she was.

Andropov craned over her, his mouth settling for seconds only on the tops of her shoulders, her mouth, the faded beauty of her breasts. He repeated her name over and over again and as he came the first time the word "Sarah" screamed from his lips like a curse.

She moaned and shifted beneath him but he was still hard. He buried his face against her belly and still the nether part of him insisted on moving against her, like a dog in heat.

"God, Dimitri, No! I can't, can't. I'm so damned sore, don't you understand? Sore!"

If the Russian understood he gave little sign. He thrust inside her hard and he was excited by his sudden virility. He allowed himself to misconstrue Sarah's writhing, her shouted protests, for passion. Spending himself in her with the force of a lover he had always dreamed, but never imagined, he might become.

Almost immediately Andropov was asleep. One leg hauled across Sarah's knees, an arm resting heavily on her breast, he lay, open-mouthed, and snored. When he awoke it was to a silence which was broken after no more than a few seconds by the sounds of someone retching outside the door. He opened his eyes and sat up, feeling stupidly over the surface of the bed to see if she were still there. He pulled on his trousers, awkward in the dark, and then a shirt; went out into the corridor and followed the sounds to the bathroom.

Sarah was kneeling before the toilet bowl as if in prayer.

Her head jerked back and then down, back and then down; the sound which came from her throat made Andropov's own stomach cold. He bent over her, went down on one knee beside her. The ends of her red hair trailed in the thick, clotted water at the bottom of the bowl and were matted together with vomit.

"Sarah. My darling Sarah."

He rubbed her back, nuzzled the cold sweat at the rear of her neck; fumbled for her hand and squeezed the fingers tight.

"Go away, away. Howard, go away."

Four years and who knows what memory dredged his name from her lips?

Andropov stayed. Finally helped her to her feet and led her to the wash basin. He took a washcloth and cleaned her face and hair as best he could, reassuring her all the while, ignoring the fact that she kept trying to pull away from him like a child caught out in the perpetration of some dreadful wrong.

Down below Millie Peterson was in the kitchen drinking tea, a hair net on her head and a quilted dressing gown belted loosely about her, the same slippers on her feet. She had obviously heard what was going on and showed no surprise when Andropov appeared. She gave him a glass of water and set out two bone china cups and saucers on a small tray, filling them from a ready-made pot and sending him back upstairs. When he was on the landing, he heard the telephone ring and realized why she had been up and awake.

Sarah was sitting in the chair facing the bed, her face completely white. She took the glass from Andropov without a word and drank it in birdlike sips, ignoring the tea. He drank both cups, waiting for her to recover.

"Who is Howard?" he asked eventually.

She didn't hesitate more than an instant. She told him

about her marriage, about the manner in which her husband's drinking had grown and grown until it had become alcoholism, about the accident which had widowed her again. Andropov listened to all this with an increasingly numb feeling taking over his limbs, spreading from his skin deep into the bones. Suddenly, he knew, even though she said nothing more, that the husband was only one of the things she had kept back from him, only one of the lies. He knew and was terrified, and for now that fear was frozen in him, a fury that would eventually break out or break him inside.

"You must sleep," he said quietly. "Sleep."

Andropov tucked the covers about her and set the cups and saucers carefully back on the tray, handling them deftly as befitted fine china; putting the glass between them and carrying them downstairs. Millie Peterson had apparently gone back to bed. Andropov stood for several minutes in the middle of the kitchen frightened at his own calmness, not trusting it. With care he took Pyle's leather case from the table. As carefully as if it were one of the bone china cups, Andropov carried it back up the stairs and closed the bedroom door softly behind him.

• CHAPTER 15 •

He had thought nothing of it at the time. One of those things which occur at the outer limits of vision and which fail to register other than subliminally. A pair of hands pushing a brown manilla envelope into a drawer and sliding it shut. Andropov didn't know which drawer that the house offered had been used, but he was certain what was in the envelope. He had seen it pass from himself to Malone, from Malone to Pyle to Peterson: the envelope held his passport.

At the time it had meant nothing, an irrelevance, a relic of a past he already considered himself having left behind. Mother Russia. In the fullness of his new country's wisdom, he would be presented with fresh papers, a clean passport—there would be a ceremony perhaps, the media of the Western world would picture his conversion to the freedom of capitalist democracy.

Andropov felt sick. Not in the same way as Sarah, but deeper, much deeper, and in his mind rather than his body. His body, too, ached, but with realization rather than pain. He wondered, from the depths of his Russian Orthodox past, from the stories his grandmother had told to him in whispered tones in the cold of her scullery, what it had been like for Paul—struck blind on the road to Damascus. Knocked from his horse by the sudden force of revelation. For Andropov himself it had come more gradually, Sarah's slurred, unsteady words spilling on to the white sheets to writhe like maggots. Scales scraped from his eyes.

For over twenty years he had lived the empty life of a fool. His every thought and action had been engendered by a belief he now knew to have been based on an emptiness of wind and water. His son a vast pregnancy that had been fertilized by hysterical need.

Except:

Except that his son was alive. Andropov's heart had clutched so tight he was afraid for an instant his blood might stop. Alive and his. His child—that part of it no lie. Andropov had Richard's address etched into his brain. Until an hour ago he would never have considered it possible that he could get so far, not on his own. But against the enormity of what he had already done—the casting aside of a country and a life for the comfort of a few lies, bought and paid for—what was this?

And something else impelled him. Out of the realization that he had offered up his life to such a sham, such a false goddess, Andropov's mind was beginning to be driven by the need to act for himself, to do what he knew to be important, to be true. He had to see Richard: all consequences now were immaterial.

Below, the telephone burped and rang.

Herb Peterson was awake by the second ring, his feet touching the carpeted floor by the third. Beside him, his wife slept on, her snoring as faint and distant as the hymns with which she celebrated each and every day. Peterson went down the stairs in bare feet, striped flannelette pajamas, rubbing his left eye clear of sleep with his opposite hand. Once the call had been taken, he would not return to bed. A pot of strong, thick tea and then out to the jetty—the tide was up and the channel full.

"Hello." Why the fuss with every two hours over this one, he didn't know. But at least there wasn't any fooling around with passwords and the like.

"Yeah," Peterson said gruffly. "Sure, sure. Everything's fine. What d'you expect?"

Without waiting for an answer, he dropped the receiver back into the cradle and started to turn away. The swing of the iron bar caught him between temple and forehead and the crack was clear and clean above the duller thud of the impact. Peterson's mouth opened to cry out as the table skittered away under his flailing, falling hand and a dozen pieces of ornate china broke across the floor. He landed on the base of his spine and his eyes blinked away not sleep but blood.

Andropov lifted the bar back over his head, over his right shoulder. Imagined Sarah's face, cold beneath him, turning away. Fragments of truth. The bar burned along his arms and his anger broke. He brought it back down. The end, ragged with rust, drove into the top of Peterson's head, exactly at the fading hairline. The length of the bar juddered inside Andropov's hands as it struck Peterson's face, buckling against cheekbone and jaw.

Andropov lifted the iron away, his breath rasping, scraping at his throat. His grip on the bar was so tight that he could no more will his fingers to loosen than he could pry Sarah's words from his mind. A sliver of pink slid thirstily between Peterson's lips and down through the stubble of his chin. Andropov leaned forward a long way, resting his weight on the bar, the bloodied tip of it pushed hard into the patterned carpet. He was still breathing loudly, with difficulty, a nerve at the side of his head beginning to race.

There were footsteps on the stairs.

He thought it would be Millie Peterson but it was Sarah. In the pale yellow of the electric light, her face was waxen, puffed out. Her hair, where it was not matted to her head by sweat and sleep, hung in straggling curls of failing color.

"Oh, God!"

Andropov ignored her, his hands already pulling at

the handles of drawers, rifling through folded papers and cloth, seeking the passport.

"Dimitri, what . . . ? My God!"

As Andropov's search became more frantic, she knelt alongside Herb Peterson, using the hem of her nightdress to wipe away the blood that was beginning to mask his face. Old yellowing newspapers were hurled across the room. Lace tableclothes and raffia table mats and boxes of faded photographs were strewn over the floor, haphazardly over Peterson's unmoving body. Sarah set her ear against his chest, the flannelette still warm. With a sweep of his arm, Andropov cleared an entire shelf of Dresden shepherdesses. Ignoring Sarah utterly, he hurried into the next room and switched on the light. After the passport there were other things, but unless he had that . . .

It was resting on top of a strip of calico, the flap of brown manilla tucked neatly inside. Andropov's fingers tore it down and pulled the passport clear. As he gazed at it prior to putting it in his inside pocket, his attention was wrenched away by a scream. He pushed the passport inside his coat, catching it twice against the lining. He kicked his way through the debris which now littered the floor.

Sarah and Millie Peterson were struggling over Peterson's body, the two of them, still in nightclothes, rocking from side to side as if performing some macrabre dance. Millie's eyes were dark and wide, her fingers dug hard into Sarah's fleshy arms, then snatched away, bringing with them an aftertow of skin. As Sarah looked towards the doorway in which Andropov now stood, Millie's hands darted back, going this time for her face. Sarah screamed as nails tore a scratch several inches long down her cheek; shouted and put up her arms in self-defense as Millie went for her eyes.

Andropov stepped clumsily over Peterson's leg and grasped the wife with both arms about her waist. Trying to haul her back, his foot pressed hard down on Peterson's outspread hand; he felt the bone give beneath his weight, knew that his balance was failing him. With a yell, half of surprise, Andropov stumbled sideways, turning Millie with him. Sarah jumped back and brushed at her cheek. Andropov glanced at her quickly, the fear on her face as strong as the anger on Millie Peterson's. The older woman waded into Andropov, punching and clawing, slapping at his mouth. He tried to fend her off and she kicked at his shins, aiming her knee into his groin. Andropov flattened himself against the glass-fronted cupboard and one of the panes of glass splintered against his elbow. Engraved cups and pieces of silver plate toppled forward as Andropov punched out at Millie Peterson's head.

"The bar, Sarah! Find the bar!"

All Sarah could do was stare at it, the blood darkening into the rust where it had gouged into the dead man's skull.

"Sarah!"

But the woman was still coming for him and Andropov's attempts to step away from the flurry of her blows only got him boxed into a corner between the trophy cupboard and an oak bookshelf. In desperation he swung his left arm in a wild sweep, his knuckles catching Millie Peterson high up on the side of her head. She jerked herself short. A sob, almost of astonishment, hung on her lips. Her eyes flickered. Andropov turned her by the arms and rocked her back towards him, before pushing her across the room as fast as he could. Her feet tripped several times as she went down, the front of her face crashing into the thick wood of the sideboard. Slowly, an oil lamp spun on its rounded base before breaking beside her.

She groaned and her head jolted sideways and then she was still.

Sarah was sobbing, her hands hard to her sides, breasts moving against the white of her nightdress. When Andropov held her, calming her, she flinched, certain that she was about to be struck. When they looked at one another, it was the look of strangers.

"How much money have you?"

Sarah was flustered, unable to think.

"Go and see. Fetch it down."

"But . . ."

"Now. There will be more here. I shall search the house."

Andropov found dollar bills in the sugar bowl, rolled into a pink and white candlestick, between the pages of a booking diary in the center room, in a tin box at the foot of the wardrobe in the Petersons' bedroom. A great deal of money. The keys to the pick-up were hanging on a hook next to a model tea clipper in the conservatory.

Sarah held out her wallet to him and he took all of the bills that were there. She had taken off her night things and hurriedly dressed, a quick comb attempting to untangle her hair.

She could scarcely bear to look at Andropov, to be in the same room with him. Sarah hardly knew him: of course, that was the truth. In her own way she had accepted the delusion of their closeness. The frightened, timid scientist who loved her from afar. Sarah turned away from Andropov and walked out of the kitchen into the next room.

Millie Peterson was no longer there.

Sarah's blood froze. Her arms, the fronts of her calves, the backs of her legs instantly turned to ice. Andropov had killed her, killed her with the same iron bar and dragged her off so that she wouldn't see.

Sarah pressed the heels of her hands hard to her face and began to cry, long racking sobs shook her body. Over her shoulder, Andropov saw what she had seen—that Millie had gone.

"Find her."

Sarah stared round at him, his face swimming inside her tears.

"Help me to find her."

"Let her go."

"No. We must find her."

The "we" reverberated around Sarah's head as she

went cautiously from room to room while Andropov checked the outside of the house. If Millie had somehow got outside, she still would not have had time to go far. The idea of picking up the phone while Andropov was out of hearing never occurred to Sarah. In one sense, she was still linked to the Russian through a multitude of irrational ties and reasons she would not have been able to understand or explain. For another, who would she call? Malone? But there was no way of contacting him until he phoned in to check that everything was still okay—and that was more than an hour and a half away. Considerably more.

She kicked a statuette accidentally along the passageway and as she did so, something seemed to echo it from beneath the floorboards. Except that it wasn't an echo.

The screen door slammed as Andropov came back into the house. Where the experience had aged her, it had made the Russian somehow younger. The lines of his face had abated; he moved with a vigor which had not been present before. The adrenalin was still coursing through his body and the mixture of fear and excitement was driving him on without reflection.

"You've found her," Andropov said, almost shouted.

Sarah looked at him, her mouth opening, saying nothing.

"Where is she, then? Where is she?" His fingers were pressing into the muscles of her arms, hurting her. "Where?"

A similar sound to the one Sarah had heard alerted him. He hesitated and his eyes searched the floor. Sarah knew that he was looking for the iron bar. When it was not immediately there, he started for the cellar, one hand still tight on Sarah's arm. She struggled and grabbed at a mahogany chair. Andropov pulled her clear, the chair twisting and falling noisily.

"Come with me!"

"No!"

"Come with me. I may need your help."

The instant Andropov opened the cellar door, an object exploded against the underside of the heavy wood as he levered it over his head. Something bounced off his shoulder and glass shattered close to his face. Shards pricked his skin. Andropov flung up an arm before his face and hurried Sarah through before him. A tin box rattled against the wall close by them and then Andropov was also through and the door slammed shut behind him. A maze of thick dust rose around them.

The cellar was a cornucopia of junk. Dried flowers, chipped enamel pots, broken gardenings tools and lengths of fishing line hung from the walls. Hooks had been sunk into the floor joists above and from these were suspended sacks of clothing, newspapers and remnants of material. More tools hung alongside half-made model boats and eyeless rag dolls. Most of the floor was covered with wooden crates, tin boxes whose lids refused to close, kettles and saucepans, small jars crammed with every size and shape of screw and nail. One shelf at the side of the cellar held a menagerie of stuffed animals and birds, drab-coated and glassy-eyed. Above it, smaller glass jars contained the results of some visiting biologist's experiments, pickled for cobwebbed years in solutions of formaldehyde.

Millie Peterson, her thick, rose-patterned nightdress torn where it had snagged on one of the crates, crouched deep into the far corner. Her heart was pumping hard, her breath straining; she was certain that each sound her body made must be magnified a hundred times in that confined space.

Andropov began to walk slowly between the obstacles, the containers, his eyes flicking to left and right. He motioned for Sarah to remain close to the door, worried that he would somehow miss the woman and that she would make a dash for the short flight of wooden steps.

The time raced through Andropov's mind, the two hours he had sought to gain were being lost again to this stupid, this pig of a woman. He hated her, with her tuneless singing and her cups of tea and that shuffling walk about the house. Hated her.

Something hit him across the legs so hard that his initial thought was that he had been cut, slashed across the shins with a blade. As he fell he felt downwards, searching for the blood. Millie Peterson scrabbled from hiding and hurled the broom handle towards his face.

Andropov ducked and parried it away with his arms, at the same time calling to Sarah to stop her. But she stood paralyzed, arms outstretched. She felt unable either to comply with Andropov's orders or deny them; she could do nothing. Like a headless chicken, Millie ran straight into her arms and the pair of them fell on to the steps, both shouting wordlessly. Sarah was grabbing handfuls of Millie's gray hair without really being aware of what she was doing. Millie banged elbows and knees against her, trying to climb up her and force the cellar door open and escape. A foot landed in Sarah's belly and she screamed and bit into the flabbiness of the older woman's arm.

Andropov watched them rolling from side to side, his eyes glancing away every alternate moment, seeking out a weapon.

"Dimit . . ."

"Little bitch!"

Millie Peterson forced her knee between Sarah's breasts and seized her hair with both hands. She began to slam Sarah's head back against the edge of one step, over and over and over, hauling it off and throwing it back down as if she were pounding bread dough off a board.

Andropov ran from six yards back, his arms raised above his head. Three feet short of the women he stumbled, one hand coming away for balance. As his head pitched down in the direction of Millie Peterson's neck, the implement in his right hand swung past it. Millie released Sarah and arched downwards, fingers clawing behind her as Andropov collapsed to his knees alongside the steps. Sarah wriggled out from underneath

Millie's squirming, the front of her white nightdress, the lower part of her face, speckled red.

Somehow, Millie was on her feet.

Not quite able to believe it, Andropov and Sarah watched as she staggered haphazardly from one obstruction to another, the sickle protruding from her back like some metal wing.

Fingers, hands sought and held, and thus joined the lovers continued to watch as Millie Peterson spilled forward, hands high, into the wall. Glass cases, jars, burst about her feet. Like a sudden child, she clutched a stiffened rabbit to her arms. The cellar stank of formalin. Something putty-white and unidentifiable slithered down the front of Millie's dress and came to rest in her sagging lap. The broken handle of the sickle perched above her shoulder, forced between her body and the rough cast of the wall.

Sarah squeezed Andropov's fingers hard; by now it was useless even to cry. "*We must find her. We.*" Well, they had found her: together. Andropov pryed himself free from her locking grasp and began to climb the stairs. In a slow daze, Sarah levered herself from the ground and, trying desperately not to look across the cellar at Millie, she began to follow in his wake. At the head of the steps Andropov turned and stared down. All those years. The heavy wooden door unleashed another shower of dust as it slammed into place. Choking, Sarah staggered back, not even able to call out until she heard the bolts slide home.

Then she fell across the steps, arms wound about her face, hands blocking her eyes, her nose, ears. She didn't hear the pick-up fire at the second attempt, the ugly clash of gears as it began to climb the dirt track towards the road.

· CHAPTER 16 ·

The twist of shell, pinky-brown, lay in the palm of Malone's hand. The spiralling surface was rough against his thumb, the inside smooth as pearl. Water lapped casually close to his feet. Up by the jetty a twenty-footer was mooring, men in black ribbed sweaters, heavy denim work jeans and seaboots securing her. The crates that would carry the equipment from the outbuilding were already in the boathouse. Later, it would be the bodies.

A bird detached itself from the mass of green at the channel's end and hung on a downward curve of air.

"Everybody's allowed to foul up the once."

Duvall walked down the slope of the shore carefully, as if frightened something slippery that stung would slide out from under a flecked brown stone, a shell. He approached Malone with caution, deference. There was no way of knowing exactly what the senior officer would be feeling, but the way Malone stood, his shoulders hunched, coat collar pulled high, both hands jammed deep into his pockets, showed him enough.

"Sir."

Malone turned and looked at him, through him.

"Sir, we . . ."

"What is it?" Malone's voice had the cold snap of death at its back.

"Pyle and myself, sir, we made the airport check you ordered and . . ."

Under Malone's stare the young Southerner's voice faltered and faded to nothing. Pyle was standing on the planking which led up to the boathouse, one hand resting on the Moose Head sign. He was wearing a green and brown pea jacket and a tight brown knitted hat, hacking with one of his boot heels at the uneven surface of the wood.

"He's got through," Malone said abruptly, just when Duvall thought his attention had faded away altogether.

"Yes. Yes, sir. I don't understand how, but . . ."

"Of course he did. Of course he damn well did!"

Malone was striding back towards the house, pebbles flying out from under his boots as he went. Duvall came scrambling along at his back. At the foot of the track, Malone paused and glanced over towards Pyle. Two men from the vessel opened the boathouse door from the inside.

Malone pointed: "See to them, Pyle. And . . ." He nodded at Duvall. ". . . take him with you."

Pyle grunted and got on with the task of supervision while Malone climbed up the steps to the conservatory. The linen blinds had been raised and a bright sun, orange-yellow, was reflecting in the sails of an armada of ships.

Sarah Jarrett was sitting in the kitchen; it was the only room downstairs left unstained by blood. *"Lemuel has shipped his oars, the oars trail in the water. The night is strewn with absurd . . ."* Malone had brought more brandy with him. He took it now from the inside pocket of his coat and lifted two tumblers from one of the shelves. Someone had made Sarah coffee and it sat untouched by her elbow. She was still to get properly dressed; she had pulled a sweater over the top of her nightdress, a raincoat—Malone didn't know whose—was draped over her shoulders. For the first time since he had seen her, Malone thought she looked her age. Older. The bright blue of her eyes a thing of the past, forced out by what had happened in the other room, down in the cellar. He knew that what she saw sitting there was not neat rows of plates and cups and glasses, jars of flour, sugar and herbs. Malone couldn't know exactly what it was, but he knew enough.

He wondered if she realized he had entered the room.

He also wondered, for the first time, if what they had paid her could ever have been enough.

In the center of the house the banging of the screen door told him that the bodies were being removed by the janitors, tarpaulin and blankets, the arms of men who had done it before and would do it again. "*This tangle of gray bodies.*" Malone refilled the kettle and lit the gas. There was instant coffee between the sugar and some jars of home-made jam, labelled in a clear but shaky hand. "*They lie together in a heap, in the night. They are far out in the bay.*" "Coffee?" "*The night is strewn with absurd . . .*"

They sat across the breakfast table like survivors from some natural disaster in which the lives of those they knew only faintly had been lost. After several minutes Malone took Sarah's hand and set her fingers round the warmth of the cup; he held the tumbler of brandy to her mouth and tipped it back. The liquid ran from her lips and down her chin and she choked. He tried again and this time she drank. She took the glass from him and drank. Then the coffee.

Malone might have looked at his watch, but he knew the time to the second: "*everybody's allowed to foul up the once.*"

"Sarah, we have to talk."

"Already . . ." Her eyes fixed on him helplessly, then slid away.

"Again," he said, drinking a little of his own coffee, hot and tasteless.

"No!" She shook her head wildly and he reached forward and took her face between his hands.

"I must know," Malone said, his voice calm and

low, his hands still round her face. "I must know what you told him."

Sarah struggled for control; he could feel it beneath his fingers, see it in the faded brilliance of her eyes. "I don't know," she said.

"Yes, you do. Try to remember."

"No." She tried to twist her face away and he let her go, moving his chair round to her side of the table, glancing through the window as he went, down towards the business being carried out at the boathouse.

"Sarah, after he asked you about Richard, what else?"

She leaned against his shoulder and looked up at him like a child. She wanted to remember, she did, she did. Malone put his arm around her and she began to snuggle against him, then stiffened, almost rigid.

"It's okay," he said softly, beginning to stroke her hair.

Neither of them spoke for some time. Malone felt her body warming against his own, the pressure of her leg and the scent of sweat and fear and tears that rose from her skin. He knew how easy it would be for him to want her, then.

"The letters, Sarah, did he ask you about the letters?"

"I think . . . yes, I'm sure. The letters."

"He knows it wasn't your idea to write them. Not in the beginning."

She nodded against his sleeve.

"He knows that it was us? Our idea?"

"I suppose . . ."

"And when you said you wanted him to come to you, to you and Richard, you told him that was what we told you to say?"

Sarah lifted her head away and looked at him. He could feel that she was starting to shake with some new fear, though as yet she could not define what it was.

She touched the front of his jacket. "I don't know."

Malone leaned far enough away to be able to take the small leather case from his pocket. The slight judder of head and hands, the quick dilation of the eyes was enough to tell him, but he asked anyway.

"Before he talked to you, Sarah, did he use this?" Malone snapped the case open. "Did he inject you with something from here?"

Her mouth opened fractionally but there was no sound; she swallowed and stared and Malone closed the case and looked away. He put the case back into his pocket, finished his brandy and stood up.

"Malone." Her hand reached for his and he gave her a quick squeeze and stepped away, setting the heavy wooden table between them.

"Finish your coffee," he said and started for the door.

"Malone!"

He turned back towards her, evading her arms. Without looking into her eyes, he kissed her on the mouth.

Pyle looked up as Malone came down the steps, brisk now and business-like. The two men spoke quietly, though there was little enough to say. Pyle nodded and went over to his car. Malone carried on down towards the boat.

Inside the kitchen Sarah was drinking the brandy Malone had left and shivering a little. Tears ran soundlessly. She was beginning, now, to feel the first moments of relief. Her mind fought for it, clung to it. Twenty years of lies and deception and now it was finished. Over. She wouldn't have to write another letter, pretend another loving word. The glass fell from her hand and she rocked against the table, crying openly now, loudly and freely. Jesus Christ! It was over!

She heard a noise outside the door and turned, her face bright again with tears.

"Malone."

But it wasn't Malone.

· CHAPTER 17 ·

Through the high plate glass to his left, Fedin watched the color of the sky changing above and between the buildings. A yellow that was almost bright became suffused with pink and immediately a line of purple, straight like the end of a blind, drew down on to it, flattening, darkening. He bit into the stickiness of his orange gateau, so thick on the shaped tine of the pastry fork. When he looked again only the narrowest of golden lines remained, bordered in deepest purple.

He ordered another cappuccino but the waitress told him they were closing. The bookshop with which the coffee house shared the building was already ushering out its customers. Fedin had waited three days for the call from Van Holst, telling him that payment had come through. The arrangement was always the same: one third paid into a bank in Geneva, a third—Fedin smiled—into the funds of an organization of his choice, the remaining amount paid over in cash, notes of differing currencies and denominations and with no decipherable sequence. Van Holst called him at his apartment opposite the flea market with the information that his consignment of models was ready. An hour later it was in his hand.

Fedin forked the remaining cake from its plate. Three days had passed in which his telephone had not rung and during which time he had been scrupulous in keeping well clear of the shop on the Amstel. Three days and he was fast losing patience. He ignored the girl hovering by the table, waiting to clear it away, and checked his watch. There was a fall-back in case telephone communication was for any reason dangerous. Fedin knew it, but had never used it. The waitress reached in front of his face and picked up the plate and the empty cup. Fedin glowered. When he stood up the sky through the window was quite dark.

He paid his bill at the counter and left the coffee shop. A short walk along Spui, weaving his slender body between a host of people busily returning from work, and he reached the Athenaeum Boekhandel. Outside a young man wearing rimless spectacles was pushing up the orange and yellow blinds with a wooden pole. A student in long, tweed skirts, a white knitted scarf wound about her neck, was unfastening a padlock and chain from the rear wheel of her bicycle. Another assistant was stacking up paperback books which had been on display outside.

Fedin walked in through the right-hand door and headed for the section labelled "Mystery," halfway down the stairs towards the basement. He spent several minutes browsing along the titles, fingering the spines. A thickly bearded man, with a shapeless green jacket over a Fair Isle pullover, came out from behind the downstairs counter and coughed loudly in Fedin's direction.

"You have Nebel?" asked Fedin.

The man coughed again into a red and white spotted handkerchief, then flattened himself against the wall to permit one of the other assistants to pass down the stairs, arms laden with books.

"Nebel," Fedin repeated, irritability creeping into his voice unbidden, "the Gregg Press edition."

The bearded man wiped his mouth, missing a little moisture which hung to the underside of his moustache. He grumbled something that might have been, "Let me see,'' and turned away. Fedin watched him for several moments, as he ferreted around beneath the counters.

''No,'' he said finally, having referred to a stock sheet and several folders. ''Nothing. No Gregg Press. No Nebel.''

Fedin fidgeted with the silver ring on his right hand, twisting it around and around. ''You can get one?'' he asked.

The man shrugged and his neck disappeared completely so that his beard seemed to be sprouting from the V of his pullover, leaving his round face squatting between his shoulders.

''Tomorrow,'' Fedin said shortly. ''If I am passing at the same time . . .''

The head rose up high enough to shake from side to side. ''Sorry, it is out of the question.'' The man blinked. ''I can do nothing for you.''

A pair of women pressed between them, shopping bags in both hands. When the stairway was clear again, the bearded man had turned back to his business and was checking through the till roll as if Fedin no longer existed.

Fedin pushed a hand through his hair and it settled back outside his collar. He nearly barged a man out of the way getting clear of the shop. Walking across Spui, he caused a red Mazda hatchback to brake sharply; a young woman with dark hair leaned out of the window on the driver's side and presented him with the middle finger of her left hand. Fedin yelled something that was lost in the noise. A few minutes later he was crossing back over the wide street, making ground as fast as he could towards the north-east of the city.

Through the thin bamboo of the blinds, Van Holst could see the silhouettes of passers-by as they headed in both directions along the pavement. Occasionally someone would pause outside the door and peer past the closed sign at the displays mounted inside the shop.

Marie sat on a high stool close by the counter, wrapping individual pieces of an order in beige tissue paper before resting them carefully in a narrow box and settling polystyrene chips around them. She held a Dutch colonel of rifles up towards the shaded light and pursed her lips to blow dust from the gold braid of the kepi. Even though she had been working in the shop for some time, the nature of the models continued to delight her—this one with his fingers gripping a pair of leather gloves exactly so, the sloping angle of the cross-strap which held his waistbelt in place.

Van Holst smiled at the girl's fascination. She was—he avoided looking at the pressure of her breasts against the green of her sweater—so much like a child.

"Marie . . ."

But she was looking away from his face and did not see his lips move; it was as if he had said nothing. Van Holst touched her arm and she turned with a little start, ready to smile.

This passer-by not only paused at the door. He tried the handle and, when it refused to turn, he struck the woodwork alongside the glass with the side of his fist.

Van Holst's head jerked awkwardly round and he felt the beginnings of embarrassment, as if he had been caught out in some illicit act.

Go away, he waved exaggeratedly, can't you see we're closed.

Marie was still smiling.

The man didn't go away and, after no more than a few moments, Van Holst recognized who it was. The shape at the door took on feature and form and Van Holst knew there was no alternative but to let him enter. With a shrug towards Marie that was meant to signify his annoyance at being disturbed, Van Holst unlocked the door.

"As you see, we are closed, I . . ."

"You didn't call me."

"No, there was . . ."

"You should have called."

"Yes, but . . ." Van Holst glanced around towards

Marie, but she had returned to her work of packing the World War II models into four long boxes. ". . . there was a delay."

"What delay?"

"The shipment . . ."

"Well?"

"Our wholesalers . . ."

"What are you talking about?"

"Our wholesalers, they are experiencing some difficulty . . ."

"Difficulty, hell! My part of the contract was carried out on time. There need be no difficulty."

"But surely you see . . ."

"I see nothing." Fedin was slowly making Van Holst retreat across the room. His eyes were narrow, the expression in them bitter. He flexed the long fingers of his right hand and the knuckles cracked.

"Look," Van Holst began, standing his ground now, setting both hands, palms out, between the young man and himself. "I understand your position. Your, er, annoyance, but you must see there is nothing I can do about it. The situation is . . ."

"Beyond your control," suggested Fedin.

"Yes."

"Out of your hands," he sneered.

"Yes."

"And for three days you have done nothing."

"There was nothing I could do."

"You could have called me. Let me know what was happening."

Van Holst licked his lips, his mouth dry as worn leather. Marie turned her head momentarily and gave both men the benefit of a smile.

"The last shipment . . ." Van Holst began.

"What?" Fedin twisted the ring on his finger, moved several inches closer to Van Holst.

"The last order . . ."

"What about it?"

"There was some query . . ."

Van Holst tried to duck away, but he could do nothing to prevent Fedin's hand from gripping him by the front of his jacket; the fingers twisted the material tight.

"What query?"

"I don't know. They said, the wholesalers said . . ."

"Said what?"

"They would send a representative. By the end of the week. Something that had to be discussed."

Fedin's upper lip curled; he stared at Van Holst with distaste. He let go of his coat and for an instant the shop owner thought Fedin was going to strike him across the mouth. Instead he lunged towards the side of the small shop and swept away Custer's Seventh Cavalry together with the surrounding hordes of Indians. One of the braves struck Marie on the back of the head; a kneeling lieutenant bounced on to the lid of an open box. The girl turned quickly, rising from her seat.

"Marie, go upstairs!"

"Leave her."

"No, she will be better off."

"She can't understand a word we're saying."

Ignoring Fedin for the moment, Van Holst shooed Marie towards the rear door which led to the stairs. He patted her shoulder, make reassuring faces, calming noises that she could not hear. Once she was on the stairs, Van Holst stepped reluctantly back into the room.

"Look," he said, trying to be business-like, anxious to disguise the tremor that was appearing in his voice and not quite succeeding. "You must understand, Fedin, there is nothing I can do." He gestured outwards with his hands; stepped on to a model soldier and cursed his own clumsiness beneath his breath. "You and I, we are both in the control of others. All we can do is wait."

Fedin crashed his hand down on to another shelf and a column of Napoleon's army executed an untidy series of somersaults.

"Fedin, for God's sake!" implored Van Holst, reaching out to restrain him.

Fedin sent him spinning away, clutching at his chest where the fist had landed.

"Phone them," Fedin said.

Van Holst winced, grunted. "I can't."

"Phone them!"

Van Holst shook his head.

More models flew from the sweep of the young man's arm . . . and still more. He gathered up handsful and rained them to the ceiling, across the insides of the windows. Shouting at him to stop, Van Holst ran from wall to wall, voice and expression frantic. Finally he threw himself at Fedin, who sidestepped and pushed out his foot in the path of Van Holst's charge. The man went sprawling, scattering soldiers before him, arm and elbow crashing into the bottoms of the counter. When he picked himself up and turned back into the center of the room, Fedin was screwing the silencer on to the end of the SIG's barrel.

"Jesus!"

"Phone them."

Van Holst shook his head, mouth open, his breathing so loud that it seemed to fill his ears with sound. Without raising the gun, Fedin sent a bullet through the rigging of a Spanish man-of-war. Seamen leapt overboard as the main-sail came toppling down.

Van Holst started crawling across the floor towards where Fedin stood. "Understand," he pleaded. "Understand, for pity's sake. It is they who contact me. There is no procedure . . ."

Fedin angled the gun downwards and fired through the floor-boards, which bucked against the underside of Van Holst's body.

Fingers pawed at Fedin's slender legs, the well-cut material of his trousers.

"Please!"

The third bullet ripped through the back of Van Holst's thigh, tearing muscles and cartilage apart. His head fell forward against his left forearm and he began to sob, his shoulders shaking convulsively. Fedin dragged him up and he hobbled backwards until he was leaning against the counter, his left leg not touching the floor, a curve of dark blood running out from beside his shoe and across the boards.

"What did they say?"

"Say?"

"You must have asked them about payment. What did they say?"

Van Holst didn't want to answer. Fedin fired once more into the body of the ship which stood behind his head and Van Holst murmured. "They were dissatisfied."

"Speak up!"

"Dissatisfied."

"Louder!"

"They were dissatisfied!" Van Holst gripped the edge of the counter with both hands and yelled into Fedin's face.

The younger man spun away towards the door. Van Holst held his breath and waited for Fedin's hand to descend on to the handle of the door. Instead he turned again, athletically, his movements almost those of a trained dancer. The normally handsome face was ugly.

He said: "They are dissatisfied with the way I kill."

"I . . . I don't know."

"With the way I kill."

"I . . . Oh, God!"

Fedin braced his legs apart; his right hand readjusting its grip on the cross-hatched butt, the fingers of the other hand closing round that wrist. The sudden stink that swept the room told them both that Van Holst had lost control of his bowels, the sphincter muscle loosened in those last moments of terror. He didn't believe.

Fedin shot him once low in the left side, immediately above and inside the pelvic bone, again in the center of the chest, splintering the breast bone away. The next bullet was nine inches higher and exploded a gaping hole where Van Holst's throat had been—the fourth neatly lifted away the flap of his skull.

Marie stood in the doorway, hands clenched before

her, her doll-like blue eyes wide. Dribble ran from both sides of her mouth and she was crying.

"They are dissatisfied," Fedin said matter-of-factly, "with the way I kill."

And he raised the pistol and levelled the sights on the center of the girl's mouth. She had not understood a word he had said: she opened her mouth wide and emitted a soundless scream and Fedin aimed down into the dark hole of that mouth.

The hammer clicked on am empty breech.

Marie's fainting body slumped back across the foot of the stairs as Fedin hurried out into the night.

· CHAPTER 18 ·

It seemed to Andropov that he had been walking ever since disembarking from the plane. In fact, there had been time passed in taxi cabs, a cafe where he hurriedly ate thick pea soup and crusty bread, benches along the canal, the softly padded seats of two museums. Each occasion was tight with nervous uncertainty, his eyes shifting from one passer-by to the next as if any one of them might have his photograph imprinted clearly on their minds; as if instead of passing they might stop and a hand descend. Then there would be a scuffle, the harsh quick brakes of a large car, seats booked on the first flight east. Or would it be west?

Andropov pressed his fingertips to his scalp and felt the thinness of skin sliding across the irregular framework of bone. With his thumb he tried to trap the nerve which palpitated wildly at the side of his head. All of his thoughts, each of his agitated walks about the city, brought him back to one place and one person—back to Richard. So far he had not been able to think clearly beyond that. Beyond his son. Expectations of the future intruded like subliminal glimpses of a rotted dream. Andropov knew that other than Richard there could be nothing now. Without him, past him, the least step he took would drag the whole mildewed structure down about him.

He had placed himself—Andropov savored the phrase as something new on his tongue—out on a limb.

He had found his son's apartment only with difficulty, the name of the street odd in his mouth: Reguliersgracht. One hundred and sixteen. The people he stopped, the taxi driver, sent him along narrow passages beside canals, past the flattened humps of houseboats made strange with green plants and budding flowers. Finally it was there. Andropov's back unbent and his gloved hands slid a little awkwardly from his pockets. It was the corner house, three-story, the front doors—two of them—strangely on what appeared to be the first floor, a wide V of steps leading upwards past the gray paint of the lower level. The rest of the building was painted cream, the curved tiles of its steep roof glistening as though earlier it had been raining.

Andropov stood on the rise of the little bridge and looked at the windows, waiting for the shape that would move across them and the shift of recognition that would shake his heart. He waited until his hands, despite his woollen gloves, were cold round the black iron of the railing. Few people passed. A cat—ginger and white—rubbed its flank against the trunk of the lime tree growing outside the house, close to the canal. It arched its back in Andropov's direction, then sharpened its claws against the bark. When the Russian looked again, the animal had gone.

He knew without checking the name plates alongside the doors that the top apartment was Richard's. One of the four windows held a poster of a large bulbous whale, another was filled by a fiercely painted sun overprinted with a slogan against nuclear power. After a while, he checked anyway; ran his fingers, the glove removed, over the lightly raised lettering— "Richard Jarrett." Andropov's breathing quickened: he had not kept the name of the man Sarah married, but hers.

Rather, Andropov wished, walking away, his own.

He passed the time walking through Frederiks Plein and down to follow the broad canal until it reached the museums. One floor of the Rijks Museum passed without his seeing a single exhibit. In the Van Gogh Museum he noticed the height and light, the space and the rich green of the plants, but scarcely a brush stroke, a sunflower, a whorl of cloud and wheat and sky. His feet beginning to ache, the leather of his shoes starting to draw sharply, he returned each hour—less—to the corner house. The gray grew darker, the cream was flat and dull yet still stood out from the surrounding buildings. There was a light now in one of the rooms below and Andropov considered ringing the bell and requesting information about his son. Once his hand hovered over a cylindrical button and he rehearsed questions inside his head. He turned away, back past the tree and on to the cold of the bridge, the wind cutting now along the surface of the canal. Finally, the street lights burning, he took up position at the back of one flight of steps, huddled there against the dark building, waiting for Richard.

It never occurred to him that he might not come.

Andropov's shoulder, his left side were numb; cold had begun to seep up through his body, infiltrating his bones. He stamped his feet when they, too, grew numb. He slapped his arms across his chest and clapped his gloved hands together before thrusting them down into the pockets of his overcoat. It seemed as cold as Norway, almost as bitter as Russia. The clip of heels chipped the cold away. Andropov peered from behind the bulk of steps and saw the man walking briskly by the canal. His ungloved hands were curled up into loose fists, his breath pluming out into the air as he passed beneath the streetlamps. A sharp turn when Andropov had been convinced that he was carrying on, and he came over the bridge towards the house. One hand disappeared from sight, searching, Andropov assumed, for a key. He passed between a pair of bollards and the light at the corner showed his face in a downward rush of yellowing light.

Andropov's hands clenched together through the material of his coat and a sound little more than a guttural moan stopped on his lips.

He swayed back against the gray-black wall as if he might faint.

At that moment, inexplicably, an image of Sarah jumped into his mind; her face staring up at him, blood-freckled, the instant before he slammed the cellar door shut.

Andropov heard the steps rising above him and in a whirl of awkward movement he rushed after them. Almost at the top, key in hand, the young man turned, shouted, thrust out an arm—only to find himself engulfed in a flurry of embraces under which he lost his footing and fell back. The two men tumbled against stone, against the smooth painted wood of the door. Certain that he was being attacked, Richard struggled to shift the heavy, squirming weight off his body, but a fresh onslaught of hands pawed at his face, his arms. The man on top of him was murmuring, mumbling, calling what could only be his name.

Richard wriggled free and was on his feet quickly, easily, his arms thrust outwards towards the shadowy figure as it fell to a position that was half-sitting, half-leaning.

"Richard, Richard!"

The light from the streetlamp was inadequate; the blinds had been pulled down inside the first floor flat.

"Richard."

There were tears running down the man's face; Richard could hear them, not see them. The cold band of fear that had snapped tight about the center of Richard's body began to relax its hold. A face, almost as grainy as the few photographs he had seen, rose up towards him out of the shadow.

"Richard."

Recognition brought not feeling, but self-control. Richard glanced along the canal. No one had seen them. He forced the correct responses, buying time. He wiped away the tears from his father's cheeks with his thumbs, the backs of his hands. The two men stood, then, facing one another, not touching, breathing unsteadily. Slowly, Andropov lowered his head and leaned forward until it was resting on his son's chest. Richard allowed this, then put an arm about his shoulder and led him quickly inside.

Richard waited while Andropov washed and changed into whichever of his own clothes were the closest fit. He gave his father coffee, black, and bourbon that he had bought on his last flight from the States. He insisted on taking him out to a restaurant, assuring Andropov that a good meal was necessary for them both. That and a celebratory bottle of wine.

They went to a small place on Herens Gracht, closer to the center of the city. There were booths along the side and back walls, no more than three other tables occupied. Candles provided almost the only light. Richard ordered for them—mussels in a sauce tasting strongly of garlic, followed by a fish stew served with mashed potato and vegetables. The wine was white and dry, the slim-necked brown bottle cold to the touch.

After no more than a quarter of an hour, Andropov began to relax, to feel, somehow, as though he had come home. No longer did he glance towards the door at each fresh sound or movement; nor did the open-faced young man opposite him, listening with an attentive half-smile, seem like a well-known stranger.

Richard allowed the older man to take his time, aware of his nervousness and some of its causes, and knowing the only thing to do was allow them to subside without effort. He ate slowly, enjoying the food, permitting his father to talk as and when he wished. At first the story came in little more than fragments, scenes from a film that had yet to be spliced into some sort of order—the debriefing, the defection, the time spent with Sarah, with Richard's mother. Andropov hesitated here, reading the handsome face for signs of discomfort, disapproval. There were none: nothing more than the beginnings of a frown, the merest pause between plate and mouth. Still there were things that Andropov, instinctively, suppressed—the syringe, those awful moments in the cellar, Sarah's face as he shut fast the cellar door.

As the meal came towards its end, the two murders stepped clean and easy from Andropov's lips, as if he were recounting some story, like a child telling of enormities whose consequences it has failed to understand.

Cold inside, Richard heard, nodded, poured the last of the wine. He sensed his own fate inside his father's desperation. He forced his hand to touch his father's cheek as if to say, I understand, there was nothing else you could do.

Coffee was served in small cups, white with a gold rim.

What will you do now? was the question that hovered in Richard's mind, but he sensed that to ask it was to drive Andropov into a panic, to open up to him the consequences his actions must have unleashed.

Instead he asked, "If you hadn't found me, what would you have done?"

Even then Andropov's face teetered into doubt, his eyes widened and he pushed one hand hard to the side of his head. For several moments he sat staring emptily forward, as if the question had not really been put. But when Richard was wondering whether he dare pose it again, Andropov began to answer.

"All the time on the plane I was thinking that, just that, when Richard is not there, when he has taken a flight back to America, to some other country, when he listens to my words and shuts . . ." Andropov's eyes closed as if in sudden pain. ". . . the door in my face, what do I do? I think . . ." He was looking at Richard again, perhaps without seeing him, rather some platonic ideal of him. ". . . I should take my own life. That is the obvious thing."

As if sensing some look of disapproval, of hurt in his

son's eyes, he motioned calmingly with his hand and his tone dropped to one of reassurance.

"Of course, there have been so many times when I have thought of this. When your mother's letters failed to come, when the work I was forced to do filled me with such distaste it was all I could do to swallow my sickness and carry on. Hours alone in my small flat when every year of my life insisted on appearing before me and each one was failure. Even . . ." He set his head a little to one side and smiled. ". . . even when I received the news that you were alive, that you had been born, conceived and born. No, not even then, then most of all. That was when I came so close. The knowledge that the son I had wanted all those years, that I had mourned and missed, that he had been alive and kept from me—I walked around Moscow that day with your mother's letter in my hand, your name, new to me like a strange toy, on my lips. I walked through all of the most crowded places I could find and I wanted to shout you out to them. Scream your name into the faces of all those uncomprehending . . ."

Andropov clutched at Richard's hand and held it. The waiter came close to the table, turned and walked away.

"Everywhere I went I saw children, babies, mothers with their daughters in proud new bonnets, fathers hoisting sons aloft on their shoulders—windows full with toys."

Andropov released his son's hand.

"And already your childhood had gone. I went home and took off my things. I went into the bathroom and rolled up my sleeves, unwrapped a stainless steel blade. The water running from the taps. I looked at my face in the mirror and saw yours in its place. Without ever . . . ever having . . ."

Richard took hold of Andropov's shoulders and gripped them tight, shook them lightly. The Russian nodded and blinked a smile and both of them ignored the fact that he was crying once more.

Richard gestured with his hand and they drank more coffee.

"I think I would go back," said Andropov after a long silence.

"Back?"

"To Russia."

"But how? Why?"

Andropov shrugged and that movement made his body suddenly old in Richard's eyes. "Where else should I go?"

Richard's mind raced. "They wouldn't let you just . . . I mean, even if they were going to allow you back, you . . ."

"But, Richard, it has only been days."

"You defected."

"I changed my mind."

Richard shook his head. "You can't just walk into the airport and book a flight to Moscow."

Andropov gestured vaguely.

"They won't let you."

"The Russians?"

"The Americans."

Andropov shifted his cup round in its saucer. "I know. I know."

Richard sat on the edge of his seat, as if counting to ten under his breath. "Then how would you . . . ?"

"Get back? I don't know. Perhaps I would walk not into the airport but into the embassy. Tell them what has happened."

Even as the words left his lips, Andropov's voice betrayed the unlikelihood of what he was saying.

"Perhaps I would go back to Trondheim."

Richard shook his head. "That's impossible."

"Why so? The conference has still what, five days?"

"You would never get there."

"Unless," said Andropov, "they made arrangements."

"They? Who?"

Andropov's smile was tired; it was becoming difficult for him to keep his eyes open. "I have a friend, not a friend, a colleague. The head of the delegation. She would . . ."

But his voice drifted to nothing and he looked flatly at Richard, as though for the first time in some while he no longer knew where he was.

They travelled by taxi and when they got out it was on to the pavement in front of an apartment block, small and modern, instead of the cream and gray house. Andropov scarcely noticed. Richard's explanation that the flat of a friend would be safer, only just penetrated Andropov's overwhelming need for sleep. Richard had to half-carry his father upstairs, undress him and put him to bed. In the morning he would talk him out of his insane scheme of returning to Russia. He would put something better in its place—the chance for the two of them to stay together. Richard scarcely slept, his mind overactive with expectation.

· CHAPTER 19 ·

On a night when he might have expected to be troubled by dreams, Andropov slept without interruption. Exhaustion, the physical endeavor of what he had been through, the meeting with his son—all of these ensured that the instant his head touched the pillow of the narrow folding bed he slept. Waking now, light drifting through the windows, he suffered the abrupt shock of displacement. His head swam and his skin froze. He sat upright, both hands to the edges of the bed frame. Five, six seconds and he knew, realized where he was. It was all right. Releasing his breath in a sigh, Andropov shook his head and pushed back the covers.

"Richard."

He sat with his bare feet to the floor, wearing a pair of his son's pajamas that were too tight for him, the jacket left unbuttoned.

"Richard?"

There was no sound in the apartment other than his voice, the faint, flat echo of it falling off the walls. Cars drove along the street outside, but not yet in great numbers. Andropov looked at his watch, but it had stopped at thirteen minutes past three. He rubbed at the sleep clogging his eyes and scratched under his left arm; conscious of a need to go to the bathroom.

Returning, he saw the note Richard had left on the

table to the right of the room, propped against an empty flower vase.

"Gone for morning run! Will return with newspaper and hot rolls—make us some coffee!

Love, Richard."

Andropov stood holding the note, smiling like a fool. Finally he set it back down and started to dress. The underpants and socks Richard had lent him, Richard's shirt, tight somehow at the waist and almost impossible to button to the top. His own trousers, two small flecks of blood, dried and dark, which the promise of the morning prevented him from noticing. Andropov left the top of the checked shirt free and went through into the kitchen. Richard wanted coffee ready when he returned—Richard should have coffee.

Richard turned the corner of the Oude Schans canal, running easily, arms tucked in at the sides, loosely clenched fists making small punching movements into the air. There were two ships, bulky and tall-funnelled, in at the dock. The water drifted mist. Ahead of him as he ran, the outline of Central Station stood out firmly as if pressed from a child's pop-up book of Amsterdam. When he reached the end of the next canal, he would turn and jog back, picking up what he needed on the way.

Andropov had filled the electric kettle and already steam was beginning to emerge from the spout. He had set a filter paper in place, opened the tin of coffee—everything left ready for him so that he couldn't miss it. Through the kitchen window he looked as far as he could along the street, left and right. There was no sign, yet, of Richard returning; no point in making the coffee too soon.

Andropov switched on the small transistor radio which stood close by the kettle and was greeted by a woman speaking cheerily in Dutch. He half-listened for a minute or two, beginning to feel hungry—strange after eating so much in the restaurant the night before—and wondering whether he shouldn't find something to nibble on before Richard returned.

He clicked open the nearest of the cupboards close to his head, at the same time toying with the station control of the radio.

Jogging up and down on the spot lest he should begin to stiffen up, Richard shook out the small plastic bag he had been carrying in the pocket of his track suit. The line inside the baker's was short but moving slowly. A housewife buying bread for a large family, workmen wanting filled rolls for their lunch. Richard's breath no longer hung silver on the air; at least waiting there it was warm. A quick smile showed on his face as he imagined Andropov still wrapped in the heat of blankets and sleep. Why he'd even bothered to write a note, he didn't know. Tired as he was, the old man would sleep around the clock if left. Arms laden, the woman left the shop and Richard moved along, next in line to be served.

Andropov stopped in his search for biscuits as the radio grazed across an English voice. He looked at the green dial and jiggled the knob back again; if he couldn't find Russian, this would be better than nothing. It was the BBC European service, the voice of the newscaster stolid and reassuring as it recounted the problems of Ireland and then paused before filling in what was obviously going to be minor, more localized news.

Andropov lifted down a round tin and wobbled off the lid. A solitary cheese biscuit lay at the bottom, one corner broken off. He could smell its staleness immediately. Andropov replaced both lid and tin and resumed his search. The newsreader was saying something about a killing. At the mention of Amsterdam, Andropov's head swung around. Last night, after his premises had closed, the proprietor of a shop specializing in replica military models had been shot several times and killed. Nothing had been stolen and so far the police had discovered no motive for the murder. Andropov tried another cupboard but this one seemed to be full of basic supplies, flour, sugar and rice. The assistant, who had been working in the shop with her employer at the time, had been able to give the police an accurate description of the man who carried out the shooting.

Richard glimpsed himself in the window of De Koffiemoten, a smooth shape in a dark blue track suit passing across ornate calligraphy, gold on glass. He held the plastic bag loosely in his right hand, the morning's newspaper was folded down into the waistband of his trousers. He made a right and as he went past the front of the Rembrandt Museum he saw the maroon car parked fifty yards further along on the opposite side of the road. Breath catching, he shortened his stride, picking up speed.

". . . believed to be in his early twenties . . ." Andropov's hand jerked against one of the glass jars and it fell forward from the shelf's edge, striking the work surface by his side and splintering apart. Innumerable grains of brown rice showered and spat, rolling across the shaded formica, along the floor. Replica models.

Replica models.

It buzzed like a sudden warning light deep in Andropov's consciousness. The proprietor of a shop specializing in replica models. Models. Soldiers. Toy soldiers. Ovals of rice continued to splatter about his feet. The newscaster had moved on to something else, some other part of Europe. Andropov's mind obdurately stuck. The file he had gained access to, the question at his debriefing, the look that had shown momentarily on the face of the American with the cast in his eye. Methods of contact. Channels. Andropov raised his head, mouth open as if the air inside the room had suddenly started to run out.

Richard was sprinting now, the newspaper plucked clear and flung aside. He wove his way between people going to work, knowing without needing to see them that men had got out of the maroon car and were crossing the road, hurrying without wishing to draw too much attention to themselves, not anxious to act out there on that early-morning street.

He grabbed at the brickwork to slow himself down, glanced over his shoulder as he darted into the apartment block entrance. Two men. Richard took the stairs three at a time, the key already poised between his fingers.

Not moving, like a fish sucking life above the swiftly shifting surface, Andropov saw the bundle at the back of the shelf where it would have been shielded by the jar he had knocked away. Afraid to reach in, to touch it, that was precisely what he did. Blue-black velvet burned.

So much of him refusing to believe.

He heard a noise from the other room, beyond it. A key being turned in the door, a voice, muffled, that was shouting his name. The soft, warm material folded back about his hand and the gun was there, exposed, refusing to be denied.

The apartment door sprang open, slammed back. Andropov stood in the kitchen doorway, his mind seeming to expand and contract in waves. He saw the expression on Richard's face as the boy realized what was in his hand. He saw, above Richard's left shoulder, ranged high along a shelf, a line of model soldiers on parade.

Richard half-glanced back towards the door.

He held out his hand, demanding.

"The gun!" he shouted. "The gun!"

"Fedin." The name slid between Andropov's lips.

The pistol slid between his fingers and before it had

hit the floor, Richard darted forward, body ducking low, supple. Andropov moved clumsily away, colliding with a chair, the table. The pistol had spun beneath the base of the settee and Richard was flat to the ground, arm outstretched. Something thumped heavily against the door and then again, and Andropov flattened himself along the wall behind it, not able to see, to think, not wishing to do either.

The door crashed open with a splintering of wood down the frame, the lock bursting apart. Two men jumped into the room and Andropov bolted into their shadow, his feet sliding from the edges of the stairs, hands clutching at the bare rail of the bannister. As he fled out into the street, the sound of gunfire echoed down the empty stairwell after him.

· CHAPTER 20 ·

The flight came into Schipol airport more than fifty minutes late. Low cloud had kept them circling high above the Dutch countryside, at times swinging out over the North Sea. Malone dug his nails into his hands, ordered another plastic glass of Jack Daniels, became certain that the plane would be diverted to Orly, even back to London. He had already spent a wasted, frustrating hour and a quarter at Heathrow, changing flights. The courier who had been sent out from the embassy to brief him had insisted on brandishing his tradecraft so ostentatiously that Malone had expected Customs and Excise to step in at any moment and arrest them as members of a smuggling ring. Either that or actors in a bad movie.

Now Malone sat strapped in, waiting for the light behind the "Seat Belts On" sign to snap off and allow him to move down the gangway and then stride clear. All the way over from London the enormity of what he now knew had stuck to the back of his throat, defying digestion. The apartment on the Reguliersgracht, the smaller flat close to the Rembrandt Huis where the attempt had been made. And bungled. All the time he had spent chasing Fedin, tracking him down, and now it had been thrown away.

Malone's eyes closed momentarily. It was not only

that. He remembered the way his mind had spun when the courier at Heathrow had spoken the name. The one Fedin had been living under in Amsterdam. Malone could smell his own sweat. Andropov had bought his way out of Russia not knowing that the information he handed over would lead to his own son.

He stood up and shuffled into the slow stream of passengers. Again, he went over what little information he had. There had been shooting and the usual ensuing detritus—spent cartridge shells, bodies and blood. The ubiquitous, silent Janitors. But where the Hell was Fedin now? And where—Malone's face contorted—was Andropov? Already, he had witnessed what had happened when the truth about Sarah had been discovered. What extremes could they expect from Andropov when he realized not only that his precious son was a killer, but that he had been carrying his death warrant inside his head.

He hammered his fist into the back of the nearest seat. Someone had better have some more answers when they touched down.

Of course, it had to be Winstat. That was all Malone needed to precipitate the end of a perfect day. The information had been cross-checked using the Clan. Ops. computer in Brussels, Charlie Huron peering through his bifocals, Madame Brenard fussing about him like some latter-day Madame Defarge. Amsterdam station didn't have a field officer to fetch and carry and so who other than Winstat would serve? Another few hours of nibbled glory, out in the field again.

They sat back in the Volvo as it sped along the highway towards Amsterdam. Winstat never still, shifting against the upholstery as if his shirt was too tight, his collar pinching. Every time one of his pudgy hands fluttered close to his pockets, Malone was certain he was going to pull out a toothpick and continue a lifetime's obsession with the contents of his mouth.

"All right," said Malone, struggling to keep his

voice businesslike and hide his rising antagonism, his extreme anger. One thing for him to louse things up himself, quite another for his subordinates to do it for him. Pyle with his squint and his quaint old-fashioned ways threatening Andropov with a couple of syringes and a phial of truth serum. God! He wondered how the Russian had managed to suppress a smile when he had realized that Pyle intended to leave them at the house as a warning.

And now some officer in the SB division of Clan. Ops. had taken it into his head to mount an operation against Fedin without any sort of proper consultation and with all the finesse and planning of a six-year-old taking his first crack at a snakes and ladders board.

"All right, who was it?"

Winstat made a placatory gesture, pushed his arm along the window of the car. "Maybe that isn't the first priority."

"Don't tell me what's fucking priority!" Malone's index finger was less than six inches from the center of Winstat's face and absolutely steady. "Now name names."

Winstat gulped in air and nodded. "Steigletz," he said quietly.

"Steigletz!" exclaimed Malone. "He's not competent to organize Thanksgiving dinner."

Winstat thought of something humorous to do with cranberry sauce but it stuck in his throat.

"What happened?"

"News came through of the shooting the previous night. Van Holst. The toy soldier man. We'd been . . ."

"Yeah, yeah, come on."

"Steigletz knew Van Holst was under suspicion of being a courier for the KGB. Possibly a banker. He's got a friend in the local police here. Got hold of the description early and made the connection with the shooting in the red light district, the Polish diplomat."

Malone waved him on, anxious to hear it all. "That's

nothing. The Dutch must have got a make on that themselves."

"Sure." Winstat rolled towards the center of the car and back again as the Volvo sang around a container lorry bound for Rotterdam. "But what they didn't have access to and Steigletz did was the material in the Nido File."

"What the hell was Steigletz doing with that? It isn't his brief."

Winstat took a toothpick from his top pocket and broke the cellophane wrapper. "He requested information through normal channels."

Malone's eyes hardened. "Through Brussels."

Winstat nodded—a small movement that could have been mistaken for the car's easy sway.

"Through you," said Malone emphatically.

"I wasn't on duty at . . ."

Malone's look was enough.

"Yes," admitted Winstat. "Through me."

"And?"

Winstat balanced the slender piece of plastic between finger and thumb. "His reasons were good. He'd made a link between a KGB operative we've been looking for and two shootings in Amsterdam." Winstat inserted the end of the toothpick between his upper teeth. "Wouldn't you have given him clearance against that background?"

"I wouldn't have made him operational."

Winstat blinked, nodded; a little pouch of fat shivered below both cheeks. "No."

"Then who did?"

They were entering the outskirts of the city, suburban houses flashing past them, long neat gardens and lines of washing that turned and twisted in the northerly wind.

"He was senior officer on duty."

"Steigletz!" said Malone, unbelieving.

"Yes."

"Jesus Christ!" Malone turned away, looking over the driver's right shoulder, out along the curve of the highway. What are we doing, he thought, what are we doing when the most senior member of personnel in a European city, a whole damned European country, is a kid out of law school who still has to put on pimple cream twice a day?

"He would have had to get authorization. I mean to move the way he did. He would have had to."

Winstat's head was already nodding up and down, the toothpick bobbing much as it did when Warren Beatty picked up Faye Dunaway in *Bonnie and Clyde*. "London," he said quietly.

"I don't believe it."

"He sent in his request and Waxwing referred him to you. Check Firecrest, it said."

"And so?"

"So the boy checked Firecrest."

Malone stared at him, waiting for what was to come.

"Firecrest was in flight somewhere over Alaska."

Malone thumped his fist into the seat back; his lips were drawn tight and he was breathing deeply but through his nose. "I wasn't in a plane suddenly bereft of communications systems."

"I know. I suppose London knew."

"Then why didn't they use them?"

Winstat shifted again in his seat. A flash of blue from the first of the canals showed through his side window. "He made a case for priority. After the Van Holst thing, he claimed our man would go under cover."

"But to take him out . . ."

Winstat removed the toothpick and examined the end with some interest. "Steigletz didn't say anything about taking anyone out. Close surveillance was all."

Malone started to say something but held it down; Winstat wasn't the man. He sat forward, elbows on his knees. The remainder of the journey he neither spoke nor moved his head.

The room was furnished anonymously, the way safe houses always are. If a search party went through the place with microscopes and infra-red cameras all they would discover would be a uniform and thin layer of dust, glasses carefully washed and wiped, some copies of *Filmfan* and *Scoop*, a box of matches none of which had been struck.

Steigletz's station officer was ten years Malone's senior and he wrote as good a report as anyone else in the Agency employed overseas. His budgeting was legendary for its accuracy and it was not uncommon for aspiring administrators to be seconded to Amsterdam for service training. The man's name was Howard Beverly and in the field he made someone like Winstat look like a superspy. Malone knew that Beverly hadn't taken an active part in an operation since nineteen sixty-eight. He didn't even plan them any more; all he did was keep everything neat and tidy, sign chits, handwritten reports in meticulous copperplate and change his shirts twice a day.

"Steven, I feel . . ."

Malone stopped him with a hand flat towards his chest. "Beverly, you can stay in the room if you want, but don't waste my time saying another word. You're nothing here."

Beverly bit his pride down into his bottom lip and took a precise step back towards the wall.

Julian Steigletz had brown curly hair which could have been the result of a perm. A handsome enough face, so that some women might think him attractive and most men would glance at him no more than once. He was a couple of inches under six foot and looked light for that height, though he would certainly be fit enough. He probably played squash five mornings a week, but he looked like a professional soccer player as much as anything—apart, that is, from a lawyer.

"You're finished, Steigletz," snapped Malone, stepping towards him. "Through before you've really started. As of tomorrow morning, you'd best be phoning your family and asking for a suite of offices and a roster of nice, rich clients."

"You can't . . ."

"Boy," said Malone, "you'd better believe that I can."

Neither Howard Beverly nor Winstat contradicted him. Steigletz knew that he wanted to explain himself, to make out a case; he also knew he wasn't going to say a word until Malone asked him. And then when he did he'd be as polite and to the point as he could. Right then he didn't think he would even have the guts to ask to go to the bathroom.

"Surveillance," said Malone. "You asked for surveillance."

"Yes."

"Sent two men."

"Yes."

"Didn't go yourself."

"I was still senior officer. There was no option."

Malone swung around towards Beverly. "That so?"

"Yes," Beverly answered, his voice deeper than Steigletz's but no more composed. "I had forty-eight hours' leave. Naturally, if Julian had considered my opinion would be of value then he could always have contacted me."

Malone nodded. "It isn't very likely he'd have thought that, is it, Beverly? Not even a wimp like Steigletz here. Especially not when he thinks he's alone in the field with the chance of making a name for himself."

"I didn't . . ." Steigletz began.

"Crap!" He took a deep, slow breath. "Just crap."

"I resent your implication. I . . ."

"Resent away, boy. I can picture you wetting yourself at the thought of getting your hands on a KGB killer the section's been after for years. Sitting back at the controls, masterminding it all. You had probably already rehearsed the speech you'd make in response to your commendation when you were briefing those two poor bastards and sending them out."

Steigletz blushed, beginning to tremble as though he were standing directly in the path of the north wind. He kept opening and closing the fingers of his right hand; the left remained clenched by his side.

Malone reached around towards Winstat and received a folder into his hand. "One man," he said, flipping it open, "had been in the field for a little over a year. The other had experience in Berlin and Frankfort before getting sent to a less dangerous and active station after an incident in which a three-year-old girl was accidentally killed. There were some signs that this might have permanently affected his nerves and he was under observation."

"He was cleared for surveillance work," interrupted Beverly from behind Malone's left shoulder.

"Cleared for surveillance, maybe," Malone retorted. "Not for being sent in close on a suspected assassin with a half dozen killings to his credit. Not cleared for being sent out tooled and with instructions to stop the target if he tried to get clear."

"No!" cried Steigletz, moving fast away from the wall.

Malone squared up to him, the two men no more than a couple of feet apart and the smell of fear so strong on Steigletz's breath that it made Malone nauseous.

"Why else would they go in? Why, unless on your say-so? They must have known they'd been spotted, assessed—probably correctly—that their target was ducking clear. They went in. Fast."

Steigletz tried to protest and Malone swept him aside.

"The apartment door was kicked down, Steigletz, how the hell did that happen? Were your men leaning so heavily on the door eavesdropping that it just fell in?"

Malone slapped the folder closed. "Steigletz," he said softly. "One more thing. According to the report these two called in, there was someone else in the apartment that night. They came to the flat together not far short of midnight. The second man was older and seemed to be experiencing difficulties getting out of the taxi. Our man had to help him inside." Malone tapped the manilla folder. "Here it suggests he might have been drunk."

It was quiet in the room, three men looking at Malone and Malone's mind already driving ahead, certain who that visitor had been and wondering where he had gone. Where he had gone and how. Where in Hell he was now?

"Beverly," he spoke quietly, moving towards the door, Steigletz forgotten. "I shall need full facilities. Immediately. You see to it."

It was in no way a question. Howard Beverly mumbled assent and made an untidy gesture with his head that was almost a bow. Winstat put his hands in his jacket pockets and followed Malone through the door. Soon Julian Steigletz was alone in the anonymous room and there was no one to see him cry, nobody to try and work out whether they were tears of self-pity or rage. Whether, even, they were tears shed for the two men he had sent to their needless deaths.

It was a long time since Malone had eaten. This he insisted on doing before any more discussions took place, any more of anything. Steak, grilled medium-rare and with only a butter sauce, saute potatoes, mushrooms and broccoli. He drank a couple of glasses of mild, slightly gassy, Dutch lager and tried to avoid looking across at Winstat nervously toying with some breed of meat pie.

That necessity dispensed with, they walked through the center of Vondel Park, forcing cyclists to swerve round them with a shout.

"Andropov?" asked Winstat.

"It has to be."

"What was he doing with . . ." Winstat stopped in mid-stride, right hand grasping air as though it was a fortune cookie which, when opened, would reveal all that they wanted to know. "He didn't know it was Nido?"

"Or Fedin, the codename he knew him by."

"He thought . . ." Winstat's tongue stumbled, not quite able to pronounce what he now thought to be the truth.

"He came to Amsterdam and went looking for his son, for Richard Jarrett. Sarah had given him the address. Of course, he would have had no idea that Richard and the KGB assassin he had given us so much information about were one and the same person."

Winstat whistled through his teeth. They went through an underpass, a girl of not much more than sixteen sat cross-legged on the ground, chording a guitar with difficulty and singing John Lennon's "In My Life" in a high, sweet voice. *"Some are dead and some are living"*; the line lodged in Malone's mind.

"You think he knows now?" asked Winstat.

Malone shrugged. "It depends what happened at the apartment. Depends how much he's been able to work things out for himself."

"Poor bastard!"

That's right, thought Malone, that's so right.

"How much of it's coincidence?" asked Winstat as they followed the left-hand curve of the path between high, green bushes, the earth around them bare of all but a few flowers.

"None of it," answered Malone, uncertain. "All it takes is someone in Moscow with a finely tuned sense of irony, a feeling for the absurdity of the world. He knows that we're using Sarah to turn Andropov and so he gets to her son—their son—probably the first time he comes over to Europe when he's no more than a kid. Sixteen." Malone shook his head. "Ready made, a teenage idealist with twenty-twenty vision and a cupboard full of sharpshooter's trophies. Whoever ran this one must have laughed aloud and rubbed his hands before he gobbled them up." He paused, voice quieter. Hesitant. "Karpov?"

"You think he convinced Richard that bourgeois capitalism was an anti-ecological plot and that a Communist world would save the whale?"

"Maybe. Perhaps after a while he simply got greedy. What's certain is that the other part of it got to him somehow, the gun, the killing."

Winstat stopped and looked at Malone. "You think they gave him back to us on purpose?"

"He was becoming a nuisance. More than a nuisance. Dangerous."

"And if we took him out . . ."

"It not only saves them the trouble and expense, but it provides Andropov with the bona fides he needs to ensure we swallow all the rest of the hogwash they've been feeding him with for the past ten years."

Winstat fidgeted for a toothpick, shaking his head. "He delivers up his own son."

"And if it hadn't been for Steigletz we'd have accepted."

"You think Andropov might have worked all this out—the way they set him up and used him as a marker? For his own kid."

"He's bright enough. He might."

"In which case he'll do what?"

"Nothing's certain. We don't even know for sure if he's on his own or if he and Richard are still together—though after this last caper that's less than likely."

Winstat extracted a sliver of ragged, whitened beef and flicked it towards the grass. "But you've got an idea you like more than the rest?"

Malone didn't speak until they'd regained the road and were making a circuit which would bring them past the museums and back towards the center of the city.

"He's a man who's lived for fifty years without acting, not physically, not even making decisions that amounted to very much. What kept him going was a tissue of lies that spread from us. Back in that house in Maine, I've seen what having that tissue broken can do to him. He needed someone to hit back at and when he found himself with an iron bar in his hand that was the time. Now, if he's got this figured as far as we have, he's going to be angrier still. They haven't just shredded his own life, but his son's as well. They've turned the one against the other. If I were Andropov, right now, I'd be thinking of ways to get back home. One minute face to face with the man who set this up, even some of it, that would be enough. I reckon that'd be the only thing I wanted in the whole fucked-up world.''

At first Kulyagin was taken aback by Olga Karenova's request for direct contact with Moscow, with Karpov personally. When he recovered from that emotion, he refused the leader of the delegation point-blank. An expression several degrees this side of pain shifted, reptile-like, across the woman's face; then she opened her briefcase and showed the security officer a letter, a card. Kulyagin stammered and apologized and hoped that his error would be excused on the grounds of caution. Karenova refused to placate him with a smile; she simply waited until he had made the contact possible, until Karpov's voice had replied at the other end of the line. Then she dismissed Kulyagin from the room.

''It is safe to speak?''

''Of course.'' Karpov's voice was reassuring, in no way distant.

''I have been contacted.''

There was a long enough pause to suggest that however much of life Karpov had experienced, he was nevertheless capable of experiencing surprise.

''Our little rabbit?'' he said.

''Exactly that.''

''What does he want?''

''To return to the warren.''

''Indeed.''

There was another pause, and Olga Karenova was uncertain whether Karpov was switching on a tape recorder, lifting another telephone receiver from its cradle, reaching for a file or merely snapping the filter from one of his cigarettes prior to lighting it.

''Where is he?''

''He was in Hamburg.''

"Was?"

"Sorry, a slip of the tongue. He is still there. He will contact me on the hour."

Karpov thought. Karenova waited.

"Stockholm would be the obvious route . . ."

"You will take him back?" the woman's tone betrayed her surprise.

"Our friends will have no use for him now. He can only be an embarrassment to all concerned."

"Stockholm, then."

"No. No, there will be others interested in intercepting him before he comes home. Not merely our friends. We must bring him in more cautiously, slowly, let them think we go for speed."

She heard Karpov drawing hard on his cigarette.

"Oslo," he said after a few moments. "Tell him Oslo. There is a hotel, the, yes, the Nobel. It is on Karl Johansgate. Tell him to go there. Tell him to travel via Copenhagen. Let him know that he will be contacted at the hotel. Reassure the poor little rabbit, tell him a sea voyage will be good for him. Say to him that at the end of it I shall be waiting for him in person." Karenova was uncertain, but she thought she heard Karpov chuckle. "Tell him that and he will be sure to follow our instructions."

"Very well."

"And Olga."

"Yes?"

"You have done well in this. I commend you."

Karenova thanked him and put down the receiver. Naturally she had done what she had to do—what else did he expect?

· CHAPTER 21 ·

The coastline slid by, unending variations of blue and gray and murky green. Layers of land were arranged one behind the other, projecting back and up until the craggy horizon was finally reached. The darkest came first, thick wooded slopes which fell almost to the waterline, broken here and there by the occasional spurt of white that denoted a farm, a fisherman's house, some kind of dwelling. Beyond that, hills hunched over one another until they became mountains, their colors lightening gradually as they grew more distant and their tops pushed up into the mist. In the hollow spaces scooped out between pinnacles of rock, snow lay thick on the ground.

Andropov was reminded of a toy his grandmother had given him one Christmas. A device for looking at pictures of landscape, pairs of photographs—or were they paintings?—which his eager fingers slotted down and gazed at through apertures like those of his grandfather's binoculars. The views seemed always to have been arranged like the one he was looking at now; a deep perspective that went back, insisting on its three dimensions. Yet each part, each successive range of hills remained for him stubbornly flat, unreal, a series of stage backdrops artfully slipped into perfect place to create the required illusion.

How else could Andropov look at things, now?

He had been given a small room on the top floor of the hotel in Oslo. There was a radio whose wall controls refused to play anything but light music, one melody merging practically unnoticed into the next. There were two bottles of beer and one bottle of Coca Cola in the small refrigerator and Andropov had considered them for some time, wondering if they were a gesture of hospitality from the management or if they had been left by some previous occupant. After taking a bath, he sat on the side of the bed and opened one of the beer bottles, pouring half of its contents into a glass he had brought from the bathroom.

Through the window, the blind pulled down no more than halfway, he could see another hotel, possibly a hostel. A man sat at a table by the open window, smoking, reading a book and from time to time making small, urgent marks in the margins. Higher up, to the right, another man paced about his room, moving into and away from Andropov's sight. He was wearing only a singlet above his trousers and seemed to be reciting, rehearsing something round and round, his right hand bunching into a fist to pummel the palm of the left. Across from this window, a man and woman sat at opposite sides of a table, the woman reading a magazine, the man playing chess with himself, book open by his left elbow. Once, Andropov glimpsed a woman with dark hair sitting before her mirror, staring into it as if uncertain of what she saw there. The light went out without her seeming to move.

All of the people Andropov saw in the building across the street were Oriental; Chinese or Japanese, he could not be sure.

He sat there close by his wondow for hours, finishing both bottles of beer, staring. Somehow it seemed important that there were others going on with the unexceptional business of their lives. And he sat watching, imagining that to see was to know. He knew nothing. Even though he now knew most things, details which had been secret to him for as much as twenty years, more. Even though the lies and the duplicities, the tissue of relationships had mostly been revealed to him for what they were, he knew nothing. He could gaze across the street no longer. It was time for the pulling down of blinds, the switching off of lights and then, as he lay back on his bed, the images would come.

Herb Peterson's body slumped below him, the blood beginning to break from the top of his head until he wanted to press both hands down upon it tight and squeeze the crack closed. When, in his fantasy, he tried this, the skull broke apart like china and his hands fell through.

Sarah's face as she lay back on the bed beneath him, her eyes and the twisting corners of her mouth showing distaste as she made noises to feign her pleasure; later, calm, her eyes wide and seeing nothing as she answered his questions, every last drop of truth squeezing down; the cellar door . . .

Andropov jerked up, his body startled, a grunt coming hard and raw from his mouth like something indigestible that he was unable to swallow. He sat round and slipped his fingers between the slats of the blind. The bulilding opposite was a blank wall, dark; nothing to watch, concentrate on. He stood up, considered taking the lift downstairs, walking the streets. Foolish, and there had been his instructions. Olga Karenova's voice brittle on the telephone, unremitting. He went into the bathroom again, ran both taps and threw water up into his face. There was nothing now on the radio, not even that detestable music. He stood in the middle of the room and considered what he had done.

They came for him at a little after seven that morning and insisted on waiting in his room while he had breakfast in the first floor dining room; a slice of processed cheese and a boiled egg, all that he could manage. Some dark bread and half a cup of coffee which was already too strong. Go to the station, they said, and reserve a seat on the train to Trondheim. Wait for ten minutes in the concourse, buy a newspaper, a magazine, anything. Look at the clock and then go into the buffet just past the main ticket office. Walk straight through and out on to the street, there will be a gray Citroen waiting, a GS sedan. One of them shook hands with him, both nodded and left. There was an envelope on the table, money and traveller's cheques and a ticket for the *Kong Olav,* a coastal steamer on its way north up the Norwegian coast as far as Kirkenes.

In the railway station Andropov looked at a map of Norway which he took from amonst the many at the bookstall: Kirkenes was within walking distance of the Russian border.

There had been two men sitting in the Citroen and the engine had been quietly running. Neither of them had spoken, not until they had been on the road for almost an hour, when the man sitting next to Andropov asked him if he wanted a cigarette. He wasn't to speak again until they changed cars at a garage at the side of the road. This time it was a Fiat, smaller and with less room for Andropov's legs in the back. Only the driver proceeded on the journey with him, continuing to make a steady pace west along E76.

In the midst of all that silence, Andropov was certain that there was no boat, that the reservation was as false and useless as the train ticket he still had in the top pocket of his coat. It had been intended to reassure him, merely that. Somewhere along the road they would pull into a house. Perhaps not even that, a deserted spot would serve; there it would be all over. The nerve at the side of his head began to wreak havoc. He stared at the back of the driver's head, his neck, summoning up the courage to strike him, struggle for the wheel. Perhaps he should wait until the car was forced to slow down, throw open the door and hurl himself clear.

He knew he could not do it, neither of those things. For now he had survived his moments of action, when the rage of his discovery had merged with a pent-up anger which had astonished him with its severity. If he were ever to feel anything comparable again, it would be at the border; it would be when he came face to face with Karpov.

A seagull set itself between Andropov and the land and broke into his thoughts. For several moments he was alarmed by the size of the bird, amazed by the soft white and gray of its wings, the drop of moisture hanging from its yellow and orange beak.

Suddenly, the bird soared high on the wind and with an easy flap and turn of wings, settled on to the red-painted rim of one of the lifeboats. A separate channel had appeared closer to the shore and a low finger of brown rock merged into the blue. The trees were cleared in patches and the signs of habitation were more plentiful. Further along, he could see that the tree line had been pushed back halfway up the first slope and held. Fields hung down from beneath yellow and gray farm buildings like pale flags.

The steamer called in at villages and small towns along the way, collecting post and freight, making deliveries, taking on passengers laden down with baskets and parcels they were carrying to friends or relatives at the next port of call. Crowds jostled out around the small quays to watch and wave and mark the passing of time.

Later in the year the steamer would bear passengers who were making a holiday cruise up and down the fjords. Now there seemed to be no more than half a dozen; a mixture of German and English who nodded and smiled at each other whenever they passed on one of the decks. In the dining room they sat apart and in the evenings the English read green-backed detective stories and the Germans played cards with a lot of noise and occasional laughter.

Trusting nobody, Andropov kept to himself. The journey would take five days, four nights; time to think, to consider, remember.

The registry clerk's head held to one side as he spoke into the telephone, waited, listened.

"FA7111."

Another pause.

"Fedin."

Andropov tried now to imagine the face of the man who had been at the other end of that line, the feigned boredom, the pretense at annoyance. In his mind he saw the quick gesture of pleasure when the call was over, the last piece slotted so easily into place.

"Fedin."

Karpov had given the Americans Richard's head on a plate and he had used Andropov to deliver. Andropov had been the one to administer the kiss which signalled here, this is the man. Only the kiss had been for Richard's mother and beneath it he had felt her flinch: the first denial which had been a prelude to the truth.

Andropov half-smiled at one of the other passengers who was standing along the rail, thoughtfully peeling an apple with a penknife, the length of peel spiralling down. As the peel finally fell away, a gull swooped from the upper deck and caught it in its beak before it could hit the water.

The Russian wondered what had happened to Richard in that room, the echo of shots that became a jumble in his ears as he ran. The son he had waited for so long, granted to him for one night and taken away the following morning, suddenly somebody else, his son yet not his son. He had no idea if Richard was dead or a prisoner or if he was walking free. It scarcely seemed to matter. For Richard had grown to another father, not Sarah's hapless, drunken husband and certainly not himself, but someone who had given him guns and ideologies and money.

Let me see, thought Andropov, let me see Karpov only once—and alone.

The steamer was beginning to move out into a wide curve and pull around the channel of land into harbor. A squat lighthouse, white with a bright red top, stood four-legged on a promontory of rock. A curve of road spanned water and stone; concrete and steel held high on lean pillars and walls of light gray stone. The newness, the powerful beauty of the highway seemed out of place, an intrusion. It reminded Andropov how easily he could be reached, how vulnerable he still was.

The siren sounded and the engines cut down as the little town came more clearly into focus. A number of modern buildings close to the quay, white with painted windows, decorated and surrounded with names and signs: Paulsen, Texaco. Andropov looked for the name of the town on a sign and failed to find one. He knew they were somewhere between Stavanger and Bergen, the map had showed the deep inlet of the Hardangerfjord. His eyes kept glancing away to the new concrete highway, speeding in from the south-east. Something about it disturbed him, drew him to examine each flash of color that rushed along it, green and red and blue glimpsed between the blur of railings.

The usual collection of people had gathered on the harbor. A woman holding a small girl high in her arms and encouraging her to wave. Young men stood in groups, hands in pockets. Closer now, Andropov could see that a faint rime of frost still edged the roofs of buildings and clung here and there to the walls and roads. In the middle of the town, the spire of the church was steep and green, the houses around it painted yellow and brown and green, roofs gray or red, bordered in white.

Those who were getting off, some of the cruise passengers who were taking the chance of stretching their legs and walking around the town, waited for the gangway to be lowered and secured. Andropov toyed with the idea that he should disembark also, stroll around; there was always plenty of time before the warning siren announced departure.

Glancing aimlessly down, he saw Richard standing back along the quay, one hand raised in an uncertain salute, his head bare and his long hair moving a little in the wind. Andropov buckled backwards and a pain pushed low into his groin as if he had been kicked. The backs of his legs collided with a chair and one of the passengers, noticing his discomfort, started towards him.

Andropov warded him off with an outstretched hand, mumbled assurances. Richard was still in the same spot, still signalling his presence. He wore a leather coat over a blue, high-necked sweater, dark blue jeans. By his feet was a canvas bag. Andropov was certain what the bag contained; he knew also that remaining on board was useless; knew that he didn't want to. Seeing Richard so suddenly there, so unexpected yet expected, he wanted to talk to him, talk and listen.

He joined on at the tail of the group descending the gangway.

They shook hands like the strangers they were. Andropov struggled not to look at the bag at Richard's feet. Richard—was that the name he was there under?

"Let's walk," said this person, this strange, slim Richard, and slipped his arm easily around Andropov's shoulders and led him away from the harbor.

They passed a ships' chandlers, a couple of fish merchants' stores, a baker's with the smell of fresh loaves. Richard kept his arm across his father's shoulders, chatting about his journey as if it were no more than a drive up-country, a taking in of the sights. Opposite the church was a small park, set on the slope of a hill. Richard led Andropov to a bench seat between two yew trees and wiped away the thin coating of fresh frost with the bottom of his bag. The sun was clear and strong and there was some shelter from the wind. Andropov sat and pushed his hands into his pockets, still feeling the cold.

"You are going to Kirkenes?" Richard asked, stretching out his long legs and hooking one foot over the other.

Andropov nodded.

"You are trying to get back inside."

"Yes."

Richard shook his head. "They will not have you."

"Why do you say so?"

"A reformed defector is not the most popular of men."

Andropov pressed both hands down on to the bench, enjoying the feeling of reality that the wood grain transmitted through his skin, through the skein of cold. "Arrangements have been made," he said, his voice unemotional, distant. He heard it as he supposed Richard did, the words of someone he hardly knew.

"You trust them, these arrangements?"

Andropov shrugged and in that movement he looked old again, the shallow slope of shoulders, the expression, almost of pain, that travelled across his worn face. "Is there an alternative? I do not think so."

"The Americans."

Andropov glanced at Richard sharply and laughed till the laugh caught at the top of his throat and he bent forward coughing, tears watering his eyes and Richard patting him high on the back.

"I do not think . . . I do not think they will welcome me with such open arms this time. Not this . . ." He stopped and turned his head away and coughed sharply into the back of his hand. "No," he continued, moments later, his voice faint, "there will be no special treatment. Not any more."

"You must have information they'd think useful. Apart from them being able to make a fuss about how you'd left your Russian masters in disgust at their awful ways."

"Please don't make a joke of it, Richard."

The handsome head, the long, fine hair shook easily from side to side. "I wasn't joking."

Andropov nodded, understanding. He pulled a handkerchief from his pocket and cleared his throat into it, muffling the sound as best he could. "I already gave them," he said, "what little of worth I knew. There is nothing more. Only half-truths, lies, insubstantial details they must already know."

The canvas bag was between Richard's feet; he moved his right leg close against it, feeling the pressure; looking quickly at the digital watch on his wrist. There, in the center of the coastal town, it was as quiet, as calm and still as anywhere he could recall. Moments in his childhood when the lawn in front of his house had seemed to stretch out forever and the trees had been impossibly high and his father . . .

"It was me, wasn't it?"

Andropov's stomach clenched at the words, at the new tightness in Richard's voice. He looked at the sections of the spire, green and overlapping; down over the rooftops of the houses as they formed giant stepping stones to the harbor. At the edge of a patch of picture-book blue he could see the funnels of the boat, its flag shifting stiffly in the wind.

"They would have had to give you something the Americans wanted, something which could be easily verified. Acted upon."

Andropov wanted to answer but his throat was full, as if a fist, a stone, as if a growth had blossomed there, choking it shut. He wanted to explain, apologize, ask forgiveness; more than that, he wanted to ask Richard to explain it to him—everything. The how and the why. The irony of a young man who devoted so much of his time to conservation, restoring the balances in favor of the natural world, a young man who killed for money. Andropov's fingers gripped the sides of the bench seat; he did not need to ask how, that was something he knew for himself.

"Poor little Dimitri," Natasha Marakova had once said, fussing around him with her high, lilting voice and her cups of tea, "poor little Dimitri, he wouldn't hurt a fly." For more than twenty years he had lifted spiders out of the bathroom, gently by their wriggling legs, and dropped them through the open window rather than crush them, wash them, drowned, away.

"The men who came to the apartment . . ." Andropov

began abruptly, his throat clearing, his mind shifting direction.

"American Secret Service."

"You killed them?"

"They would have killed me."

"And now?"

Richard's mouth tightened and in that instant a glimpse of some other person, someone who existed beneath the attractive exterior, showed through. "I guess they're still trying."

"To kill you, Richard, or to capture you?"

"It makes no difference. It's all the same in the end." He put his hand on Andropov's arm. "For both of us."

"I don't understand."

"If I could find you, then so can they."

"They?"

"Whoever it is who's making you his responsibility. The CIA officer you mentioned in the restaurant."

"Malone."

"Yeah, Malone."

A rush of panic roared like waves inside Andropov's head. He hadn't thought that Malone would come here, not back to Norway. He hadn't considered it, but as soon as Richard said it would be so, he knew that it was the obvious—the only thing. And Malone would have seen the bodies at the house, the Petersons, he would know at first-hand what Andropov had done. He would—a cramp gripped the Russian's stomach and folded him forward like a twisted doll—have spoken to Sarah.

This time Richard made no attempt to assist him. He simply waited for the older man to straighten up, rubbing himself across his chest, his face white and drawn, the skin blanched and taut.

Richard stood up, not looking at Andropov, staring away.

"You did inform, didn't you?"

"Inform, I . . ."

"The details, the bits and pieces they needed to fit it all together. Van Holst and the shop in Amsterdam, the model soldiers. A confirmation of what contracts had been carried out." Without moving his hands from his sides, Richard's voice pointed down accusingly, so that Andropov felt he was wriggling and pinned. "You gave them the contents of the Fedin file."

Andropov could only nod, move his head and try to look away, somewhere past his son to where the funnels were silhouetted against that childlike patch of blue. The sound of the steamer's siren rose through the clear, frosted air. Andropov's hands tightened on the wood of the bench and then relaxed, again and again while the siren echoed and faded, rose and faded once more. If he were able to see past Richard now, he would be able to pick out the slow movement of the steamer as it headed back to sea. Down on the quay, women would be lifting their children to wave goodbye.

"I didn't," said Andropov, speaking haltingly, "I didn't know that it was you."

Richard shook his head. "No. You didn't know that."

He lifted his father's face towards him, till he could see the older man's eyes, yellowing, watery. "And if you had?"

Andropov jerked away from Richard's hand as if an electric shock had been transmitted through it. "What are you saying? I would never . . ."

"Not to get to her?"

"Her?"

"My mother. To Sarah."

Andropov's head twisted to one side and he clutched at the front of his coat, needed the reassurance of something textured and real. The slats of the bench pushed hard against his back. There in that open space, high in that air, he was finding it difficult to breathe.

"It was you. You. You were the one I wanted most of all. Surely you must know that? You do, you do."

Richard stood quite still, impervious to Andropov's pleadings. Then, when the Russian finally leaned back and spread his arms along the top of the bench, Richard nodded. "Okay then," he said. "Let's go."

· CHAPTER 22 ·

The Citroen GS had been backed into the garage and the doors locked; the steel sliding front had been pulled down and the padlock snapped shut. It had taken the police no more than seven minutes to open both garage and car and another three minutes for the inspector of the Norwegian Special Branch to leave his desk strewn with papers and take the lift down to the basement motor pool. He made three calls from the car as it sped through the almost deserted Oslo streets and he had made contact with Malone just as his driver was slowing down and approaching their destination.

"Yes," he said into the receiver, his accent clipped and slightly strained. "Yes, it seems to be the case. Yes." He lifted the phone away from his face for a moment and spoke an instruction quietly to the driver, another to the man who had appeared alongside the driver's door and who was now leaning with his head towards the open window.

"Sorry," he apologized into the phone. And then, "Of course I shall confirm, but the request was to contact you as soon as there was any sign . . ."

The inspector scratched at the inside of his right ear, nodding, listening. "Right away. One of my men will confirm and give you the address. Nothing will be touched."

Deftly, the Special Branch officer hooked the receiver diagonally across its small cradle and got out of the car. There were two uniformed men outside the garage and most of the lights of the suburban house alongside were burning. It was five minutes past three and he had not been to bed for too many hours. Now the complications of the Americans, the wretched necessity of holding hands with their CIA. The inspector stifled a sneer that threatened to spread across his face and followed one of his sergeants towards the Citroen.

The body was crammed into the corner of the rear seat, pushed up against it as if somehow attempting to escape through metal and glass, to get away from the weapon which presumably had been threatening him.

"Flashlight," said the inspector, glancing over his shoulder.

The extra light snapped on. There were two bullet holes. One above the heart, the other at the base of the neck, exactly at the point where the Adam's apple would once have been. There was a great deal of blood, dried now for the most past, though here and there it retained in the torchlight a quality of tackiness which almost tempted touch. The inspector knew from their position—one leg forced down beneath the driver's seat, the other cradled along the back, an arm pushed back against the window and another with its hand gripping the upholstery at its upper edge—that the dead man's limbs had begun to set with rigor mortis and that, already, he would be difficult to move. The exit wounds at the back would be larger and there would have been a considerable amount of blood loss there also. Without a doubt, the body would have to be pryed from the seat.

He leaned away, the stink of blood familiar enough, once it would have made him vomit. Standing at the front of the garage he lit a cigarette and dropped the lighter down into his inside pocket where it fell with a thin click against the butt of his pistol.

Malone arrived within six minutes, the rear door of the sedan swinging open once the lights of the house were in sight. He appeared tall and tired, the victim of even less sleep than the Norwegian, the color of his eyes faded now almost to nothing. Winstat, thank God, was back in Brussels conspiring with Charlie Huron and leaving a trail of broken toothpicks all over the office. Malone had been driven by a new agent from Oslo station, bright-eyed and bushy-tailed and drivelling on about the inalienable rights of democracy until Malone had told him to shut his mouth and keep his eyes on the road.

Now he stood close by the driver's door, watching as Malone shook hands with the Special Branch officer and the pair of them went to examine the contents of the parked car.

A few seconds was enough.

"He's known?" Malone said, seeking confirmation.

"That was why we called you. In the light," with a hesitant smile, "of your present difficulties."

"A courier?" asked Malone, ignoring the remark. If he were in the man's place, he guessed he'd feel the same.

The inspector shrugged. "Sometimes. There was a link with one of the attachés at the Russian embassy. Once, a burglary concerning the house of a Western diplomat. Little more."

"But," said Malone, impatience showing in his voice as he attempted to hurry the man along, in the way he rubbed his eyes without being aware of what he was doing.

"He went to the Hotel Nobel and spoke with a man who answered the description of this one you are looking for."

"One of those we are looking for."

"Precisely."

Malone turned back towards the garage. "D'you have any information on the weapon?"

"Not yet. My instructions were to touch nothing until . . ."

"Okay. Sure. Wrap it up. Let me know as soon as you can."

The Norwegian nodded. "What are you expecting?"

"A SIG 210/5. 7.65 Parabellum cartridges."

"A target pistol? At that range? From the size of the wounds, he must have fired from the door, possibly from across the front seat."

"I know," agreed Malone, "but that's the pattern."

With a backward nod of the head, the Special Branch officer said, "It was the one you were looking for, then, the second man?"

"If the ballistics check out it has to be."

"And what would he have wanted?"

"Information."

The inspector walked towards his car. "Get your driver to follow me to headquarters. We can both be contacted most easily there. In the meantime we can discuss this."

"These are my men," Malone began.

"And they are in my country," said the inspector, and slammed the car door closed behind him.

The inspector blinked himself awake, reached for the mug of coffee, looked at the American across his desk. "He was his father?"

"Is, I hope."

"And he betrayed . . ."

Malone interrupted him with a shake of the head, a quick gesture of the hand. "There was no betrayal. There couldn't be without knowledge. He gave us the information we had insisted on as a part of the deal."

"The Russians knew this?"

"The KGB knew too much. They also, I guess, had their own reasons for wanting the man they called Fedin out of the way. What better if we were the ones who solved that little problem for them."

"And now the son is chasing the father?"

"That's my guess."

"With the full knowledge of what happened?"

Malone nodded wearily.

"Then to avenge himself?"

"I don't think so."

The inspector showed tired surprise.

"Dead, Andropov is nothing and Richard Jarrett needs all the leverage he can get."

"This Andropov is no use to you now, or to the Russians."

"He's less significant, I'll agree to that. But no use at all, that I don't buy. And Richard won't be sure." Malone lifted up his mug, but it was already empty. "No, he'll try to use him, bargain as best as he can."

"With yourselves or the Russians?"

"My guess is both of us."

The telephone hiccoughed to life and the inspector lifted it to his ear. He listened, saying little, once or twice asking for something to be repeated. When he set the receiver back down a smile was showing on his face for the first time in what seemed an inordinately long while.

"You were right about the cartridges," he said, "and the pistol they were fired from."

"Well, that's . . ."

"That's not all."

Malone's pulse quickened, the sense of expectation in the Special Branch man's eyes and voice enough.

"The agent who was shot. On the afternoon prior to meeting this Andropov at the hotel, he bought a ticket for a mail steamer travelling up the coast."

"How far north?"

"Far enough."

Malone leaned back in his chair, crossed one leg over another; some of the tiredness began to seep out of his face, vestiges of blue were returning to his eyes. He followed the inspector over to a large map of Norway hanging from the outer office wall. The man's fingers traced a red line down beside one of the deep fjords, out towards the sea. He was making calculations of time and distance inside his head.

"The boat calls here," said the inspector, "and further in, here. If this Jarrett wanted to make an interception, either of these would be possible."

Malone looked at the map: Halhjem and Hatvik. The road curved cleanly away.

"If he waits later then it is Bergen and in such a place interception becomes more difficult. If he does not want to draw attention to himself."

Malone thought, nodded finally: "Okay. Can you check with the captain of the steamer?"

"Of course."

"And the only road out is . . ."

"Oh, yes."

"We can arrange an interception without the warning of a formal road block? An accident, maybe, something like that?"

The inspector looked back at him. "*I* can arrange," he said. "You will be there."

The light on the water still had the quality of early morning, although it was far later in the day; it seemed flat and motionless, muted. They drove past a number of boats with brightly painted hulls, a fishing vessel with its nets draped out behind, unmoving. It was as perfect, as unreal, as a water color.

The road moved through a left-hand incline and all sight of the fjord was lost behind a plantation of pine and spruce. Andropov leaned towards the side of the car, his eyes glancing down at the handle then through the window at the verge beyond. But Richard, his face unsmiling and silent, was driving too fast to make such an escape more than an idea, a fantasy.

Andropov had no idea where they were going, except that it was back into the interior of the country, further away from the north, from Kirkenes, from Karpov and the border.

The same old nerve was triggered off at the side of his head; did he really think Karpov would be there himself? That he would travel all those miles to greet him as he walked gingerly between frontier posts, the snow beginning to flake about his bare head. Was that what he had imagined?

Andropov allowed himself a belittling smile. Had he not kept himself alive on fantasies that were far more fantastic?

The road turned back on itself and as it led down the side of a long, sloping hill the trees were left behind and below long fields Andropov could see the fjord once more, wider and apparently deeper. At the far side, wooded hills pushed steeply towards bare rock, mountains that were ridged with snow. He stared through the windscreen at the fjord. Four huge vessels were moored there, vast and empty, their perimeters coated with the remnants of that morning's frost. The hull of the nearest was patchy with rust, orange-red in the dull, flat light.

Richard nodded towards them, spoke for the first time in miles. "VLCCs."

Andropov looked sideways at him, not understanding.

"Crude oil carriers. They keep them in the fjords in lay-up when demand is slack. Two hundred thousand tons of junk left to rust and rot at the whim of world markets." He sounded like an environmentalist again, the switch sudden and unexpected. "They put in dehumidifiers, keep them sealed, the oil companies will pay to have them serviced for just as long as they think they might be used again and no longer. Then they'll simply leave them there like grotesque bloody whales!"

Andropov listened, fascinated not so much by what Richard was saying, but the force behind it. Did he really care that much, or was he sliding back behind a mask in a gesture that was so well-learned that it was automatic? Triggered off by the sight of the carriers, the situation?

"Where are we going?" Andropov asked once Richard's anger had subsided.

His son looked at him momentarily, and maybe his

eyes flickered briefly with a wry smile that signalled if only I knew.

"If you're going to kill me . . ."

"Don't talk like a fool. What use are you to me dead?"

Andropov's eyes closed and he rocked forward. What use, he thought, have I ever been to you alive?

Richard slowed down for a bend in the road, braking and changing gear smoothly, professionally. "With you maybe I can bargain my way back into the States."

Andropov shook his head; it was almost the worst thing he could hear. "After what you've done against them, surely they would not agree? The other day, did they not try to kill you?"

"Things were different then. I didn't have you to make the package more attractive. Besides, I think someone might have been stepping out of line. They're not usually so inept."

"Then," Andropov asked slowly, trying not to look too obviously at the canvas bag sitting at the center of the rear seat, "you will contact Malone?"

"Sure," Richard agreed, "why not Malone?"

A truck passing in the opposite direction flashed its headlights at the car and the driver made a backward movement with his head.

"What's that?" asked Andropov.

Richard shrugged. "Who knows? Unless the road's closed up ahead. "An accident, maybe."

They were coming into a long, wide bend which shifted the road away from the onward direction of the fjord. There were buildings high on the left and, in front of oil storage tanks, the red and blue logo of the Norwegian State Oil company was lofted in the breeze. On the near side of the road there was a short expanse of scrub—young, failing firs, their branches thick with small red berries; amongst them the purple candles of fireweed. Beyond that were the tankers, close in now and seeming even larger, the few rowing boats secured to long ropes utterly dwarfed before them.

Richard changed down and peered ahead, seeing if he could pick out any obstruction. As the car slowed Andropov's left hand dived for the handle and his right snatched at the canvas bag on the back seat. Richard turned too slowly, totally unsuspecting. Andropov rocked his body and, as his hand depressed the handle fully, his shoulder and part of his back pushed against the center of the door hard. With Richard's shout passing through the sudden roar of the engine, the swish of tires on the road surface, Andropov fell backwards, his legs jolting up and threatening to catch.

He hit the smooth tarmac with hip and arm and thigh and all he knew was that he was rolling faster and faster, the bag clutched like a child to his belly.

Richard's head swung back from the wildly shaking door to the rear window, the steering wheel slipping between anxious hands, the back wheels of the car starting to skid as the camber of the bend threw them out of line.

Andropov had stopped rolling; he balanced on his hands and knees, fighting for breath, not sensing yet the bruises on his body, the grazings of his skin. He watched as the car Richard was driving made a squealing circle in the road and slid suddenly forward again as if it had hit a patch of grease. Richard's foot had struck the accelerator pedal and before he could correct the error or wrench the wheel round, the front of the car buried itself into one of the young trees. The pine bent and then slipped part way back, cleaving a deep V into the hood.

Andropov was running, limping, down through the scrub; he had little clear idea of where he was going, only that it was imperative to get away from Richard before they met up with Malone. Like a sharp burning, the Russian became aware of the pain in his left leg, a numbness, almost, in his hip. Branches crashed about him and once he was struck across the face by a whiplash which instantly drew a line of blood from the bridge of his nose and one cheek. The soil was hard in patches, here and there there was frost enough to make him lose his footing.

Once, when he paused, holding his side, and glanced back there seemed to be no movement from the car, no sound of pursuit through the trees.

All too soon, he realized that the cover was coming to an end; his feet splashed into the beginnings of the fjord. From where he stood the cliffs opposite were all but obliterated by the bulk of an oil tanker, vast and monumental and useless.

His fingers uncertain, becoming numb also, Andropov freed the end of the nearest rope and threw it towards the small boat, paddling after it with the canvas bag tight under his left arm. He climbed into the boat warily, almost succeeding in toppling it over. Each stroke of the oars was like pulling against an open wound, his bruises becoming real to him with a clarity which made him moan out loud.

Frost gripped the metal rungs more tightly than he did, the space between them such that he had to haul himself up and stretch awkwardly, the handles of the bag pushed over his shoulder and its contents banging hard against his kidney with each movement. As he swung from the uppermost rung a noise brought his head round and he saw Richard breaking through the scrub line onto the shore.

Andropov scrambled over and hunched down. He moved crab-like across the deck, uncertain as to whether Richard had another gun or not, and if he had whether he would use it. No, he thought, clinging to the cold metal of a ladder, there is little space left now for doubt. He leaned against a sheet of rivetted metal and struggled to forget the nagging pains, fighting to control his breathing. Down at the edge of the water, Richard was hauling one of the rowing boats towards him. Andropov turned his back and hurried through the carrier, searching for somewhere secure to hide. Ideas buzzed and hatched in his head like maggots wriggling, white and blind. The doors were all locked fast, windows and hatchways sealed. There were only levels of the deck and sheer metal plating, seared with frost. Once, Andropov fell, and as his head was jolted upwards he saw the tops of mountains at his back, their crevices clogged with snow, seeming to fall slowly towards him.

Richard's boat was out of sight.

Andropov squeezed behind a flight of steps and unzipped the bag; the pistol was in the same velvet cloth he had found by chance in Amsterdam. It fell open as warmly to his touch. The butt of the gun beneath it was cross-hatched and cold. He found the safety catch below the barrel end and thumbed it down.

"Andropov! Andropov! You're being a fool."

His hands tightened about the gun; his tongue floated dead in his mouth.

"If you'd got back to the border, they'd have shot you down, you know that."

Richard's words echoed strangely around the hollow tanker, sounded resonant of emptiness and waste. Andropov's back and legs were cold and only part of that was through fear. If only, he thought, it were possible simply to remain here until the cold spreads through me far enough and deep enough so that there will be nothing else to feel. No one else to face.

Not ever again.

The pistol had become a part of his hands, annealed to them. He was staring at the barrel, the smooth curve of metal at the end, the circle dark beneath the arch of the front sight. There was something beautiful about it, some quality of perfection.

"Andropov."

The voice boomed and faded but the footsteps were coming closer. For the first time Andropov's finger pressed itself to the metal of the trigger; he was staring at the barrel end. He was thinking of that morning so many years ago when a young man had turned his head and been caught up in a flame of red hair and the fresh, young face of an American girl. *Sarah staggered back beneath the shower of dust, the heavy slamming of the cellar door, the sliding firm of metal bolts, hard into place. Shut in that cellar with the stench of blood and formalin and now the dark.*

"Andropov!"

A step rang out so close to him that Andropov jerked his head away too fast and struck the edge of the step, breaking the skin.

All my life: waiting.

Another footfall.

"Dimitri!"

Another.

Slamming shut.

Richard was there before him, blocking the light. Andropov twisted the pistol and fired, his finger depressing too soon into a roar of an explosion that was both too close and too loud. Andropov was conscious of a rending scream as metal tore against metal and then he was burrowing back like a rabbit, frantic to escape, tunneling deeper and deeper until there was nowhere else, no room for maneuver.

He broke through the tight space at the far side of the steps and began to run. Half a dozen paces on, his left leg gave way beneath him and he spun to the deck. He called out and the gun threatened to slip away from his grasp but he recovered and realized that his eyes were closed. When he opened them Richard was coming towards him, only slowly, walking as though wounded. A dark patch showed on the left leg of his trousers and Andropov knew that somehow his hasty, useless shot had ricocheted into Richard. Stupid irony for a marksman to be shot in such a way! Andropov felt that he wanted to laugh.

A stitch bit into his side and he was aware that his sight of Richard was only hazy, a young, untroubled face that seemed to bear down upon him, a mouth that opened and closed without Andropov hearing any sound. Instead there was a roaring in his ears and he was unsure if it was the water or if somehow the great engines of the tanker had come throbbing to life. He felt cold along his spine, cold in his bones; the tops of the mountains were still covered with snow and they still seemed to be falling on him.

Richard's hand was extended, asking for the gun.

Andropov saw a window full of toys. Colored monkeys, hoops and a ball. The son he'd never known.

"Okay, Dad."

As the fingers closed about the muzzle, the gun fired. Richard was hurled back, one arm high, his legs skidding wide. He hit the deck, and there, almost sitting, he rocked for several moments, head and trunk swaying unnaturally forwards and back, head and trunk darkening, darkening. Then the legs kicked out and the rest of the body slumped sideways and all that seemed to remain was a misarrangement of limbs leaking blood.

Andropov's eyes opened again and it was later, it had grown much dimmer; the chill had started to consume him. The pistol was still in his hand and there was no way in which he could rid himself of it now. He clambered to his feet, noticing that his left side was clumsy and throbbed. Distantly, with pain and in the back of his mind, he wondered why. As he walked forward, splay-legged, he noticed a bundle of arms and legs folded in upon itself and unmoving. Andropov glanced at it curiously and tried for a short while to understand what it was. What it was doing there. He shuffled along the deck, heading haphazardly towards the side. He knew they had docked and it was time to disembark. People he had to see. Business. His mind furred. Was it the conference, was that it? The rest of the delegation. He wondered where he had left his notes. At the rail he stopped and looked down to the edge of the water and, yes, there, the welcoming committee. The man standing straight and tall, now with his hands extended. Andropov began to smile and raised his right hand to wave.

Malone shot him twice: head and heart. Arms akimbo, Andropov hovered on the brink, stumbled back as if something was driving him, as if he knew there was something, someone he still had to reach. Already dead, he plunged over the rail, twisting and spiralling like a child's discarded toy. Malone's pistol was already back in its holster, away from sight. Men began to move forward through the trees.

Karpov gazed out over Gorki Park. The big wheel was turning slowly around and the colored lights glittered and spun. He snapped away the filter from one of his cigarettes. The report was by his hand. It was not, of course, a satisfactory conclusion, but then the last move was rarely that. The essence was in the game itself, advantages gained or lost. Pieces moved across a board. He turned away from the window so that the lights were behind him, flickering faintly over his shoulder as the interior of the room slowly darkened. There was a new consignment of wine, a muscadet, that needed to be sampled.

The report between his fingers, he began to walk towards his desk.